# Vampire League

## Book II

## To the Last Drop

I0651929

# Vampire League
## Book II
## To the Last Drop

## by Luiza Dobrzynska

PAPERBACK ISBN: 978-1-7353456-1-1
EPUB ISBN: 978-1-3937722-1-7

\*\*\*

WRITTEN BY LUIZA DOBRZYNSKA
PUBLISHED BY ROYAL HAWAIIAN PRESS
COVER ART BY TYRONE ROSHANTHA
TRANSLATED BY RAFAL STACHOWSKY
PUBLISHING ASSISTANCE: DOROTA RESZKE

\*\*\*

FOR MORE WORKS BY THIS AUTHOR, PLEASE VISIT:
WWW.ROYALHAWAIIANPRESS.COM

\*\*\*

VERSION NUMBER 1.00

# Part 1 - The Hunt

Commissioner Serrano was returning from work angry and embittered. Everything seemed to state that Philemon Scapedi will escape justice again. Despite the enormous effort put into preparing the indictment and gathering evidence. This has been the case for years. The Sicilian police were working super-hard. But the evidence and the witnesses would always disappear. Sometimes even the judge was disappearing. And the members of *Capo di Famiglia Scapedi* were always fired. This time the witness was alive, she was not intimidated and expressed her desire to testify. Except that the Commissioner had no illusions. If he tried to take her to the court in Rome, the case would end like the previous ones.

He wanted to put don Scapedi behind bars with all his heart. But he didn't want to have Gina Ricci on his conscience - the daughter of a close friend. The girl who's the only fault was that she saw too much. This was a serious dilemma indeed. Pondering, he began to open the door to his apartment and stiffened, feeling it was not locked. He thought for a moment, then pushed the door open and fell inside by unlocking his gun. And he froze.

In the living room, three men unknown to him and a young girl played bridge, while on the table was a plate full of steaming pasta with bacon and tomato sauce, covered with a glass cover...

"Please have dinner, Commissioner, we'll talk later," the girl encouraged him. He saw her for the first time in his life, like the men, but it was she who drew his attention the most. Because she looked so inconspicuous and defenseless.

Men could be mercenaries. All three wore black leather jackets and trousers, and they looked confident. She did not. A small, skinny woman in a simple, loose knee-length dress. She had peculiar hair - dark brown, red at the ends, seemed like burned. She didn't look like a hired murderess. He knew very well how misleading it might be at first glance. But after so many years in the police force, he had an instinct. He felt that this girl did pose no threat to him. But those men, it was a different matter...

He was silent, eyes rolling from one to the other.

"Octavio di Mauro introduced us, partly..." said the one who looked like the leader of the group. Long-haired, with eastern appearance and eyes resembling the eyes of a wild cat, he was irresistibly associated with India. He also had a strong, foreign accent. "I'm Sinclair Radhjaleah, this is Theo Lebrigadon, Gerard Phil and Augusta Monteloupi. Apparently, we are supposed to protect the daughter of a certain Vito Ricci until the trial and bring her safely to the courtroom, where she will testify. Because we know that you don't trust anyone, I say straight away that Vito Ricci is our countryman, and more precisely we are on the same diet."

He tapped a finger on one of his teeth, slightly longer and more pointed than it should be.

Luigi Serrano hesitated for a moment, but he came to the conclusion that if Camorra wanted to eliminate him, they would find a simpler way. As a bachelor, he usually dined in bars, and here a home-cooked meal awaited him, in addition, smelling so good that he would eat it even on full stomach. He decided to postpone the explanation. He sat down and mechanically began to eat without taking his eyes off the uninvited guests.

"Enjoy your meal," the girl said kindly, "You can trust us."

The commissioner nodded, without interrupting his dinner, prepared very well, he estimated.

"Indeed, this is usually a problem, because the police have snitches," he said with full mouth. "But someone has to help me in the end, because I can't do it all by myself. I've been banging my head against the wall from the beginning of this hellish matter..."

"Three spades," Gerard said.

"Contra," Theo responded.

He had a deep, seductive voice. A policeman looked at him and wrinkled his forehead, trying in vain to remind himself how he knows this guy. He chewed for a moment in silence.

"Gina Ricci is at the Carmelite convent in Palermo," he said finally.

"Probably that's why she's still alive, because they don't know about it. But I think they will find out. If the little one doesn't testify, Philemon Scapedi will get away again and continue to murder. So far, I haven't been able to pin him down, and believe me, I tried very hard. The matter is complicated by the fact that he can afford the best lawyers, he also has many judges in his pocket and more than half of local carabineers.

"Damn bad luck," Oggy muttered disgustedly. She looked at her cards and put them away reluctantly. "No bid"

"In this situation, you tell me "no bid"?" Gerard got angry. Features and attitude really resembled the actor whose name he wore and for a moment Serrano wondered if it was an accident or not. He postponed clarifying this matter.

"Each time Scapedi plays a victim of defamation in front of journalists, a modest businessman, and his insolence pushed for the fact that during the trial he moves to one of the hotels of the cheap Demarco chain so that, as he claims, it's not said that he was hiding. And to emphasize that he is not as rich as they say."

"Is he that rich?" Theo looked at the commissioner and raised his eyebrows slightly.

"He could burn a hundred-dollar bills in a fireplace, and he wouldn't even feel a loss."

"He is as bold as bull."

"Yes, but makes sure that he is safe. Almost everyone around him is either intimidated or bribed."

"We'll be back to bridge later, at a better time," Radhjaleah decided, taking Gerard's cards. "Fanfan, don't get angry, it's just a game."

"Yes, as long as you lose and I'm doing well."

"There now. There are more important matters now. Commissioner, where can we find Gina? I don't want to scare you, but we must act quickly. Mafia or *Camorra*, whatever, won't be messing around."

"She is in the monastery, as I said, I will give you the address in a moment. She bears the religious name of Sister Angela. Tell her I sent you. Do you have any idea what to do?"

"I think I have," Gerard finally stopped sulking. "I just figured it out. It's a little risky, but it should work."

"Wait, we'll talk about it later," a third member of a group joined the conversation (and this one also reminded them of someone). "We still need a photo of a girl, a firearms license valid in this area, and two inconspicuous cars. Is this possible to get?

"Of course. But I must warn you: you'll probably die."

"Ha-ha," the leader of the group laughed, showing frighteningly sharp teeth, giving the impression that they were very many, too many…

"They will be on their guard," Oggy added contemptuously.

"Here's the address," the commissioner stopped scraping the remains of pasta from the bottom of the plate and reached into the drawer for a notebook. "Will you… have problems with entering the consecrated land?"

This question caused crazy gaiety among his guests.

"Don't worry," the Indian finally calmed him down. "Don't believe in nonsense about vampires spread around the world. But will she want to talk to us?"

"She'll want to, she knows who her father has become, so that won't be a problem. You will have a problem with those who want to get her. Be careful: the right hand of Philemon Scapedi is Gianni Satriani, nickname El Commendante, a bastard like no other. Remember this name."

"And what, is he a primadonna in this theater?" Gerard asked nonchalantly. He stood leaning on the edge of the table, his hands in his pockets, and chewed on his drinking straw. It was hanging from the corner of his mouth like a thin cigarette.

"The worst scum," Serrano replied, "murder, kidnapping, drugs, and women trafficking. A brut and wife beater. I used to help one of his forced lovers, apparently he beats for good morning, for no reason. He has no morals."

"When he saw us, he won't have a head for brutality," Theo muttered.

Now the commissar remembered where he knew him from - he was strikingly similar to a young man from the French adventure series, broadcast in the sixties. This resemblance may not have been accidental...

"Have you ever fought the Black Prince?" he asked in the most natural voice possible.

"What? Oh, yes. Call me "Fronda" like everyone else. I fought him. Over six hundred years ago. Although, to tell you the truth, I saw him only a few times closely and talked once. The writers unnecessarily blew the whole thing out of proportions."

"Theo, what did the Black Prince tell you?" Gerard asked.

"He said: "Hang that bastard." Short words, maybe unsophisticated, but straight from the heart," his friend laughed, as if it was the best joke.

Serrano finally finished the spaghetti, wiped the mustache of the sauce and pushed the plate away. He sighed deeply, with obvious satisfaction.

"I haven't had such a good dinner since my divorce," he confessed. "I had no idea that vamp... those like you... could cook."

"You should thank Oggy. She is not a vampire. We do not really cook, for obvious reasons we have no need." Radhjaleah scratched his ear thoughtfully. "Do you realize that this girl will probably die anyway? Mafia will not forgive her."

"Camorra." He corrected him. "Yes, I know that Gina can be murdered. She knows it too, but is ready to take the risk. Courage is her family trait. She believes that it is worth giving her life for truth and justice, and I will not convince her that she is wrong."

"Because she's not wrong either," Theo muttered.

The commissar looked at him sadly.

"You were a knight, right? And so easily reconcile with the death of a lady?"

Fronda shrugged.

"You don't know anything about knights. And I do not agree. Maybe we can think of something to save her, but if she knows the truth, she should confess it to court. Or maybe you prefer us to liquidate this Scapedi. We are not paid killers, but it could be done."

The policeman shook his head.

"It's not enough. If Gina testifies, she will sink half the family, practically paralyze their activities. If you kill a *don*, another, maybe even worse, will come. No, no, this hydra needs us to tear off all the heads and burn the necks."

Theo spread his hands in a theatrical gesture of helplessness.

"So the matter is resolved and there is nothing to talk about. You can stop reference to my past."

Serrano looked at him hard.

"Man is his past. You should know this best. Come back to... well, where you stayed and come back tomorrow after dark. I will have everything you want."

As friends left the Commissioner's apartment, they habitually looked around closely to see if anyone was following them. They easily discovered two lads watching the house. One was smoking a cigarette, the other was listening to music on the headphones.

"Supper?" whispered Never.

Theo nodded slightly.

"I already have an idea how to stage a fight."

Throughout the centuries of wandering around the world he has developed a system of masking the traces of his feasts. If he has already killed, it would always be so that it looks like an accident or rumble among the social dregs. And he has come to perfection in this.

\*\*\*\*\*

"Funny things are written about vampires," Gerard said, lifting his head from reading, "I wonder where the writers get such a macabre."

"That's what you should ask our friend Freud," Never replied without taking his eyes off the screen of the small TV. "Why do you even read this nonsense? It's enough that Fronda does it. He will not miss any horror."

"I'm just beginning to understand his point of view. Reading these rubbish, one ceases to be surprised that so few people believe in our existence," the actor turned the next page of the book.

"Possible, but there is no word of truth and it pisses me off," the Indian snorted contemptuously. "Have you tried to fly yet? Or penetrate through the keyhole? It would be nice to turn into a bat, though I can't imagine the technical possibility of such a transformation. I got some zoological knowledge, and in the end what are we, if not animals?"

"What a philosopher," Frond shouted with a laugh from the bathroom where he was just changing. "And Oggy? How will the professor explain this transformation?"

"I don't explain it. I just take note of it." He answered.

Theo came out of the bathroom, adjusting his clean shirt. His face was smooth, his hair carefully combed, and the smell of good cologne was discernible from him.

"Have you shaved a second time? What is her name?" Never asked sarcastically, looking at him out of the corner of his eye.

His friend shrugged.

"We're going to a monastery, if you don't recall."

"I understand," Gerard flipped the next page of the book he read. "Though they are in habits, but still they are women. You are impossible, Casanova."

"And you are wicked," he cut off. "I wouldn't pick up a nun... especially not in Lent. What do you take me for?"

"What does Lent have to do with this? It probably doesn't concern us. Don't be offended. It shouldn't concern you either."

Fronda gave him a heavy look.

"If you are going to mock my religion, then better give it up, because I will get angry."

He was extremely touchy about his faith in a form derived directly from the Middle Ages. In this small group of friends he was the only Catholic - Gerard did not believe at all, Oggy was an agnostic, and Never professed Shaivism[1]. Usually, they tried to avoid religious topics in conversations, so as not to provoke arguments, but from time to time one of them controlled the spirit of mischief and a verbal scuffle began.

---

1 One of the main branches of Hinduism.

"Fronda fasts, instead of blood he sucks fruit and vegetable juice," Never mocked. "Because meatless blood probably wasn't invented? You would have to ask Octavio."

"Do you want a smack in the face?"

"Just calm down and tell me, will you go with Easter basket on Holy Saturday?"

"Easter basket?" Gerard asked.

"It is a custom practiced in the Balkan countries. Lambdon Tygier once told us. He is Polish."

"And what it's all about?" Gerard tried to remember if he had ever heard of such a thing. Probably not, although his mother was from this part of Europe.

"You put various food in a special basket, goes to church, and the priest sprinkles it solemnly with holy water."

The actor digested for a moment what he heard.

"Looks like paganism to me," he uncertainly murmured. He grunted when Theo slapped him sharply on his neck. "What are you doing?!"

"I warned you, right?!"

"Calm down!" Never boomed. "We don't need skirmishes in our company, damn! What it is, a kindergarten?!"

The door slammed open and Oggy ran into the room with a small package in her hand.

"Did I make it? That's good."

She unrolled the package and took a large piece of raw meat out of it. With a grunt of contentment, she sunk her teeth in it.

"I don't like to go to action on an empty stomach." She explained between one bite and the other. "When I'm hungry, I can give in to my original urges during the fight."

"We rather wouldn't want that," Gerard muttered, rubbing his neck surreptitiously. Fronda had a heavy hand, of which he was not fully aware, and his pokes, even the friendliest, were painful.

"No, no" Never agreed. "Let's all of us tank up before leaving. We will need full strength. Mafia or *Camorra*, it doesn't matter to me. Both are rather unpleasant people."

"I believe so," Gerard tried to remember everything he had heard about mafia structures. "How are we standing with weapons?"

"Not so bad. It would be better, however, if we didn't have to use it," Oggy murmured, her mouth full. "Believe me, I grew up here, I've seen a lot, and heard more. *Famiglia* Scapedi is not familiar to me, but I knew other similar families. Since childhood I was warned with whom not to hang out and from whom to get out of the way, although to tell the truth, when the time of my transformation came, it ceased to matter. I was the one who you should be afraid of."

"And this is all about us. We are not ordinary people. It is true that we are far from the skills that human fantasy attributes to vampires, but we still have more options than the average John Smith." Never pulled a neat chest from under the bed and opened it. "As a support we got a side weapon. Magnum pistols, but Oggy is right, we only use them when absolutely necessary. We have to fight these people mainly with our brains, because when it comes to firepower, we have nothing to compare."

He took four identical weapons, additional magazines, and some papers from the briefcase.

"These are legal permits issued to the four of us. In case of carabineers control. As a side note: they may be corrupt, so be careful."

"Gerard's plan seems risky to me," Oggy finished the meat, threw the bloodstained paper in the bin, and washed her hands. "If something goes wrong, it will be nasty."

"No risk, no fun," Theo chuckled.

The phone rang in the room. Never picked up the phone, listened for a moment, and then looked at his friends. His golden eyes glistened, his pupils narrowed dangerously.

"Cars are on the way," he said.

Friends jumped up without a word and followed him, closing the door behind them.

"Why do we actually need two cars?" Gerard asked as the old Fiat Mirafiori sped down the night highway. The other, driven by Never, kept some distance.

"You'll know when it's needed," answered Theo. "For now, enjoy the ride on a beautiful night."

He put his hand out the window and threw a small pebble on the surface of the pond just passed, glistening on the side of the highway.

"Wake up fishes! It's a waste of time to sleep!" He shouted cheerfully.

"Calm down. Anyway, there can be no more than tadpoles in such a small pond," Oggy murmured, a little sleepy. The journey already lasted two hours, she had to nap from boredom.

"And skies, and bedbugs, and little frogs," Fronda said. "Every piece of our planet is full of life. I didn't think about it at all back then."

"Back then? You mean when?"

"When I was an ordinary man. The first time I felt it was as I walked through the desert, hiding in the daytime under a thick canvas of black, rubberized tree roots buried in the sand. I was starving terribly then, by the way. One morning, when I looked from under this damn cover at the shining world, I noticed a small viper, and then a fennec who ran near me. I saw how he stopped and ate the captured scorpion, then he kept on running. Then for the first time I felt that I was not alone, because all around me are the children of Mother Nature. It was a nice feeling."

"I think you'd get along famously with Allain, my stepson. He could talk about animals for days." Gerard sighed sadly, as always when he recalled his lost life. "He once got the winning prize in the school biological Olympiad. I wonder what's happening to him now..."

"We will try to find out in our free time," his friend consoled him. "Do not think too often about what was. We've all lost something or someone, and we have to live with it. There is no other choice."

He was right, and yet the actor still felt an unhealed wound in his heart. Sometimes he missed his past life so much that he felt like hiding in a corner and crying, and there was no indication that this condition would pass.

It was past midnight when they found the monastery, a grim building from the eighteenth century, fenced by a high wall. They parked the cars some distance away, in a place that would suggest to an outside observer that their destination was completely different from what it was. They reached the monastery on foot, hiding in the deepest darkness and not lighting the flashlights. They jumped over the wall without any difficulty - up close it turned out to be moss-overgrown and rugged, covered with thick ivy. One by one they jumped into the dark courtyard, looking around vigilantly. They were expecting an ambush, but there was only uninterrupted silence.

Even the faintest light did not reflect in the monastery windows. The chapel built next to it also remained in silence and darkness. Oggy, who squat a bit to the ground after a fall off the wall, sniffed for a moment, then straightened and nodded.

"I think we're safe," she whispered.

"Okay, now what?" Asked Theo. "Are ring at the gate or enter through the window? I remind you that since Romeo and Juliet it has been the most popular way to bypass detectors."

"Shakespeare wrote the play when a vase fell out of window to the street and hit him. It turned out that it was a Julia who threw it at her husband Romeo on the first anniversary of their wedding. It was Shakespeare's literary revenge." Gerard remembered the anecdote circulating in the world of theater and had to quote it.

"You are terrible," said the girl resentfully.

A friend playfully pulled one of her black-n-red strands, then turned to Never:

"So what next, Rajah?"

"We're still implementing your plan. Oggy and I will take Gina to the safe place, and you and Fronda will take care of the chase."

"Wait a minute. How do you know that there will be a chase?"

Never, with an ironic smile, handed him a military night visor slung over his shoulder, then pointed at the nearby gate. The actor hesitated, then set up the device and directed it at the thickets visible behind the gate. When he understood how to interpret the colored patches appearing in his eyes, he realized that two cars and several people were hidden there. So the Scapedi people already knew where the main witness was. It seemed that if they wanted to save Gina Ricci, they were barely on time. A cold shiver went through him.

"My turn." Fronda took his night visor and looked through it himself. "What pig heads! My hands are itching to grab them..."

"Don't you dare," Never hit him with an open hand on the back. "They never saw us sneaking in here, they have no idea about us and for now let it stay that way. Now follow me quietly."

He shrugged, but returned off the night visor and obeyed.

The door of the monastery building was closed with a lock, with which one of Fronda's lock picks managed open already on the first try. Theo shook his head irritably, muttering about the unreliable recklessness of Carmelite nuns, then pushed the door gently, careful not to creak. Although, following his example, everyone tried to be as quiet as possible, the nun sleeping in the room next to the entrance woke up and looked out into the corridor, shining a flashlight. At the sight of unexpected guests she froze with half-open mouth.

"Praised be, sister. We need to talk to sister Angela urgently, where is she?" Fronda asked her, bowing respectfully.

The nun, coming to her senses, screamed weakly, then her nerves refused to obey her, and she fainted collapsing in the faint into Gerard's arms. He held her instinctively.

"What's going on?" He was surprised. He patted the woman's cheek. "Hey, sister, please wake up. Are you afraid of Fronda? Such a handsome boy?"

"What is going on here?" A strong, demanding voice sounded from the depth of the corridor and someone turned on the overhead light.

After a while, an elderly woman appeared in a large dressing gown, heading for the group of confused friends, nervously pinning the cornet on her head.

"Oh, it's probably the abbess," said Theo. "Praised be. We need to talk to Sister Angela urgently. Commissioner Serrano sent us."

The nun looked him up and down, then nodded understandingly.

"Forever and ever. It is good that you are here because there have been suspicious types around the monastery since yesterday." She said. "I support Angela's desire to act as an honest citizen, but I would not like her to pay for it with her life."

"It won't happen as long as I have anything to say," he assured her solemnly.

"Could you lead us to Sister Angela?" Never said impatiently. "And what shall we do with this fainted sister? I will go crazy from this word "sister" every five minutes..."

"Take Beatrice to her cell and put her to bed," the abbess ordered a little nervously. "And follow me. I will show you where the parlor is and I'll bring Angela there immediately."

Theo helped Gerard move the nun into her room. He placed her carefully on the narrow bed and began to fan her with a brochure taken from the bedside table.

"Somehow I feel stupid here," Gerard confessed, embarrassed as he looked around at the spartan cell.

"My parents wanted me to become a priest." Theo whispered.

"Reverend Fronda, what an idea." Never raised his eyes with obvious mischief.

"Indeed, it would be quite difficult to imagine such a combination," Oggy admitted, forcibly refraining from growling. Her sixth sense warned her of the growing danger and with some difficulty kept the human form.

"It was just an idea, and it was a great deal at the time, although there would be no tournaments."

"Theo, and maybe now for a change you would take part in the American wrestling tournament, if you miss it so much?" Never maliciously asked him.

"Gee whiz, don't give him such ideas!" shrunk Oggy in horror. "He's crazy enough to do that."

The parlor was located in the further part of the monastery, right behind the side gate. It was intended for people visiting Carmelite women in some private matters. It didn't make a good impression. A small room with no windows, divided into two parts by a carved wooden grille. On each side of it stood a table and two chairs. There was no more equipment.

"Crap, looks like a prison," Gerard muttered.

"Monasteries do not differ much, regardless of religion. They are just barracks for the army of gods." Never sat on one of the chairs, put his legs on the table and began to whistle.

Fronda frowned threateningly, but did not react to this disrespect for the holy place when the door on the other side of the grille opened. From behind them came a young, dark-skinned girl in a habit.

"Are you from Commissioner Serrano?" She asked, coming to the table. She sat behind it, resting her hands on the table.

She was not so much pretty, but incredibly delicate, like a Chinese porcelain figurine. She had large, gentle eyes and black curls slipping out from under the cornet. She was only postulant since her hair had not yet been cut.

"Yes, sister," Fronda said warmly.

"Does it mean that you know the matter exactly?"

"More or less. You can talk to us openly, your father and I, we are... how to say it? Very, very similar." Never tried to speak in general, because he was not sure if the walls in this monastery had ears.

"It's even better. I would be afraid if it were otherwise. Understand me, I love my father regardless of... everything."

"This "everything" is probably quite difficult for you."

"You and my father are not, as you say, standard, as compared to the people of Scapedi," Gina shook slightly. "You do not even know what they are capable of. It is very noble of you that you want to help me, and very brave that you oppose... such people."

"Whoa, miss," the Indian interrupted her vigorously. "Let's not exaggerate. Don't make us noble gunslingers. Whatever we do, we are paid for it. And when it comes to the mafia or *Camorra*, we don't care of them. Let people solve their own problems, we have a lot of our own. We would probably not interfere in this matter were it not for your father, who is one of us. Fronda, put out that act of Don Quixote! Run to the car and drive it to the gate as soon as you can. Just don't get noticed!"

"No worries. I was doing more difficult hare and hounds when even your grandparents were not in the plans."

Gina Ricci smiled at Theo, who actually took on his face an expression as if he was playing the role of an unhappy admirer in costume drama. She liked him, it was visible that he was flattered.

"Let it be that, and I am grateful to you anyway. Do you know what to do?"

"Of course we know. We are not amateurs. Take these rags off, miss, and change into something human," Oggy said sharply. She did not like this girl, like anyone, at whom Fronda looked at with such a gleam in his eyes.

A few minutes later, Gerard, with the help of Sister Angela, already dressed in civilian clothes, put a veil and a cornet on his head. He felt extremely stupid and wasn't sure if their enemies would be fooled. He was definitely taller than the petite Italian. Suddenly he lost all faith in his plan.

"Curl up a bit and run," Never whispered him.

"I'll try," he murmured without conviction.

He did not feel well as a nun. Acting training helped him pretend female movements, delicate features could deceive the untrained eye, but height remained a problem. Fortunately, it was still night, and they did not intend to give the men watching the monastery time to closely watch the refugees.

The Indian grabbed his hand and pulled him, not giving him time to hesitate. They sped through the dark courtyard, run out of the gate just as Fronda approached one of the gates. He pulled his younger colleague into the back seat and tugged at the gear lever. The car started off like a race car, miraculously avoided collision with trees on the side of the road and in full speed went out onto the road.

"All right," Theo muttered cheerfully, watching the lights of the cars chasing them in the rearview mirror.

"I think it's only you who think so," Gerard hurriedly undressed from his habit, not taking his frightened eyes off the speedometer. The hand apparently tried to jump out of scale, and yet the lights behind the car were not far away.

"Slow down, Fronda!" He screamed finally. "We'll crash soon!"

"Don't be such a chicken!" A friend yelled back cheerfully.

He drove with a steady hand, although the car was just over every speed limit. Everything pointed to the fact that the battered Mirafiori with inconspicuous appearance can give much more than it would seem at first glance. No doubt the engine came from some better and faster model. The cars chasing them - two Maseratis and one Lancia Stratos - were still lagging behind.

Something rattled at the body of a Fiat, like a handful of gravel. One of the panes cracked radially.

"They're shooting at us!" Gerard squeaked, feeling the hair grow at his neck.

"Thanks, I wouldn't have guessed without you," Theo turned off the lights he could do without it.

"Open the door," he commanded the actor. "There's a gorge nearby. Jump on my signal, you have to make it before we reach it."

"I'll kill myself!" Gerard grabbed the door handle in horror with both hands.

"Who asked you for your opinion?! Jump when I say!" Foronda's voice suddenly appeared so angry that the actor didn't dare to object.

He waited a moment, then at the signal of a friend opened the door and jumped, convinced that he would not come out alive. However, to his surprise, nothing bad happened - his body hit the soft ground on a gentle slope and rolled down somewhere. Catching his breath, he realized that except for a few harmless bruises he wouldn't have any major injuries. His body became more resilient than before. Maybe not all vampire stories were fairy tales.

He lay there, unsure what to do when a roar sounded nearby and the darkness lit up with the orange flame. He had not worried yet, when Fronda appeared next to him, also safe and sound, though in a heavily soiled shirt.

"Be quiet until they leave for good," Gerard warned in a whisper.

They both looked up at the highway. Nearby, chase cars braked with squeal of tires, from which dark figures stepped out. The bandits lighted the hillside with the flashlights, thankfully avoiding both friends. They didn't pay much attention to the side of the road, rather they were interested in the area around the burning wreck. Then one of them went down a few steps and came back after a moment with a message they did not hear. A few minutes later, the men got into their cars and drove away.

"Are you ok?" Fronda asked and having received confirmation, added. "I activated the transmitter, so Never and the company should find us quickly. Brrr, what bastards. Harass a defenseless girl, in addition a nun..."

"What are we doing now?" Gerard asked reluctantly, for he felt he was a little bit bruised, and in addition he bit his tongue painfully during the jump.

"Nothing at the moment," said Theo. "If what Serrano said about the mafia plants in the police station is true, they'll learn from the report that no one was killed here. They will look for Gina further, and it is up to us to hide her so that they do not find anything. If this plan, which you conceived, be a success, then I think I will proclaim you a knight with joy."

"Many thanks. I will do without this honor, moreover, there is no place for knights here nowadays." Gerard finally stood up and looked at his hands scratched on the stones.

Theo winced slightly.

"To tell you the truth, knights lost it when the guns came to existence," he confessed openly, "the nobility, especially ours, didn't want to acknowledge it. Many good knights died in senseless cannon rounds. However, their ideals are alive to this day, don't you think?"

"Maybe... Anyway, something has survived, and there are also enthusiasts who organize tournaments in old castles..."

"I would like to take part in it if I could, sometime..." Theo pondered and only the sound of a car approaching brought him out of his dreamy state.

The friends fell to the ground again, but the one who appeared on the slope was Never.

"Get in," he said shortly, opening the door wide.

The second part of the plan could be started.

\*\*\*\*\*

"I don't understand you, Gianni," Philemon Scapedi's voice was calm, though threatening. Someone who didn't know him might not even see it, but Gianni Satriani heard it well. "You've never let me down, and now what? Suddenly all your boys can't find one barely grown girl?"

The big man lowered his head like a scolded child. He knew well that he had wrecked the case and what his boss was like, despite his good-natured appearance. Handsome, slim, with slightly graying temples, always dressed with English sophistication, he could easily be considered a representative of the former aristocracy. An outside observer would swear that someone with such a gentle face and such a nice smile would not hurt a fly. Employees of companies belonging to him praised him as a forgiving and generous boss.

But Scapedi had a second personality. He was ruthless, hard enough to keep his and his "family" position. He would not have won it by allowing himself to be forgiving or indulging in someone's ineptitude. He always got rid of colleagues who disappointed him in something, and the head of his soldiers, called by the subordinates of El Commendante, did just that. He did not understand how it happened, but he failed. This hellish girl, a nun with the appearance of a shrinking violet, tricked his best people and literally dissolved in the air. There is no trace of her left to be found, except for the burned wreck of the Fiat Mirafiori at the bottom of the gorge next to the highway. Empty.

"Or maybe you just sold me to the prosecutor's office, Gianni?" Scapedi asked gently, without taking his piercing gaze from his gray eyes..."

"Boss, what are you talking? It never occurred to me." This time Satriani was really scared. "We still have an emergency plan. This girl won't testify, I swear."

"I hope so, because in case not only I will go behind bars," Philemon Scapedi suddenly hit the wall with his fist. "Can't you silence those roars somehow? Every night the same. Who let such cattle in here?!"

From the next apartment came the muffled sounds of guitar music and young people's voices. They sang something in English, in a language that he honestly hated.

"I'll see in a moment," Gianni took the opportunity eagerly and eased himself out of the room.

Music from behind the wall upset him no less than his boss, but this time he blessed the troublesome neighbors.

As he learned at the reception, the band was called "The Flower Power" and came from Chicago only for a week. They were supposed to give a few concerts, but where exactly the receptionist could not say. He was already tired of complaints about Americans' behavior. They didn't care about hotel regulations, and they couldn't be removed because they had paid in advance, and quite a lot. If they demanded a return of the money they had paid, it could come to light that they were charged twice as much as other guests - a common trick played by small hoteliers on visitors from overseas.

Satriani tried to intervene by phone to the owner of the Demarco chain himself, who only throw up his hands helplessly. He stated that he could not evict these people, it would be a terrible advertisement for a hotel and the strategic investor (the chain has recently fallen into financial trouble) strongly disagreed. It would be difficult to convince him and it would take a lot of time. The influence of the Scapedi family did not reach Rome.

"I should have forced a trial in Syracuse," Don Philemon muttered to himself and lay down on the couch.

He hoped that his man would silence somehow noisy neighbors, and he will be able to sleep soundly. Living across the wall with such people was a nuisance. Scapedi would have preferred to move to another hotel or to the home of one of his friends if it hadn't been for the facade. Here was the easiest way to play his role, the role of a modest businessman, a victim of police persecution. The modest hotel suited this image better than any of the better and more expensive ones. Anyway, he always stayed here and didn't like to change his habits.

"They'll calm down immediately if what I told them got to them at all," El Commendante reported, returning to the boss. "The room smells of some herbs, so it can be different. Why they let such a people into a decent hotel..."

Loud music behind the wall died down, apparently band members understood what they heard - whatever it was.

"I will have it behind tomorrow unless you fail. I wouldn't want to be in your skin then." Scapedi stretched with a sigh of relief and closed his eyes. He was an old fashion man, and music referring to the hippie era irritated him immeasurably.

Gianni went out into the corridor again and called his people.

"The trial is tomorrow," he said. "You know the plan: you take all entrances and if you see this woman from the photo, you shoot without warning at her and everyone who will be with her. Then of course you run a mile. In the event of a screw-up, you keep your gob shut, and the boss will take care of the rest. And remember, you must not screw this up.

Despite stitching everything up, he was tormented by uncertainty, as if he were balancing on a thin rope over the precipice. He could not imagine that his opponent in this game is one frail girl, in addition deprived of protection of any protector. Carmelite... This one hurt him a little, since childhood he was raised in respect for the "Holy Church and all his servants," as his mother used to say. He would rather not touch a pious nun, but ultimately she she'll only have herself to blame. It was necessary to stay in the monastery and pray in confinement, nothing would threaten her then.

Plan B, or placing the assassins in front of the court building, was a coarse provocation, but only that remained. In principle, it could even be effective. No one will get testimony from the corpse, and before the police dig through the paperwork, there will be enough time to wipe all traces. He has worked for his *Padrino*[2] for very long time and worst things were already done.

He was sure of one thing: it would be a tiring day, and he couldn't afford to go to sleep. He was responsible for supervising everything, spotting police undercover agents, checking the spacing of cars with assassins - quite a few for one person. In addition, he had the absurd impression that he was being watched all the time. This was not supported by any observations or evidence, just a strong conviction that he could not cope with. Practiced in "losing the tail" from an early age, he was not afraid of detectives, but now he could not even spot the stalker. In the end he decided that it's only his nerves, and he decided to ignore his feelings, focusing only on his task. He only had one night to refine everything so that nothing would surprise him.

Preparations for the big day took him so long that he barely made it to the building of Palazzo di Giustizia, where the trial was to take place. His boss's limousine was already in the parking lot in front of the main entrance. A driver sat inside and pretended to be completely absorbed in reading the newspaper. Gianni gave him a given signal mean that everything was under control and looked for his people.

None of them came inside, their role was after all something else. They probably regretted not being able to witness the Scapedi family lawyer defending the Don and massacring the prosecution. Pietro Lualdi was known for his intelligence and dexterity, so there would

---

2 *(it.)* Godfather.

certainly be something to listen to. El Commendante also had to give up this fascinating spectacle, because he preferred to keep an eye on everything that would happen around the court building. He did not trust his people enough to give them a completely free hand. The principle of limited trust was one of his primates.

"Do you know what to do?" He asked rhetorically those who, by chance, were near him.

He knew each of them not only by name, but also from his entire biography and considered them the best, two were dressed as taxi drivers, four as sweepers, and one as a drunkard standing in the corner. He counted on him most. A pupil of the family, the best soldier, ruthlessly faithful and obedient, and at the same time intelligent enough to work efficiently even when he had to improvise.

"For now, everything looks as if Gina Ricci just gave up the testimony, but be vigilant."

"Maybe she came to her senses?" Carlo Cesar muttered, pushing his taxi driver's cap deeper over his eyes.

"Much better for the girl." Dressed as a sweeper Paulo Visconti waved the broom on the sidewalk. "I'd rather not have a nun on my conscience. She's not just a whore that you smash without stopping."

Satriani would never admit that this point of this case also spoils his good mood. Raised in a Catholic family, he had respect for the clergy and shooting the "servant of God" was not something he could accept with enthusiasm. If necessary, he would not hesitate for a moment, but he felt carefully hidden relief at the thought that maybe there would be no such need.

"Don't be a wimp, Paulo," he growled scolding.

"After all, I'm Catholic and you're not? She is a person dedicated to God."

"Then you will show her the way to heaven! She would only have herself to blame, we warned her. End of conversation, everyone in position!"

Paul's words annoyed him. If he wasn't absolutely sure that he could trust this boy... He was sure, but the soldier's scruples were an unpleasant surprise for him. He shouldn't have them. When it's all over, he'll have to talk to him. He wiped his sweaty forehead with his sleeve and looked at the huge edifice. All the entrances were constantly pouring in and out the stream of people, nobody paying attention to those whom Satriani had placed along the street. They blended perfectly with the crowd.

He walked slowly to a spot where the carved bay window gave some shade. It was going to be a record hot day, and he felt like a chicken on a grill in his expensive navy wool suit. If he were in his villa now, the air-conditioning would be at its highest speed, the chilled beer would be waiting in the fridge, and he would be lying in front of the TV waiting for Sophia to bring him a shrimp cocktail.

He winced at the thought of this slut. Saucy, bratty bitch. Why is he still keeping her, though she was irritating him so much? Well, the reason would be... beautiful, you have to admit, though, and it's true that there are hundreds of them. Shapely, athletic, without inhibitions. Hardly anyone knows how to please a guy in any way. Besides, only she stayed with him for more than two months and there was no indication that she was going to escape. He chuckled almost silently. Wonder how long the daughter of Vito Ricci would survive with him...

Suddenly he budged. An armored van and two carabineers, a tall man and a fairly small girl, arrived in front of the court building and dragged a handcuffed young woman with loose blond hair. After floral pants and a blouse, hung with tinsel, he recognized the singer of The Flower Power. She laughed noisily and sang aloud snippets of hippie songs, no matter how much she made a spectacle of herself.

"She was drunk as a skunk," he muttered to himself, not without satisfaction. "I wonder what she did, too, that they had to handcuff her."

The policemen pulled the hippie into the courthouse through one of the side entrances, regardless of the resistance and screams from her. El Commendante watched the scene, leaning against the wall, smiling ironically under a prominent nose.

The thought that flashed beneath his skull was so sudden, so absurd, and at the same time simple, that he jumped out of his shady asylum in a bay window like crazy. He rushed to the court door, pushing the guards who had blocked his way, demanding to show his ID. At a record pace, he ran through the red-paved corridors and fell into the room where his boss's trial was just taking place.

The lawyer was ending a sublime speech, which clearly showed that the prosecution had only slander and not a single tangible proof. From the side door, reserved for court employees, two policemen led the American singer, removing her handcuffs on the way. Before dazed Gianni managed to reach for the weapon, he was expertly overpowered by civilian *carabinieri*, guarding the hall. All that was left was to look powerlessly.

Everyone in the room - the accused, his lawyers, the public and the judges - froze.

"What's that supposed to mean?" The trial judge asked severely. "Who is this lady?"

The girl rubbed her wrists and took off a light wig, from which black curls spilled out.

"I am Gina Ricci, Your Honor, your prosecution witness," she said in a calm, even voice. She took a packet of cosmetic tissues from her pocket and began to wipe the coarsely makeup from her face.

The room rustled, and the lawyer of the Scapedi family dropped into place, as if he had something heavy land on his head.

"Forgive us for this masquerade, Your Honor," said a small policewoman. "We didn't do it for fun, but simply out of necessity. We were worried about Miss Ricci's life, and given who she was to testify against, our fears were not unfounded.

"That's ridiculous," Pietro Lualdi protested. He pointed his index finger at Gina's escort. "Explicit evidence that the police are trying to discredit my client."

"As if!" a second carabineer, a tall, dark man, reminiscent of an Indian, interrupted him politely. "We're not policemen and forgive us for abusing a uniform, Your Honor. We didn't do it for fun."

"Not only have you had friends, *don* Scapedi," his companion added maliciously.

"Enough!" The judge hit the table with a gavel. "Ten minutes break! The prosecutor and you, whoever you are, to me."

They obediently approached the table.

"I don't understand something here," the judge leaned forward slightly. "You decided to secure the witness, okay. But where did you finally hide her that no one found her, neither the accused nor the prosecution?"

"It was easy, Your Honor," the girl in the police uniform pulled off her hat and shook her tousled, black-red hair like dog fur. "Our friend rightly noticed that the darkest place is under the light. So, we pretended to be a hippie music band at guest appearances, and we stayed in the same hotel as Scapedi. Literally door to door. Killers would have come across any other hideout by accident, no one even considered this one."

"They characterized me so that even my mother would not recognize me." Gina added. "We spent the day recording the album in a music studio, and at nights we played up. There were even some complaints about us."

The judge smiled despite his will.

"Aren't you afraid they would throw you out of this hotel?"

The Indian shook his head laughing.

"No. They charged us so much that they wouldn't risk losing that sum. And Scapedi's men were looking for Gina everywhere, but not in the apartment next to their boss's headquarters. I also don't know if they would recognize the devout Carmelite in the drugged hippie for the price of their lives."

The man in the gown smiled again.

"So, you're not from the police? A great loss to our forensics," he said. "All right, return to your place please. We are continuing the trial."

Don Philemon, watching the scene from the bench, accused his teeth of helpless rage.

"They must die. All of them," he whispered to his bodyguards.

"Quiet please," his lawyer grimaced in disgust. The moment was too serious to plan revenge and not think about the threat. The testimony of Gina Ricci, plus evidence collected by the police, could be enough to send his client to prison for many years.

While the hearing was in court, in parked two streets away Renault, Gerard Phil bit his fingers in nervousness. He had a terrible time, the car was horribly stuffy, and the shortwave radio on the dashboard was silent. Forced inaction drove the actor crazy. The darkened windows protected from direct sunlight, but the sheet was so hot that it was impossible to touch it, although the sun was already setting.

Theo, indifferent to everything, sat with his legs rolled up in the driver's seat and read the astronomy manual by shining a flashlight. Recently, he had trouble distinguishing between print in dim light.

"Do you understand anything of it?" Gerard asked him when silence became unbearable for him.

"Almost nothing," Fronda said lightly. "But it's very interesting. For example, this chapter: "Dynamics of the Oort cloud". At last, I know where comets come from and what it actually is. In my life I wouldn't have guessed that a comet is just a piece of dirty snow.

"So, what?" Gerard asked in an unpleasant voice. "Why do you need such information?"

"Maybe for nothing, but they write here that if one of the bigger ones crashed in Europe, there would be nothing to collect. Fortunately, Jupiter draws on almost all space debris flying around our system. You know, it's interesting: ancient astronomers gave the name of the father of gods to this planet, without which comets would collide with Earth every thousand years on average. Surviving alive in these conditions would be impossible. What do you think?"

"Only that I'd love to see at least one comet. I'll be crazy..."

"Gerard paused, because the walkie-talkie just chattered sharply.

"Action, guys!" Never's voice squawked in it.

Theo quickly threw the book into the corner, sat behind the wheel and turned the keys in the ignition. Seeing in the rearview mirror that Never, Gina and Oggy were running out of the court building, he got in their way. He shielded them so that it seemed to the outside viewer that a pair of fugitives got into their car. Meanwhile, their friends hid in a camper parked on the side of the road, while the dark gray Renault moved forward, cheating the *mafioso* pursuit.

"Hold on, it will be a ride!" Fronda shouted and pressed the accelerator with all his might.

He had to pull the pursuit as far as possible and believed that he could handle it. The carabineer's commander from Sicily could not compete with them. Nobody dared to know that he hired them, and besides that day he was unexpectedly sent to Naples. Scapedi probably pulled on the right strings, hoping that Serrano was protecting the main witness. He miscalculated.

For Fronda or Never, it actually didn't matter, they both got used to dealing in any situation without foreign help, but Gerard, a young vampire, would gladly accept police help. However, he was frightened of the gangsters chasing them as much as the reckless ride of Fronda, who seemed to treat it all as good fun. He even shouted cheerfully, maneuvering among other carts like a cowboy in a cheap western. It's his "yuppie ki-yay!" and "yahoo!" it would upset someone even calmer than Gerard. He clenched his hands and mumbled such words that it was good that Theo could not hear him. In addition, Fronda took turns so sharply that his companion's stomach drove up to his throat and only with great difficulty he could stop nausea.

About five miles out of town, the car's engine choked suddenly, then smoked violently and Renault refused to continue driving.

"Off," Theo jumped to the side of the road and opened the door wide. "The radiator is down, we will go on foot."

"Damn!" Gerard staggered out of the wagon and added something else, but bullets whistled densely above their heads, forcing them to flee. The chase was coming in full power.

They rushed between the thickets. They had the advantage of chasing the bandits that they could see perfectly in the dark, but all their weapons were two magnum pistols with spare magazines. It would be hard to shoot accurately on the run, in addition towards the back, so they had to stand up for a moment, turn around and fall to the ground. It did not help much, because they had no time to aim and sent bullets into the air, but at least forced the gangsters to stop. For a moment there was a fire exchange like in a movie western, which Fronda seemed to enjoy.

Gerard had quite different feelings. He not only shot badly, but he also had great moral resistance to it. He didn't want to kill anyone, not even one of such low-life. He was squeezing his pistol in his hand and pulling the trigger correctly, but his hand was shaking so badly that he would not hit the barn. When police cars signaled from afar, they were close, and he would lower his weapon in a sense of sudden relief.

"Hopeless," Theo scolded. "Think it's just an air pistol. Just a toy."

"It's easy for you to say. I was an actor, not a warrior," Gerard choked, wiping his wet face with his shirt sleeve.

"Imagine, then, that we are on the fourteenth of July and there is a game of paintball shooting. Let's just not get lost in these bushes... And what the hell is growling here?"

"Theo, don't move... They are dogs. We've entered somebody's land," whispered Gerard in the deepest terror, grasping his elbow.

"Oh, come on, actor from the burned theater. If they were dogs, they would already tear us apart." Fronda looked around and pointed to a small loudspeaker hung under the crown of one of the trees. "Oh, there you are. This is a trick for misers, which is a shame to feed a live animal. But we are actually on someone's territory."

This was to be expected. In the end, they fled almost blindly, breaking through the bushes and jumping over fences, which, as you know, do not grow by themselves.

Theo parted the bushes and shouted:

"Come on! There is a path here, just watch out for the wires on both sides. They probably are under voltage, and when the electricity once shock me, I still remember it. I saw all the stars without a telescope and an amplifier."

Gerard obediently followed his instructions, trying to follow the geometric center of the path and pouring cold sweat every time he accidentally nudged a branch. The path and the bushes ended after about ten minutes of walking, and friends found themselves in front of a classical building, bearing a large plaque with the inscription "Museum of Italian land and art." Two yawning guards were walking around the area, the sight of which reminded Gerard that he was terribly hungry.

"Oh, supper!" Said Fronda, who was obviously thinking the same.

Obedient to the gesture of his older colleague, he sneaked to the left and waited for one of the sentries to close sufficiently. Then, at the sign given to him, he attacked, hammering a narrow blade into the guard's neck, which he always wore behind the shirt cuff. Out of the corner of his eye, he noticed that at exactly the same moment,

Theo had caught up with another. They both enjoyed the taste of fresh blood for a long moment, and it was only the crackling of the trampled branches by people that broke them from this trance.

They came to their senses and abandoned their victims, hiding in the shadow of the colonnade. Several armed men came out into the open space, sweeping the area with flashlights. One knelt down and examined the guards lying motionless, looking for some wounds on their body. He found nothing because both friends made sure to lick the wounds after the cuts, which caused rapid sealing.

"Someone stunned them," the gangster reported, getting up.

"Then look for them. They must be here somewhere." Came the answer.

"I don't understand anything, the carabineers didn't pick them up?" Gerard asked in a whisper.

"Serrano said that some of them are corrupt. Apparently he was right." Theo raised his magnum and immediately smashed all the flashlights with a series of accurate shots. Armed men responded blindly with fire, trying to find the shooter.

"Damn, it's my fault. You couldn't count on the police," Fronda muttered. He backed deeper into the shadows, pulling his friend with him.

The gangsters set up quickly throughout the whole area. First, they tried to find those hunted with the help of flashlights, then one of them somehow sneaked into the switchboard and turned on the gala lighting. Large floodlights flooded everything with streams of bright light.

Fronda leaned out of his shelter and fired a few shots. However, this did not improve the situation, but rather made it worse, if possible. The bright light, far too bright for the vampire's eyes, glared him so that he could hardly aim. The columns gave minimal coverage, but there were simply too many bandits. They were also hiding where they could, apparently waiting for their victims to shoot all the bullets. They were definitely not new to their trade.

"Shoot in the floodlights. Even a novice like you should hit, just aim where you can't look." Fronda gave the extra clip to Gerard and bent down to collect pebbles.

He still carried a Roman slingshot, a weapon maybe not on time, but still dangerous in his hands. Although the conditions were not favorable for firing with a slingshot, Theo was considered an expert in this field. Obedient to his words, Gerard fired, trying to hit the floodlights without even trying to figure out what his friend was going to do. He could not imagine that with the help of a leather belt and a few pebbles someone could harm killers armed with firearms.

Meanwhile, Fronda knew what he was doing. With an incredibly long battle preparation behind him, he could assess the situation at a glance, and reflexes practiced for centuries made him a moving target that was difficult to hit.

Few today realize that a stone, thrown out of a Roman slingshot, can be as deadly as a bullet. And Theo knew how to operate this simple instrument with dexterity, which arouses admiration even among his contemporaries. He eliminated one of the gangsters by hitting his forehead before Gerard removed the first floodlit. The other, taking advantage of the confusion, came from behind and knocked his neck. He was about to take his weapon, but the noise caught the attention of the other thug, and it was necessary to quickly run. These killers were definitely not amateurs. He barely dodged the bullet and hid in the shadow, again covering the half of the courtyard.

He smiled to himself with satisfaction, seeing that he had misled the opponent. He was putting another pebble into the slingshot when the shots fired again, and he heard Gerard's desperate scream. Regardless of danger, he turned between columns and caught a friend writhing on the ground.

"Only without hysteria," he growled sharply, ripping the blood-soaked sleeve of his shirt.

A bullet ricocheted from one of the pillars and hit Gerard in the shoulder, ripping the muscles and artery. Blood soaked the entire shirt in a flash and flowed unstoppably like from a source. Theo, experienced in such cases, quickly seized the first piece of wood, wrapped it with a strip of fabric torn from his shirt, and put on a professional tourniquet. Meanwhile, the gangsters realized that they had an advantage because they had abandoned their shelters and were dangerously close. He heard their footsteps and single words.

He picked up Gerard's magnum from the ground and quickly changed the clip. The killers did not go to the certainty - knowing more or less where they hid the ones they hunt, they tried not to get the shoot. He tried to remove one of them, but the action failed. He didn't miss, but the man hit in the stomach just staggered and immediately regained his balance.

"They've got bulletproof vests," Fronda guessed. "Damn it."

The case really looked hopeless when something appeared that looked like dense, consolidated into one shape dense darkness between the hunted and their pursuers. Two shafts of yellow light blazed ominously from the creeping darkness, each cut with a vertical line like a blind reptile. There was a whistling, modulated sound in the air, like the hiss of thousands of angry snakes or the demonic whisper in some unknown language.

The assassins who remained at Camorra's service were not afraid of anything material, but this view proved to be beyond their strength. With a bloodcurdling scream, they rushed with panic. Massive as a pitch, the darkness followed them in the air, pulling out their spectral tentacles until the last car disappeared in the distance. Then it snickered with satisfaction and returned to friends.

"What's with him?" he asked in a voice like a whistling wind, bending his dark figure over Gerard.

"He lost a lot of blood," Theo told him. "Damaged artery and several smaller blood vessels, but it will grow by itself. Worse with blood loss. It's too significant. In addition, it's already dawn. Really, Shadow, you arrived at the most appropriate moment."

"The pleasure is all mine. He, he, they flew away like hares, and what could I do to them? At most a philosophical lecture."

"But where did you get here?"

"Octavio asked me to keep an eye on you. You know, thanks to my structure, nobody will do anything to me, and I will slide everywhere. I don't know why I'm so different, but I like it. And, as you can see, I can be useful. Some cannot sleep because of the very fact of my existence, for example, Octavio for a month tried to figure out who I was, but he almost went crazy and gave himself up." The Shadow laughed again, but soon became serious. "What will happen to you now?"

Theo considered looking at his friend. Gerard looked very bad, gasped and pale.

"Find Never and tell him where we are," he asked. "But look for a shelter for us before, because the sun will rise soon. I don't really like it."

Shadow curled up in place and flashed near the ground, circling the building. After a few minutes he was back.

"There is an exit to the underground building storehouse around the corner," he reported. "But closed."

"Does not matter. Run away now and find Rajah. If he doesn't take us away quickly, we may be in trouble."

Fronda lifted the semi-conscious Gerard off the ground and moved in the direction indicated.

The flap that Shadow found was heavily decayed and strewn with withered leaves, and the staple that closed it was quite rusted. He broke it without hitting the heel, then carried his friend down some rickety ladder. The room under the flap was unbelievably dusty, cluttered with junk and musty. Nobody has been coming here clearly for years. He placed Gerard on the trashy floor and examined his pulse with his fingers.

"Almost a hundred and fifty," he whispered. "There is nothing to wait for."

He removed his inseparable haversack from his shoulder and took out an object from it, wrapped in paper and khaki canvas.

"What is it?" Gerard asked weakly.

"Field transfusion set. During the war I underwent training for field paramedics and kept a few souvenirs. Unfortunately, only that can save you. If I don't give you intravenous blood, you have ten minutes to live. The drink one will not be able to absorb.

Gerard shuddered violently. He didn't know what terrified him more - the announcement itself or Fronda's dispassionate tone. He didn't waste time. He checked the wires and small container filled with sterile glucose solution by the light of the torch, inserted one of the needles into the vein at Gerard's elbow flexion, and stuck the other needle into his own arm. He unscrewed the miniature faucet, praying that the apparatus, which already been past the date for a long time, would endure. As soon as blood began to flow from his body to his friend's veins, he sat down and leaned his back against the chest. He gently pressed the plastic container with his fingers, forcing the flow of life-giving fluid.

"It'll be okay," he said.

The actor sighed, feeling his head slowly light up.

"It won't hurt you?" He asked.

"I don't know? If we does not check, we will not know. Anyway, it's a chance," Theo answered him calmly.

"You are not afraid of death?"

"No. I used to be scared until I realized that it didn't make sense. I have a chance to live a long time, but of course I am aware that somewhere... that someday..."

"I'm afraid of it. I'm so scared," whispered Gerard.

"Unnecessarily, Fear of death is usually the result of misinterpretation of religious dogmas. Islam and Christianity scare people with various atrocities from birth to death, so it's no wonder that fear of death is so common in these societies. Buddhism or Hinduism treat these matters completely differently. No, my little one, I tell you there is nothing to fear of death. Worse is the fear of it than itself, the Elder Sister of Mercy, not a grim reaper with a scythe, as it is most often depicted."

He softly whistled the theme from Gunoud's Ave Maria."

"Were you once close to death after your transformation?" Gerard asked after a moment. He spoke with difficulty, but did not want to let silence fall. It frightened him.

"More than once," Theo laughed freely. "I used to try to kill myself, but it was childishness. During the French Revolution I would have been almost guillotine. And in Napoleon's time I was put in a firing squad and I got seven bullets."

"Oh..."

"The emperor ordered to throw me into the prepared grave and cover, though the bastard saw, that I was still breathing. I had enough strength to put myself in a trance and that saved me. I will teach you one day, this is a very useful skill. Never saved me then and by the way he hated Napoleon. I too had to hear from him what kind of donkey I am that I let myself be arranged like that. Sometime later when he read in the newspaper that the English had poisoned the emperor, he turned purple like a peony and roared: "It's good for him!""

Gerard closed his eyes. Blood slowly running down his veins, gave him strength, though very, very slowly. He did not know whether he was worried or whether he was happy that from now on Fronda's blood would circulate in his body, at least for some time joining them with an invisible link. He had no idea what the effects might be, and something was telling him that Theo didn't know either. He was impulsive, usually acted without thinking, but he was also extremely lucky - he always came out unscathed from the trouble he got himself. Maybe he knew what he was doing now?

Anyway, his story calmed the wounded one somehow. Fronda had the gift that even by telling the most dramatic events of his life he could dull the blade of horror and color everything with humor. And he had these stories in his repertoire and liked to reach for them.

"Tell me something else," he asked. "Something happy if you can. I don't want to fall asleep now, I'm afraid I won't wake up anymore."

"OK. Well, once, when I was still a man, I had to escape literally from under the gallows. My friends attacked the guards when I was led out of the tower. They broke my bonds, but I still had to deal with myself. I ran that there was only dust, but the city guards were on my heels. It was fragile with me when suddenly, bang! The door of the city brothel opened and one of the girls pulled me inside..." he stopped, hearing the distant sound of footsteps. "Quiet... There's someone upstairs."

"Maybe it's ours people?"

"Impossible. Too fast. This is someone else. Don't say anything and let me listen."

He strained his hearing. The steps came and went. Someone was saying something, but too quiet to be able to distinguish individual words. The sound of the engine blending into one with a moaning signal. Closer voices.

"Devi avvisare i carabinieri..."[3]

"Il telefono è in ufficio."[4]

"Cosa potrebbe succedere qui?"[5]

---

3 *(it.)* You have to notify the carabinieri.
4 *(it.)* The phone is in the office.
5 *(it.)* What could happen here?

"They found the guards we bite," he whispered to Gerard. "They called an ambulance and their police would be here soon. Damn, we can sit here till evening."

He looked at the transfusion device while trying to calculate how much blood he had already transfused. The set was not very efficient, and according to his knowledge, the wounded needed at least one and a half liters to stabilize.

"Maybe it is better." He muttered without conviction. "You will manage to regenerate and even if Shadow does not bring Rajah, we will be able to escape from here alone."

"Why not bring him back?" Gerard rubbed his forehead and eyes with his free hand. He felt as if he had partially lost his sight and was slowly overcome by unspeakable fatigue."

"He may just not find him. Shadow can do a lot, but he doesn't always succeed. Hell, I hope nobody looks here. We would have a little trouble. Can you sit down? Or better get up? I'd rather not separate us."

"I think so," Gerard rose from the floor and staggered to his feet, leaning against the chest.

Theo grabbed a metal pipe in the corner, about two meters long, and skillfully propped the flap up from the inside.

"We are lucky that it opens down, not up." He muttered. "At least now no one will surprise us."

"What if it opened up?"

"No worries, I'd think of something too. It would just be harder. I hope dark will come soon."

\*\*\*\*\*

"Did you know that it could kill you both?" Never sternly said, bandaging Gerard's arm.

"Your equipment has expired in the time of Stalin, it could transmit air," added Oggy. "A clot in heart can kill as effectively as bleeding. What if bacteria causing sepsis developed in glucose, what then?"

"Septic encephalitis even kills vampires," Indian nodded.

Fronda shrugged nonchalantly.

"But everything went well, so what's the scream for? I just lost all this silly things," he said casually.

Friends sat in a four-person room rented for the action, happy that they finally had it all behind them, and sipped blood from half-liter containers with pleasure...

"And if this needle grew to Gerard's bone, not to the wall of the vein, what would it be?" Never grumbled. "Have you forgotten that young vampire organisms in critical situations try to absorb literally everything? What if "vampire embolization" happened? Have you ever heard of this phenomenon?"

"No, what is this?" Theo looked at him with interest.

"This is the case when, with just such a combination of two blood circulation, the one in need begins to rapidly and aggressively draw blood from the other. It can end quite badly. Where your sense at, Fronda?"

"I was supposed to stand and wait for my friend to pop off? What else, don't expect such things from me?"

"Give him a break, Rajah. He saved my life," Gerard interjected.

He was still weak and dizzy, but after emptying two full bottles of blood he felt much better. He was full of gratitude to the medieval knight who did not hesitate to take the risk to save him. It was amazing. Gerard already knew how much vampire's attachment to life and fear of death increases with age. The stories of vampires who got tired of life are just a lie - so when someone "settled" exposes himself in a matter, it really has great moral value. Risks not a dozen or several dozen, but hundreds of years that can survive in full vitality.

The former movie and theater star did not know that yet, but of all the bloodsucking population, only Fronda was such a risk taker. Never, though brave, sometimes even crazy, was much more pragmatic and careful in this respect. When the need arose, he knew how to take on a heroic reflex, but always preferred to find another way out.

"In any case, we almost get Gina Ricci's case over," Indian said after a moment, changing the awkward subject. "All we have to do is take her to Naples and give her over to her father. She cannot return to the monastery because she would not only endanger herself. Scapedi people are looking for her everywhere."

"Are they very angry?"

"What do you think? Their Don is in a big house thanks to Gina's testimony. It would even saints led to fury, not talking about bandits like them." He examined the pulse of Gerard with his fingers and carefully examined his eyes, lifting his eyelids with his thumb in turn.

"You should recover in a day or two. You had more luck than Fronda had reason."

"Exactly, Fronda," Oggy reminded herself. "I received a letter to you from the main mail. From Lenor."

"Give it to me," Theo livened up.

He tore open the envelope and began to read.

"Who exactly is this Lenor?" Oggy looked questioningly at Never. "You never said what connected her to Fronda and how you met."

"Oh, now you suddenly reminded it? After all those years?"

"Oh, just like that. Before, I didn't want to think about her, I was probably jealous of their intimacy. I tried to get her out of my mind."

Never smiled forgivingly.

"Well, she is a former lover of our panty dropper. She entertained him very unkindly, which, moreover, was predictable. For a Frenchman it is not safe to enter into any alliances with the English."

"You are a mean type, Rajah. But you are right, it is indeed so," Theo said agreeably, looking up from his letter.

"Have you been to England often?" Gerard looked at him questioningly. He lay out on the bed and tried not to sleep.

"Only once, but quite a long time, because a few years. In the meantime, when I was having an affair with Lenor, I cut myself into a completely crazy group of English Hunters. They were druids and wanted to sacrifice me at the tomb of the Black Prince. It was a bit scary, but even funnier, because they got to the point completely unprofessional."

"Professionally or not, and you were lucky enough that Lenor interfere with this," Never reminded him. "It was she who brought the police to those fanatics."

"Well, I suppose so... But overall it turns out badly for me," Theo sighed.

"Why?" Gerard looked up from the pillow.

"Because the dumbo felt obliged to repay her," Never snorted, seeing that the embarrassed Fronda was not going to answer. "When Lenor fell into dangerous typhus, he saved her with his blood and made her a vampire. And then she chased him away like a dog."

"I beg your pardon" Oggy growled.

"Sorry, honey, I didn't mean you."

The girl huffed and turned her back to him, feeling her resentment even more than ever before.

Theo put the letter back on the table and put his arm around her.

"Don't worry," he said comfortingly. "Something more is needed to break me. It was not my first unsuccessful affair, and not the last. I'm not lucky with women, actually."

"You?!" Gerard exclaimed in amazement.

"You crawl to them too much. When a woman feels that she has power over a man, then she sticks her heel in him with satisfaction." Never took another bottle of canned blood out of the fridge.

Theo shrugged.

"I can't do otherwise. For me, every woman is a lady and I treat her as well."

"Surprising that you are still alive." Never took the letter from the table without question and began to study it diligently. "Looks like Hunters still doing research in England. They can camouflage perfectly. Lenor has nasty problems with them and writes that inside man in the enemy camp would be useful. Will we take care of it?"

"I don't want," Gerard said. "I am an ordinary, calm actor, and I have no predisposition for a secret agent. I've never even played one before."

"Speaking of secret, give your passports. I need to get a visa to spare." Never put down the letter and looked out the window, scanning the street diligently.

"In the night?" Oggy was surprised, archaizing her speech following Fronda's example.

Theo usually used colloquial language, but in moments of emotion he began to use medieval wording and syntax. Oggy found it extremely elegant and original, and often imitated him despite her will.

The leader gave her a lenient look with his golden eyes.

"Just in the night. How else will I get to the official seal? On the day the embassy is full of consuls, diplomats and such other scum."

"Where are we going now?"

"It depends on Octavio. First to him. As soon as we leave Gina at her father."

They already knew that Vito Ricci now lives in the mountainous part of Andalusia, in a vampire commune there. They had no idea what a young Carmelite girl would be like in such a place. They didn't delve into the topic, not wanting to embarrass Gina, but the dilemma was interesting. She could not stay in Italy, and even outside the country had to guard herself, because *Camorra*, as is known, has its people around the world. The girl had no intention of giving up her calling, so how was her father going to solve the case?

"Are there any monasteries missing here?" Vito Ricci laughed when less than a week later they had the opportunity to ask him this question directly.

Misleading the Scapedi thugs turned out to be easier than it probably would have been in a gangster novel or film. The so-called "Octopus" has long tentacles, but fortunately does not employ clairvoyants. Friends and their protégé crossed the border not disturbed by anyone.

Vito Ricci turned out to be a cheerful, handsome man, looking slightly older than his daughter. Hugging Gina, he turned to her guardians with warm thanks, flooding them with a stream of quick words that they only understood a third of what he just said. Never interrupted him.

"OK, OK. From now on you are responsible for this young lady and you better take it to your heart. They will hunt her."

"Let them try. My friends are not the ordinary guys, it's better for these people not to get in on us."

Never looked convinced, but he said nothing. Every young vampire must go through puberty, in which he is deeply convinced that he is able to conquer the whole world. You can see Gina's father has not left this phase yet. He looked at her with concern. Over the past days, she has shown remarkable patience and calmness, sitting quietly in the corner of their motorhome and moving the rosary beads in her fingers almost all the time. He liked her. For all her gentleness, she must have been hard as iron.

"Take care, Gina," he said. "If you ever need help again, contact through Octavio."

"You not join us?" Vito was surprised.

"Another time. Now... we have an appointment. Forgive us."

"Appointment" may be said too much. During a telephone conversation, Octavio di Mauro hinted that his laboratory, hidden near Granada, has a gift for Never's team that would make it easier for them all to continue their business. However, he immediately stated that he would decide on the time and manner of contact, and that it would not happen too quickly. The four friends were simply to live in a roadside motel and wait for further instructions. Maybe if such a condition were set by someone else, they would not agree, but Octavio was not just biggie. In the vampire underworld he enjoyed enough respect for them to agree to wait patiently.

They now had enough money to rent rooms in a good hotel, but the dingy motel guaranteed them what they needed most - almost complete anonymity. The owners of the suspicious shrine, the neglected middle-aged dark-haired girl, were completely uninterested in who her guests were. If they paid and did not disturb the peace, they could even introduce themselves as a band of Charlie Manson. Octavio showed them this motel. He had to know it well and know that they would be safe there.

On the first day they found out that he was right. This place was not visited by so-called "decent people". The guests were usually lorry drivers who used the opportunity to stop refueling and sleep in relatively clean bedding. Many did not even speak Spanish, which did not prevent them from bringing a roadside prostitute into the room.

"I don't know about you, but I slept in worse places," said Fronda, returning from a night trip. "We have roof over our heads, nobody will look for us here, and you can eat without trouble."

"As in the vicinity of every hellhole," Never looked out the window, which was as dirty as holy ground, overlooking a garbage dump collapsed to the brim, in which several rats were bursting. "I don't have problem with this place. I think only our movie star would mind."

Gerard snorted contemptuously.

"Come on. I went through this and that in my life and spent the night in various burrows. Sure, I'm far from your experience, but I'm not wimping out of such a trivial reason."

I wonder how long we'll be here," Oggy stretched out on the bed and yawned widely. "I'd go for a walk."

"We can all go," suggested the actor. "What do we finally have to do? Sit here and stare at cockroaches?"

Never looked away from the view outside the window.

"Maybe it's right. We will explore the area. Fronda has already eaten, maybe we will hunt something."

Gerard grimaced reluctantly. He didn't like to hunt. When the situation required it, of course he had to, but he definitely preferred canned food.

"We don't have even a drop anymore," Indian warned his question. "Either we will find donors or we will be hungry. And you know what it threatens."

"Yes I know. All right, let's go..."

Over the next few days, such night walks became the only available form of entertainment for friends. It is true that Fronda still offered a trip to the Alhambra, but Never did not like museums, and Gerard felt some stupid, unreasonable fear of the old Moorish fortress. Sensitivity of vampires is a real bane for them in the first decades after consolidation. They are not yet able to distinguish well between what they really feel and the feelings of the surrounding people. What takes away their sensitive nervous system is sometimes real torture.

Gerard was a more sensitive "receiver" than others, thanks to his artistic talents and for the time being it caused him a lot of pain. He could not yet control the hypersensitive after consolidating the senses and take advantage of the fact that he feels more than the average person. He avoided human clusters as much as he could and looked at Fronda with horror, who stubbornly attended holiday services wherever they were. This was unusual because even Never avoided churches.

"It has nothing to do with religion." He explained. "There is simply too much emotion in the temples. It is better not to go there if you are someone like us."

Willy-nilly, Fronda went to the Alhambra only in the company of Oggy. Gerard and Never locked themselves in a room and, with nothing better to do, played chess until midnight. Punctually at twelve o'clock the door opened and Theo burst into the room with Oggy. The girl held a large piece of liver in her hand and bit it with great satisfaction.

"We found a convenience store at night," she said. "And in the museum, the curator gave us a message from Octavio. We are to explore the area and enjoy the views, and he will find us when he finds it appropriate."

"What?" Never frowned and looked at Theo.

"Yes," he confirmed. "Looks like he and his buddies are wary."

The Indian scooped the figures into the box with a loud noise.

"I'm starting to get tired of it," he said angrily. "We've worked for them more than once, and they are still so unconfident. It's offensive."

"I do not know." Gerard muttered. "You were more open and how it finished for you?"

Oggy finished eating and licked her fingers carefully. They couldn't unlearn her, just like a few other annoying habits.

"He's right," she said, deliciously munching.

"An egg smarter than a chicken was found," Never reluctantly murmured.

"What came first, the chicken or the egg?" The actor asked, putting his hands under his head. He didn't know where that question came from.

"Egg," Never categorically said. "If the theory of evolution is correct, of course. The first was an egg from female X and male Y, containing a set of XY genes + random mutation... Do you have any reason to ask, are you just bored?"

"I think it's the second one," he said after reflection.

He couldn't help thinking that if he was bored now, what would happen next if he had a potentially very long life ahead of him? He could not deny the facts. He was forced to be idle, although it lasted only a few days, and what was worse, he saw no goal in front of him. It was clear that he couldn't cope without his friends: a demonic Indian, a knight from the hundred year's war and a werewolf girl with a warm look.

"Why don't they really trust us?" Fronda looked out the window and out of habit he looked around the garbage bin, if nobody was lurking there. "We worked for them some time ago. Did we do something wrong?"

"Maybe they have a type of vampire xenophobia?" Never chuckled grimly. "Anyway, I'll talk to this curator tomorrow night. End of stalking, she must know something."

He started walking around the room nervously.

"If you're going to break the record for a hundred in walking, maybe we'd better go to the Alhambra," Gerard suggested.

"We should do it. That bitch, who gave the message to Fronda, must know something..."

"I can scare her. The bravest ones are sometimes afraid of dogs." Oggy volunteered, wiping her hands on the dress. They couldn't unlearn her that either.

"An idea worth noting," Never nodded appreciatively and went to the bathroom to take a shower before bed.

They left as soon as it started dusk, not caring about the flashlight. They didn't need them, they didn't even have to turn on the motorhome headlights. Their eyes were perfectly adapted to seeing in the dark, and in addition this warm spring night was not too dark at all. It was lit up by a full moon and thousands of stars blinking above. Probably even an ordinary man in this light could drive the car on Andalusian roads, not talking about them, "the children of the night".

The ride was a nice pastime for them, but they felt even more pleasant when they got off near the Alhambra and were able to walk around the semi-wild park. Magnolias, jasmine and lilacs smelled sweet. There were ancient ruins in the distance, a favorite meeting place for local low-lives and lovers trying to hide from the world. It was easy to hunt for something, according to Fronda's favorite expression.

Despite their troubling feelings of anxiety, friends succumbed to the charm of the night and stared at it, forgetting why they had come here and even hunting. They walked slowly among the trees and bushes, enjoying the night air and a sense of freedom, which they rarely have recently available. Oggy was dancing happily across the grass, running forward, and then turning back to the men, like a puppy on a walk. Theo had a hard time controlling himself, not to shove her with a stick and call out: "Fetch!" It would be inappropriate, at least, since she was still in human form. He wasn't the only one who had similar dilemmas.

"Sometimes I don't know is she a girl in a dog, or a dog in a girl," Gerard confided to his friends, watching the bright dress flashing in front of them.

Never picked one of the magnolia flowers and stuck it in his hair, just above his left ear. Somehow it suited what would have been immediately taken away by another man's appearance - hair braided in a long braid, thick eyelashes over excessively elongated temples, strange eyes... And the flowers in which he sometimes dressed up like a kid. Despite these seemingly effeminate accents, the Indian vampire always looked like a 100% man.

"Maybe it is not worth considering...?" He began and paused.

A strange figure loomed near friends: a tall girl in a long, flowing dress. Were it not for the slight movement of the material and her long hair in gusts of wind, she would look like a statue. Next to her was a car, a sportster Ford."

"What a devil?" Said Theo in an undertone.

Oggy fell into his hand, snarling wildly as always when she was scared of something.

"Let's find out."

Never accelerated his pace and came closer to the girl, clearly waiting for the four of them.

Up close it was clear that her hair was light red, and the dress was white, old-fashioned, with wide sleeves and a high collar instead of a collar, at the waist compressed with a wide sash with a braided buckle. He immediately realized that he was dealing with "one of them". The girl's eyes glowed slightly in the dark, her face was as smooth as marble and still. There was peace from her like a puma resting after hunting.

"Aap aur main ek khoon hain.[6]" He spoke password reflexively in Sanskrit, borrowed at the end of the nineteenth century from Kipling's Jungle Book and used by vampires around the world.

"Tumhaara khoon mera khoon hai, mera khoon tumhaara hai."[7] The girl replied.

Never nodded at friends to come closer. He saw their hesitation and knew they were surprised. He also knew why.

The unknown beauty was red. People with this hair color are usually resistant to the transformation factor, no one knows why, and she was undoubtedly a vampire, and quite old.

"You were looking for contact with my brother," she said as they approached. "If you're still interested in this, get in the car."

---

[6] *(hindi)* Me and you are one blood.
[7] *(hindi)* Your blood is my blood, my blood is yours.

"Just like that?" Gerard was surprised.

"Either like that or not at all," she cut short.

"It would be good to introduce yourself." Growled Oggy, eyeing her the more unfriendly that Fronda was obviously very interested in the new friend.

"I am Mercedes Aurora Beatrice Luciana di Mauro y Vasquez. I know almost everything about you, so you don't have to introduce yourself to me," the girl replied dryly, opening the Ford door and indicating the place in the middle with the movement of the blood queen.

Gerard, Never and Oggy crowded in the back seat, and Theo took his seat next to the driver and smiled charmingly.

"The lady is probably sitting behind the wheel for the first time. Is it already differentiating between the accelerator and brake?" He asked sweetly.

"If I am not sure about the meaning of something, I will dismantle it and give you a consultation request." Mercedes apparently was not of those women who were easily upset and give up.

Never laughed slightly, a little nervously, as if he was afraid that the knight's behavior would ask them all problems. It would not be the first time.

"Don't worry about Fronda," he said. "He's a fierce anti-feminist, but he's actually a good boy."

Mercedes smiled dismissively and turned the Ford onto the highway.

"Why do you call him so strange?" She asked after a moment.

"Like Fronda? Because, he extremely skillfully uses the Roman slingshot." Indian explained to her.

"That toy?"

"He says you don't need permission, won't make noise, and there are plenty of stones everywhere."

"Not bad thought," she admitted.

The car sped along the highway, but after about half an hour it turned into a side road that was clearly rarely used. After the next quarter of an hour it stood in a secluded place where unlit, low buildings loomed vaguely. As they got off, they realized that there must be a concrete bunker from the war, the one Octavio had told them about. At first glance, there was no indication - the buildings were secured in a modern way, and after opening the entrance they found a small museum of souvenirs from the time of General Franco. They looked around uncertainly.

Mercedes did not allow them to contemplate too long. She went to the wall hung with documents, and then touched it in several places. The wall, which looked like a solid concrete slab, slid open quietly like on well-lubricated hinges. The resulting crack was quite narrow, so that they squeezed with some difficulty. It closed behind them immediately. They found themselves in an empty, musty room with no windows, so dark that even they could see nothing.

Oggy squeaked fearfully, clinging to Gerard's side, which was closest to her. He embraced her involuntarily, though he couldn't stop trembling himself. Mercedes roared soothingly and, judging by the sounds, jerked something heavy. Just before friends opened silently flap, through which the dim light fell...

"Gosh. Like in a spy movie, " the actor muttered, following his friends down the narrow rungs, leading somewhere down.

Mercedes was last one, closing the tailgate carefully behind her. They were now in a corridor that looked like a duct, but clean and poured sand. Spotlights on the walls and ceiling lit it. The corridor was closed by an armored door, devoid of anything like a castle. The red guide opened them, tapping a short, fast rhythm on the disc with her fingers. She led them through six more sluices and only after opening the seventh door did they see what looked like the hall of a super modern institute from a superhero comic.

"I'm sorry," Never sighed, looking around the walls, lined with white plastic and glistening dark glass. The finishes were made of bright, polished metal, probably aluminum.

"What's this space station?" Asked Fronda, dazzled.

"Almost," said Mercedes, not without pride.

They descended from the main hall to a lower level by one of several elevators. There were no stairs - or maybe they just didn't see them.

The lower level, as sterile white and silver as the hall, was one series of closed laboratories with information boards. Some of them also had orange warning lights above the door. Several open rooms were of an office nature, and they were just introduced into one of them. Above the desk full of papers sat a young, clean-shaven man whose hair was blazing the same golden copper as Mercedes's hair. Only when he looked up they recognized Octavio in him.

"Hello," he said warmly, standing up. "Don't make so big eyes, have my horns grown or something?"

"You are red..." Theo choked in surprise. The last time they saw him, he was a fiery dark-haired man with a dark complexion and short hair.

Octavio laughed.

"Oh, yes. Forgive me those dress-ups, I wasn't sure I could trust you. I have confirmed information that the Vanhelsingians have at least two "bloodhounds" at their disposal. At least, and that means that there could be more. They will do everything to destroy us."

"Does that mean... what they have?" Oggy bristled as always when there was talk about dogs.

"Vampires turned up to track down their brothers," he explained to her." That's why we don't trust anyone until we check several times that he deserves credit. Even to you."

They looked at him incredulously. Now that he got rid of the wig and makeup, his appearance pointed to Slavic rather than Iberian origin. The fair complexion dotted with freckles, gray-blue eyes and a short, slightly upturned nose over friendly smiling lips with a slightly shorter upper lip - all this did not bring to mind a native Spaniard. He looks like a vampire, more than a thousand years old.

"I heard you declared a holy war on the Vanhelsingians. You don't lack courage." He continued with appreciation. "Can... can Gusto Vanderbelt really be a traitor?"

"Unfortunately yes. Fortunately, I have copies of his old notes. I knew where they were, so I took them with me and carried them all the time. I didn't want Gusto's work to be lost. You will be able to make proper use of them."

Never gave Octavio two thick notebooks in a green cover. The Spaniard began to browse them greedily and for a moment completely forgot about the guests. They shortened their time looking around the studio or rather the office.

"What are you working on here?" Gerard asked, studying the cardboard boards hanging on the walls with curiosity. They presented various graphs, chemical formula strings and tables with sets of data he did not understand.

"Anything I can," Octavio told him without interrupting his notebooks. "This is the vestibule of the biochemical laboratory, its archive and, so to speak, the conceptual work room. In addition, we have various departments: paleo-biology, solid state and elementary physics, hydroponics, astronomy and so on."

"Astronomy? Do you build horoscopes or are you looking for green people?" Oggy asked, poking her head over Fronda's shoulder.

"Astronomy, not astrology. We explore the universe based on the data that flows into us, because unfortunately we do not have a decent telescope. In fact, we don't have any."

"What is your opinion about UFOs?" Theo joined his friend, who had been interested extraterrestrial life since he heard about it.

Octavio shrugged, genuinely amused.

"I have no opinion on this. The scientist should not speak about something that he did not see with his own eyes, and I... I was studying the Roswell case and everything I could see there was a purely earthly product. The human imagination is immeasurable and everything can be so embellished that the bare fact would not know itself in the mirror."

"What finally crashed up in Roswell?" Oggy asked, clearly disappointed.

"Soviet espionage equipment. No wonder the army then cut off the area. Unfortunately, during the period of my interest in ufology I didn't find anything that could be considered as a trace of newcomers from another planet. Believe me, I wanted it so badly. Anyway, I'm afraid that the visits of aliens to our dusty planet are highly unlikely," concluded Octavio with obvious regret.

"Old Indian Vedas..." Never began, but the Spaniard interrupted him immediately.

"I know what the Vedas say. I researched all the texts available to me. For them, I learned the old variety of Sanskrit, and it was hard work. These Hindu gods are indeed more like aliens than honest deities, and it's hard to do anything about it. It is not only a matter of interpretation, but also strikingly accurate, even precise descriptions."

"And so?"

"What... the devil knows, maybe it was a remnant of some highly developed civilization wandering the galaxy in a multigenerational ship? This is the only acceptable solution, because I assure you that all Hollywood movies in which a ship the size of a sports light aircraft freely flies from Earth to Alfa Small Dog and back are poppycock. The laws of physics apply not only to our good old globe."

"But why is this impossible?" Fronda moaned in disappointment. He had now been facing a child to whom candy was taken away.

"Distance factor, first of all. We can assume, at least theoretically, that there is a fuel we don't yet know. However, the ship will not be able to develop certain accelerations with living entities on board. And even if it developed them and somehow did not kill the crew at the same time, a trip to us from the environment of the star closest to us, around which the planet can theoretically orbit, would take at least four years. This star is Proxima Centauri and we still don't know if there is a planet from the Goldilocks zone around it."

"Excuse me?" Gerard snapped, clearly stunned by this lecture.

"The Goldilocks zone, i.e. the conventional zone of space around the parent star, which is neither too cold nor too hot, and in which conditions that can sustain life generally prevail." He explained to him. "For example, Mars, Earth and Venus are in this zone, although only the Earth has optimal conditions today. Other planets are not suitable for life as we know it. And then there is the most important question: why the hell aliens would do it?"

"Colonization? Research?" Theo replied. Octavio shook his head no.

"Colonization would make sense only if "They" came from a similar planet like Earth. Minimal change in basic physicochemical conditions, such as gravity, the level of background radiation or the proportion of gases in the atmosphere, and the flop. The resulting life could not adapt to earthly conditions. Even if the invaders survived somehow, different living conditions would have a disastrous effect on their future generation. A civilization developed sufficiently to be able to travel without risk in space would have to know that. They wouldn't risk it."

"People, however, see UFOs," Oggy muttered, clearly disappointed.

"People, my miss, have to believe in something. This is an indispensable element of their psyche. When they can't accept God anymore, they believe in UFOs and are not bothered by the fact that radio telescopes penetrate the firmament of days and nights, and the results of this search are nothing.

Octavio gave his four friends a warm look. He decided they were all right, and suddenly he suddenly regretted his initial suspicion.

"Would you like to watch the station?" He asked.

"Oh, yes!" Cried Fronda enthusiastically. "Is it big?"

"Sixteen levels," he answered proudly. "This bunker was prepared for the Frankish government, and we adapted and expanded it in accordance with our needs. It was a crazy job, but worth every effort. At each level there are laboratories suitable for the science department represented there. At the very bottom there is a reactor that gives us electricity and an isotope lab. A small cyclotron runs around, in which our physicists study elementary particles. Fifteen years of construction, a trifle, right?"

"As your reactor shatters someday, it will be a catastrophe of the century," Gerard remarked bitterly.

"We know. That's why we took it a hundred meters underground... Come and see. This level is mainly conceptual labs, but I will show you preparations. Then we'll go lower, there are laboratories." Octavio finally put away his precious notebooks in a drawer and came out from behind the desk.

The first door to which he led his friends was labeled "Anthropology and Anthropometry". There was a large room behind them, filled with display cases, like some medical museum. Formalin, fossils, artificial organ and bone models stood on dozens of shelves. In the next room, complete skeletons of various dimensions hung on plates, bearing plates. According to the descriptions, they were not only strictly human bones, but simply a whole gallery of hominids and human apes. The only exception was the skeleton of the gibbon[8], probably placed there for contrast or a sense of humor.

---

[8] Gibbon is the only one ape which is not included in the family hominidae.

"Are you studying here...? Earthlings? For lack of aliens?" Never asked, examining the preparations with focused attention and raised eyebrows.

Octavio didn't seem to get his irony.

"Yes," he replied. "The alien is hard to reach, so we focused on Homo sapiens and related species, and once there were quite a few of them."

"You're screwing up!" Theo raised his voice despite his will. He could believe the revelations about aliens, he even liked them, but the preaching of teachings on the origin of man contrary to the Bible aroused strong opposition.

"Shut up Fronda." Never waved his hand impatiently and turned to Octavio. "Keep talking, it's exciting. Are you saying that there was more than one kind of man on Earth?"

"Yes. Exactly. Why in our time only Homo Sapiens of the Cro Magnon species survived, we do not know it, but in the distant past there were others: Homo Sapiens Neandertalis for example, but also Australopithecus, contrary to appearances, a separate branch of our evolutionary tree, not our immediate ancestor. There is also the mystery of dwarf skeletons from thirteen thousand years ago, found in China..."

"And you don't have a centaur skeleton?" Theo couldn't stand it again. "Or maybe the devil with dumplings?"

Octavio smiled indulgently.

"Not this one," he replied calmly. "But I have something here that will definitely interest you."

He opened one of the cases and took out a long wooden box. A feather lay on the velvet lining, certainly not from any known bird species. It was long and wide, glistening with rainbow colors, as if applied to gold, and obscured by a diamond coating on the surface. They had never seen anything like it before.

The unusual reflections fascinated Oggy so that she couldn't help herself and touched the feather.

"Gee, like silk!" She was delighted.

"What is it?" Asked Never. He was the least fascinated by the strange object, but from the scientific point of view it seemed undoubtedly interesting.

"Apparently Angel's feather," Octavio answered calmly. "A Sandoval, a drunkard and a mythomaniac brought them to an employee of our station, so I don't know if this is true. This is a local low-life, for money for a bottle he would sell everyone and everything. However, there is a reason to consider his words."

He lit a Bunsen burner on the laboratory table and inserted the tip of the feather into the yellowish portion of the flame. He held the feather like that for a moment, then touched it with Fronda's hand, who couldn't stop a slight cry of surprise. The feather was cool and silky, even untouched by the fire. Then Octavio opened the Devara container with liquid nitrogen and immersed the feather in the liquid evaporating with vapors so cold that they cut off their breath. The result of the test was exactly the same. The beautiful item has been left untouched. The iridescent quill remained crystal clear, as did the seemingly delicate stack. The delicious rainbow flag growing out of it was still soft and silky[9], the tactile impression also remained unchanged.

The Spaniard allowed his friends to touch the wonderful object for a moment, so that each of them personally found out how things were.

"It is unbelievable, of course, because such a thing has no right to exist." He continued after a while. "Whatever has such resistance to extreme conditions, it certainly is not one of the species known so far.

---

[9] A bird's feather consists of a quill, a rachis and a flag.

Maybe if it were possible to live on Io, one of Jupiter's moons, then there..."

"I know," Oggy said to him. "Io has a temperature close to absolute zero, but the tectonic movements caused by Jupiter's attraction heat its interior so that the lava flowing out of the volcanoes is as fluid as oil. I read about it in the scientific quarterly, received from Fronda. I'm also interested in such things."

He nodded approvingly and carefully put the artifact back into the display case.

"Well done, miss. You have a strict mind, as you can see. You will definitely be happy to talk to our specs of stars." He first looked at her more closely and frowned. "Wait... you don't look like a vampire to me."

"Probably because I'm a werewolf." The girl explained to him seriously.

Octavio jumped.

"Really?!" He shouted. "Great for me! There has never been a lycanthrope here! Oh my, what a chance... Let us do some basic research. You know, skeletal x-ray, blood and hair test.... These samples will be invaluable to us."

"Wait a minute!" Never interrupted him. "Oggy is not a guinea pig! What are you thinking?"

Di Mauro squeezed his arm lightly.

"Brother, I don't want to hurt her." He assured. "It's just few basic research. You see, lycanthropes are a subgroup of allomorphs, people who can take animal forms. We have been asked twice to help us master this process, but we did not have comparative material. Thanks to this girl we can push tests forward and maybe we will finally find the right medicine."

"All right, I agree, but only if Theo will be with me all the time," Oggy decided.

"Well, it's been agreed. This will not escape us, so let's go further."

They saw other laboratories, mainly natural and geological ones, pledged with cataloged specimens. Then they took one of the elevators to the lower level. It smelled of chemicals and everywhere people in white aprons hung, often stained and burned with acids.

"I understand now why you have checked us so long. If this Parisian traitor knew the location of this place... "Never flinched at the thought.

"We would be massacred and our work destroyed. But be calm, he is not here. Probably..." Octavio was obviously not entirely sure.

"It's awful to think that someone like us can hunt us like a tame wolf in the wild," Gerard sighed.

"That's why we call these" bloodhounds," Octavio explained to him.

"Or maybe it's not a vampire, it's some kind of half-vampire? I read such an American comic..." Theo began, but Never interrupted him with disgust:

"Don't babble, Fronda. There are no half vampires. Either someone is a vampire or man, there is no third choice. It's like searching for the missing link between a monkey and a human. No sense. One of the two things. Either an animal or a man, you can't be a little this and a little that."

"But archaeologists supposedly found something..." Oggy squeaked. "Some skull, and they called it Lucy."

Octavio shrugged.

"Another monkey, what's the difference? In this matter, I share the opinion of Rajah."

He pressed a button to open another door. The room behind them looked like a university library - it was full of books and manuscripts, and huge boards hung on the walls.

"This is where human species behaviorism is studied," he said. "Ruben Shaffner tries to decipher the relationship between biological material and the mind, Jeff Cody eagerly studies human history, and

Irka Kralowa is a geneticist, and, dear, a high-class geneticist. And then we have their laboratory."

The inner door swung open, and a tall blond man with ponytail came out, taking off his coat on the way.

"Tygier!" Never shouted cheerfully. "Lambdon Tygier! Is that where you resisted?"

"That's you?! I thought they were already killing you!" The Pole hugged him effusively and rushed to greet the others. "Servus servorum Gala rex, knight! Oh, our star, you look great! And you, baby, how's it going? Are you still hanging out with these outcasts of society?"

"Lambdon's surety is due to me letting you in at all," Octavio explained to the end.

"Sit down," Tygier suggested to his friends several tripod stools. "And what, Theo, have you already had the opportunity to watch "your" series? Nice, huh."

"I saw several episodes. They are a little prate, but you can watch. Anyway, what I care about now... There are more serious matters."

"I know. Have you heard who turned out to be a traitor?"

Tygier took a bulky bottle out of the cupboard and poured some light ruby blend smelling of rum into his glasses.

"I'm not sure of anything anymore," Fronda sipped and nodded approvingly. "Good. You know, Lambdon, I just want to put him down, no matter who he is. Much worse is the fact that he does not work alone, but on a leash of Hunters."

"Yes. IVH branches are everywhere now. I had signals that one was open even near Warsaw... You know, it's in Poland." Added the lab technician, remembering that his Parisian friend is very poorly oriented in geography.

"I've been there before," Theo said lightly. "A beautiful country, but they are still fighting there, and with everybody, and if they are no longer with whom, then among themselves."

"Not Poland's fault, that history has dealt with them so much. Wars, annexation, partitions..."

"We had exactly the same thing in France," Fronda laughed. "You won't impress me. I don't like your fashion either. Your kontush... maybe it's pretty, in itself, but even the most handsome man looks like a pregnant nun."

"Behave yourself, who now wears kontush? We have now twentieth century, my friend!"

"Leave fashion discussions for a better time," Never interrupted. "Lambdon, Octavio wants to test Oggy's blood and hair, and you're a damn skillful lab technician. Get from her what you need, and it'll be past her. She will trust you more than someone she does not yet know."

"Why not?" The girl agreed not eagerly, grabbing Fronda by the elbow.

Theo put his arm around her, and they followed Tygier together. After a while, a squeak came from the next room:

"Oh, it hurts!"

And reassuring Tygier's persuasion:

"It's nothing but a slight prick. Give me a hand, baby."

"I just hope you don't have a vivisection studio here," Gerard said, shuddering despite his will.

"Any of those things," said Octavio. "We do not accept such methods. We don't do experiments on animals at all, because the value of most of them equals zero. Man is not a dog or a rat, despite appearances and not a monkey. What will prove to be helpful in treating those species can even harm a person. And besides... what are these poor beings guilty of, say, some bitch wants to paint like a wall and need to test a new lipstick?"

"That's right, but on the other hand, if Pasteur reasoned like you, we would not have the vaccine for rabies or smallpox to this day," objected the actor. He took a sip from his glass. "And your humanistic views don't seem to concern people, judging by some exhibits."

He took the dried-up head of a Houcan warrior from the shelf and looked at it with a mixture of disgust and curiosity.

"It's an auxiliary exhibit," Octavio said calmly. "Tygier describes various cases in his spare time, so he brought here a few small things. You know, he wants to educate himself in the direction of Jeff Cody and help him in his research. This is crazy work."

"And what does he do it for?" Gerard was surprised. He put the head back on the shelf and drank some more.

"Such a passion."

"Passion? Does this mean that you work for the sport of it?" Never got up from the stool and began to watch closely the boards hung on the walls.

"Not exactly. After all, we live on patents and doing black work for some scientists from renowned institutes. We have developed many small inventions attributed to large corporations, and we have the money necessary for the functioning of our facility. The apparatus costs, reagents too, not to mention other things. Only electricity is free because of the reactor."

"Are you not afraid of it? I thought that after Hiroshima and Nagasaki everyone would be more careful." Gerard clearly was not convinced by such devices.

"Nuclear power is clean. Of course, it can do damn damage, but it can do anything if it runs out of supervision. Humanity is doomed to reactors, because mineral resources are running out. Sooner or later everyone will have to deal with it."

"Brrr. I'd rather not have a nuclear power plant near the house." Gerard shook himself.

Octavio smiled with some contempt of a well-informed person towards the layman.

"You have very narrow views, but in the end it justifies you that you are a very young vampire," he said. "You have to think in perspective. There are more and more people and less and less energy, something has to be done before we all find ourselves in a forced situation. We see it well, better than others. Hiroshima has nothing to do with it, let's not confuse the concepts. Nuclear power is just a tool, and nothing comes out of the tool. It all depends on what you use it for."

"Interesting, Fronda said the same thing," Gerard mused.

Octavio nodded.

"I heard he has an interesting philosophy. Tygier talked a lot about him."

Oggy and Theo left the analytical lab. The girl wiped her eyes with the sleeve of her dress, Fronda embraced her frail arms.

"Well, I guess it wasn't too bad," Gerard patted Oggy comfortingly on the back.

"I hate needles," she stammered through tears.

"She has the right. One does not like this, and the other one something else, is not a crime." Theo, as always, defended her, maybe a little exaggerated. He carefully examined her hand and fixed the bandage in the bend of the elbow.

"Continue sightseeing?" Octavio asked, but was interrupted by a long, modulated sound that seemed to come from all sides.

Friends, amazed and disturbed, wanted to ask what it was, but the Spaniard stopped them with a wave of his hand. After a moment the loudspeakers placed under the ceiling clicked and calmly pronounced words were heard:

"Third stage alarm. Employees are asked not to leave the station under any circumstances until further notice."

"Probably some teenagers are roaming the bunkers again, delighted that they have fled their parents," Octavio sighed, not showing too much fear. "So, we'll wait. Anyway, visiting our station will take you some time, so there is no misfortune."

Tygier, who apparently didn't pay attention to the alarm, jumped out of the laboratory, delighted as if he had discovered a vein of gold.

"Man, this girl is a treasure!" He shouted. "The skeleton x-ray shows such deviations from the norm that only finger-licking good! She is one in a billion!"

"You don't have to tell me that," Theo smiled.

"Don't let him look at me like a lab specimen." Oggy demanded tearfully, grabbing Fronda's sleeve again.

"But, miss, I didn't even think about it." The Pole controlled himself a bit and was clearly embarrassed. "You are simply a treasure for science, but that doesn't mean I treat you like a two-headed calf. I am infinitely grateful to you for your agreement to basic research, that's all."

She smiled at him at the speech. Tygier nevertheless made a positive impression on her - tall, athletically built, with thick blond hair and a round face shaded by three-day beard, he could be liked. He had bright eyes and a nice smile, though his teeth were a bit too big. Strongly pointed fangs indicated that it had to be fixed quite a long time ago, at a time when he was "biting", as historians of vampirism used to say. She decided that she liked him.

"Lambdon will be your guide for now," Octavio said. "I need to talk to Mercedes. You can ask him anything, he knows more about this station than anyone else."

"Right," said Tygier. "I used to work here before, even before I left for Paris. Do you have any questions?"

"Where can you smoke here?" Gerard started poking around his pockets nervously for cigarettes. "I really can't take it anymore."

\*\*\*\*\*

The station was built with real panache and it took a long time to learn about it. Four friends visited all the studios in turn, admiring the state-of-the-art equipment, mostly constructed by the station employees themselves. This institution was actually a replica and extension of previous institutes, which were the work of Octavio. This very old, more than a thousand years old vampire was initially an alchemist and as such was perpetuated, transferring in his vampire existence a passion for science in all its manifestations. He gained his education in various ways, studying professional literature the most, but also attending lectures. He used the fact that he is a "marten", which meant less sensitivity to the rays of the sun. His knowledge exceeded all possible boundaries.

"Tell me one thing. You are a believer like me. How do you reconcile science with faith?" Theo asked him as they were leaving the paleobiology lab.

Octavio looked thoughtful.

"Just without God, there's nothing doing," he said after a moment. "Maybe I would lose my faith after so many centuries of dabbling in scientific experiments and deliberations, if I was not tormented by one undeniable evidence of the Act of Creation."

"What proof?" Gerard asked. As a petrified atheist, he was very curious to see if this could be done.

"Simple. That everything exists. I know that the official theory speaks of the Big Bang, but even if we assume the existence of this pra-atom, from which everything was supposed to hatch... it would have to be big, by the way... where would it come from? From nowhere? Only zero can result from zero, that's what mathematics teaches us, and I believe it. If there was nothing, then nothing could be, and if something was, where did it come from? Vicious circle."

The actor shook his head silently. He could not agree with the Spaniard, but he could not find any arguments against his theses. He reached for his pack of Gaulois and stepped aside. Of the four, only he adhered to this purely human addiction - Oggy and Fronda did not smoke at all, Never very rarely and only narghile. Fortunately for him, some of Octavio's colleagues were also smokers, so at every level of the station they saved a place where one could freely indulge in addiction.

When he left the smoking room, his comrades were just finishing a lively discussion with Octavio, who at his sight suggested:

"How about eating something? The canteen is behind the sports department, which in turn is behind the conservatory. It's there. I will have a nap for a moment, and when you come back we will go on sightseeing."

He really looked tired. In the heat of scientific work, institute vampires often forgot about bedtime and worked until they dropped. Usually, they slept a day or two later to stand back to the murderous grind.

"Okay," Never said, "it's time to eat."

"Wait for Lambdon there. For sure, he will end soon."

Tygier, who was to act as their guide, was now checking the results of Oggy's research, but the route to the canteen was so marked that they could do without additional hints. It was enough to follow the arrows, it was impossible to make a mistake.

First they went through a conservatory, full of tropical plants and hummingbirds flying between them - they looked like animated gems. Parrots swung on the branches of the dwarf trees, mainly arakangs and South Zealand kea, although they were noisy by all means fist-sized parrots. Behind this tiny paradise was the sports department. They passed gyms, a fairly large court, where two mixed pairs played a friendly doubles, and a chlorine-smelling swimming pool. Several vampires of both sexes practiced jumping from the trampoline under the watchful eye of a pretty, heavily muscled trainer.

There was a canteen behind the swimming pool. The nice girl behind the buffet handed four canned blood bottles and glasses to friends.

"Not for me. I'm a werewolf," Oggy told her with some embarrassment, feeling her stomach grumble.

"Maybe you want raw beef, honey?" Suggested buffet. "I have a lot of meat for our doctors' dogs in the cold store."

"I didn't know there were dogs here," Theo brightened vividly. She liked animals.

"Dogs, cats, rabbits... Almost every employee has a favorite here. But all this sits in a residential complex. And that animals must eat, we imported meat for them."

"Nice!" Pleased Oggy, who had already prepared for forced fasting and was very dissatisfied with it. She was able to persevere without eating a week, but it was not a pleasure.

Having received quite a bit of rawness, she began to jerk her teeth with a murmur of satisfaction, while the men sipped blood with the addition of orange liqueur. After a while, the buffet sat down to them.

"You must be a group of Rajah," she said. "Shadow told me about you."

"Is Shadow here?" Never was surprised.

"He is. He work in security. Doctors from the paranormal affairs department examined him in every possible way, but they failed to discover what or who this freak is actually."

"Silly question. Shadow is Shadow... Pure intelligence... I think." Indian said uncertainly.

"The current state of science probably excludes the existence of such a thing," Gerard muttered, looking at the light almost black in the glow of blood fluorescent in his glass.

"Science used to exclude the existence of a vacuum," Fronda snorted dismissively. "I remember it very well. Only experience with the Magdeburg hemispheres proved its existence. Maybe, over time, the existence of a Shadow will not be considered something extraordinary at all? After all, science is still going forward. A revolution is taking place in our eyes in medicine and technology, and above all in the way people think. We, theoretically immortals, can best judge this."

"And why aren't we getting older?" Asked Gerard after a moment. "I mean, what is the scientific justification for it?"

"This is a very interesting issue," at the table Tygier grew up and pulled up a chair for himself. "The biostatic agent found in vampire DNA probably blocks a hypothetical enzyme that causes living cells ageing. Although, for example, there are those who thinks that RNA, not DNA is responsible for that."

Theo looked at him wandering eye.

"What's the difference?" He asked helplessly. "Have mercy, Lambdon, I don't even have a high school diploma. I believe in stars and planets because I can see them, but chromosomes, atoms, DNA, forgive me..."

Tygier laughed.

"You may not stare your black eyes like that," he said. "It's actually very simple. DNA is planning protein structure, and RNA is a contractor, like a construction team. Understand? Genetics deals with this department. Vampire RNA must be somehow 'smarter' than human RNA because it does not reduplicate errors that may occur in DNA sequences. The factor of vampirism, conditioning the transformation, are probably plasmoids, such pieces of RNA strand, surrounded by a capsid mantle. Or maybe viroids, looped pieces of thread, even without capsid. Just such creations are responsible for the so-called drug resistance of bacterial strains. By connecting with bacteria, they kind of transfer their information content inside, and thanks to that doctors have a nice trouble."

Fronda shook his head like a man dazed by a blunt blow to the dark.

"I won't deny it because I have no idea what you're talking about," he said and drank straight from the bottle, draining it to the bottom.

Tygier waved a hand at him and changed the subject:

"There's a film up there, that's all the commotion. Within a few days, our bodyguards should know when you can leave safely. For now, you will be our guests. You don't want to sleep?"

Never shook his head and looked questioningly at his companions. Gerard repeated his gesture without a word, because as an actor he was used to sleepless nights and a long day at work.

"It's enough for Octavio to go sleep," Theo said without interrupting his sweet eyes to the buffet.

"A workaholic, like all of them," laughed Tygier. "Crazy scientists."

Despite these critical words, he was no better - he often forgot about bedtime and meals, especially since he worked in all laboratories in turn and felt at home everywhere. He wasn't the only one subject to such rotation. Doctors and associate professors (these degrees were obtained in absentia at renowned universities), the station had more than enough talented lab technicians, unfortunately, much less and were at a premium. Several scientists also worked on a rotational basis, trying to create something like the department of nexialism - applied allism, a scientific discipline described by Van Voght in the "Interplanetary Mission".

Their experiment did not have a great future, as it could not serve people. The average length of human life, especially life understood as full ability to learn and work, is painfully short. Vampires have time that is not given to people, moreover, they are not afraid of typically human degenerative diseases. Probably for this reason, their institute was ahead of this type of institution by an entire era.

They moved on after the meal.

"Actually, why don't you do UFO research?" Gerard asked after a moment, looking around at the studios he passed. "That would suit you."

Tygier interrupted his lecture on the importance of hydroponics for feeding future generations and looked at him indulgently.

"Mainly because we haven't found a single proof of such a problem so far," he replied. "Science doesn't deal with 'one lady said another lady' reports."

"There are eyewitness accounts." Oggy interrupted shyly.

The Pole laughed heartily at this remark.

"Oh, honey," he said, wrapping his arm around her confidently. "In Fronda's time, every other man, regardless of education and social status, was ready to swear before the altar that he saw an angel, a saint, or on the contrary, a witch on a broom and a devil with horns. I am also strangely sure that the vast majority of these people would successfully pass polygraph examinations. Such evidence sucks. Unfortunately. I would give a lot to see an alien."

"When I read the testimony of the woman the aliens abducted," the girl continued. "They did her various tests, and then she couldn't explain where she was."

"Exactly," Theo supported her. "Talk what you want, there is evidence. And not just in the form of testimonies. Although they are also interesting, in all of them there appears the theme of "getting lost" a few hours and conducted research. They leave quite tangible traces, my dear."

"Missing time." Tygier nodded. "It's easy to get it, just give the patient something as banal as opium. You don't even need hypnosis. As for research, Dr. Svanson from the paranormal department put forward a reasonable hypothesis on this subject. He came to the conclusion that the research as such took place, except that they were neither carried out aboard the flying saucer nor were they done by aliens. If in a given area there was a leak, say, some super-secret biological or chemical weapon, and then how to examine selected residents without arousing suspicion? You have to characterize yourself, kidnap a person and give him some drug to cause confusion. Then everything will be blamed on UFOs and finish. The government and army do not have to explain themselves."

"I have a question," Gerard said. They were just in the medical department, and the sight of the research and treatment equipment made him sad memories. "What the hell is pushing scholars and all minds being a vampire? After all, they should not even believe in such a thing as the possibility of consolidation."

He looked at the table, cluttered with test tubes and beakers, trying to guess what they were actually studying. It was, however, beyond his strength.

"What do you think?" Tygier answered him. "Faust syndrome, my dear. Fixation allows you to work any amount of time, not to worry about illness and old age. A dream for a scientist. Let's go further."

Friends went to the workshop, whose central place was taken by a huge saltwater aquarium. The chubby blonde in a white apron was feeding sea anemones with manipulators, being careful not to immerse her hands in water. This caution was advisable by all means, as apart from the anemones, there was a young Medusa of the sea wasp species and several rockfishes in the tank.

"It's Dr. Tamara Kawrechkin, a toxicologist. How's it going, Tamara Siemionowna?" Tygier turned kindly to the girl.

"I've already isolated a few factors that could harm us, but I have a long way to go. For now, it is better not to step on any of these creatures." The doctor answered him, interweaving French words with Russian. At times, they could hardly understand her.

"Are we susceptible to poisons?" Gerard asked with some surprise.

"Some types of venom, yes," replied Dr. Kawrechkin. "For example, the venom of certain snakes or spiders. For example, phoneutria, fortunately extremely rare, seventy times more venomous than the king cobra. Not just her. Everything that causes hemolysis harms us. I recommend my work on American linyphiidae."

"What is this devil?" Fronda asked, coming up to the table something was walking around.

He jumped back with a slight cry of disgust, after a moment. On the table, fenced with strips nailed to the edge, the spider salmon pink bird-eater majestic moved, even huge for its species - it was almost the size of a plate, brown, covered with silky hair.

"What kind of reptile is that?!" Theo shouted, unable to hide his chills.

"You don't have eyes? It's not a reptile, it's a spider. Arthropod." The Russian came to the table and put her hand to the salmon pink bird-eater, on which the giant climbed nimbly up to her shoulder. "Where have you been hiding that you don't know such things? Chikita is a giant salmon pink bird-eater, quite rare and extremely intelligent."

"I hate spiders, intelligent or not. She's lucky I didn't smash her with shoe." Fronda still couldn't shake the impression.

"You're the lucky one because I would tear you apart. Where did you go from the Middle Ages?"

He looked at her with dignity and resentment.

"As a matter of fact. However, I am not at all backward: I know that it is necessary to protect rainforests, segregate waste and fight so that various paid in millions hookers do not wear fur from protected animals. However, I just loathe of spiders and will not cry when one day these nasties disappear from the face of the Earth. You can't convince me here."

"I'm not going to do that either. Think what you want. If you were to disappear, there would be nothing to regret, that's for sure." The doctor was clearly angry and her gray eyes were fluttering anger.

Tygier laughed, amused.

"Give him a break, Tamara," he asked. "Don't require him to understand things like your fascination with all filth. You probably don't know, my dear, but Tamara also conducts research on collective consciousness in some insects, such as ants and bees."

"Collective consciousness? Does that mean that a swarm of bees is as wise as a man?" Gerard looked at Dr. Kawrechkin completely surprised.

She snorted angrily.

"Their intelligence is not growing exponentially. They just have collective consciousness... but you won't understand it anyway."

"I'm not an idiot, although I may look like that," said Theo.

"And yes, you do," confirmed Dr. Kawrechkin.

"Blah blah blah. I hate insects anyway."

"Mercy! Spiders are not insects!"

"Insects will survive us all," Oggy said. "They even survive nuclear annihilation because they have chitin armor."

"I don't know about chitin, but I used to wear armor myself... sometimes even armor," Theo dreamed.

"And what, they put you on a horse with a crane?" Asked Gerard, who saw a similar scene in one of the films.

He looked at him pityingly and tapped his forehead with a bent finger.

"No, where did this idea come from? The armor weighed over a dozen kilograms, but we were able to move in them quite efficiently. Otherwise, it would have been pointless. The knight, as you know, had to have big muscles..."

"And an empty head, it can be seen even today." The doctor said to him, stroking the spider curled on her shoulder with one finger.

Tygier, laughing, pulled the Frenchman ready for some sharp answer to the corridor. He was about to explain to him that Tamara

Siemionowna was unparalleled in fencing when her friends' attention was caught by something else.

High in the corridor wall, a vent hole blew, once securely guarded, now exposed by oblivion. A small mulatto in a red overall stood under this hole, crying tearfully:

"Sparky! Kitty! Come here, kitty!"

Ventilation suited her with furious mewing and snorting.

"Can I help you, lady?" Knightly Fronda, as always, was near her in a moment.

"Sparky got into the vent, when the rotors turn on, it will be his end." The girl moaned.

"Help me, Rajah," Fronda said to Never.

"You'd better be careful. This Sparky is a caracal, not a domestic kitty, and he is crazy." Tygier warned him, but Theo just waved his hand and climbed the vent on the Indian's back.

"Gee whiz, how lovely he is!" He called with delight.

"Be careful, he is very nervous," Mulatto asked, stepping nervously from foot to foot.

"Say better crazy bully," said Tygier unsatisfied. "Oh, Trelawny, can't you just set up an aquarium or buy a hamster? And why is Sparky here? It was said that pets are to stick to the housing department."

"Don't whine. Sometimes you act like an old woman in a student dormitory." Theo reached into the hole in the wall without fear and pulled out a fawn tomcat who was defending himself fiercely. "Please, miss, here is the loss."

The cat flicked its short tail and leapt into Trelawny's arms with excruciating mew. The girl climbed on her fingers, kissed Fronda's cheek in thanks and disappeared into the elevator.

"This crazy girl is from the engineering department. She's crazy about various clever cameras and the crazy little cat. She probably pulled him out of all the sensitive points of our institute, because he is still running away. Well, let's go further. Here we have..." Tiger stopped, because the door, bearing the inscription "Weight room" suddenly opened right in front of his nose and a young man in a lab coat came out, like a glove matching the stereotype of the "crazy scientist". He was quite short, gray, with lush hair protruding in all directions and untidy hair. He didn't look encouraging, but Fronda glowed like the sun seeing him.

"Simon!" He shouted. "And you are here?! In life, I would not expect!"

"How are you, Thierry?" The scientist hugged him cheerfully. "I thought after the revolution that you're dead, but as you can see, it is not easy to harm you."

"Let me, he is my old friend, Simon Mage once called him," Theo turned to his friends.

"Can you make magic?" Oggy asked shyly.

He shook his head with a smile.

"I wouldn't want to disappoint you, child, but I can't even get a banal rabbit out of my hat. Simply put, in the olden days people thought of magic everything they didn't understand. What are you doing here? Do you want to work scientifically?"

"God save me," Fronda said. "I have been here recently and already have a claustrophobic attack. I prefer to act on the surface. How do you withstand this seal underground?"

"Somehow," Simon said dismissively. "Come to my studio later, maybe I will have an interesting offer for you."

Oggy tugged on Fronda's shirt sleeve.

"Why is he addressing you per Thierry?" She asked quietly.

"It's a popular Celtic form of the ancient Greek name Theodoric," her friend explained. "Another form is Gallic Astheorix, yes, my dear. Names are a funny thing, but ultimately everyone must have one."

"You blow smoke up my ass as usual," she nudged him lightly under the rib.

The tour of the station continued, and they watched its subsequent levels with growing admiration. It was really huge. The first users expanded the underground Frankist bunker, pierced the corridors into the network of suburban canals that had not been used for years, and created an almost self-sufficient city. On sixteen levels, there were a total of one hundred and twenty studios, fifteen libraries, a residential department, a cinema and a recreation and sports complex. Over one hundred scientists of both sexes and technical staff worked there permanently. The size and modern equipment of the station could be staggering, especially when someone realized that it was all underground, in the middle of Europe, near the unsuspecting city.

"I'm surprised that you wanted to do all this." Fronda summed up when they finally finished the inspection and returned to the paranormal department, or rather, as the corresponding "Considered paranormal" plaque said. There they found Octavio, discussing fiercely with Simon on an apparently serious topic.

"It's good you are here," di Mauro said at the sight of them. "We have a case for you... actually two cases."

"Nice," Fronda said, looking around the studio. "Hey, apparently you don't deal with UFOs!" He roared after a moment. "And what it is? Chopped liver?!"

Everyone burst out laughing because the sight of Fronda, triumphantly waving a flying saucer model, was extremely comical.

"Unfortunately, my poor friend," Simon said when he could speak calmly. "It's just a model of an experimental American rotor. The project was abandoned because the fuel consumption with this hull shape is fifty percent higher than in traditional models. This shape can work in a vacuum of space, but not in an atmosphere as dense as Earth's. I have to disappoint you: there really isn't a single confirmed information about UFOs. Each observation has the most earthly explanation, from swamp fires to secret prototypes of military fighters, although UFOnauts do not want to acknowledge this."

Clearly dissatisfied with his reply, Fronda began to watch the boards hanging on the walls.

"Simon, what are these charts?" He asked after a moment.

"This? Tricia hanged it, my lab worker. On the left you have the theoretical scheme of fuel production based on single-atom hydrogen. If we could implement this, we would have the most ecological fuel on Earth. And on the right," the alchemist came to see better. "Ah, yes. It is also a theoretical chart. It concerns the matter of so-called spontaneous ignition of the human body. There were reports of such cases in the cobblestones, but I personally do not believe that this would be possible. The human body consists mainly of water."

Fronda looked at both charts curiously.

"And water is mainly hydrogen, right? If he were to split hydrogen in the living organism with water into this monatomic..."

"Thierry, please! The tripe falls over when I hear such nonsense," Simon interrupted him with disgust. "Do you even know what you are saying? Monatomic hydrogen is difficult to obtain and unstable. If someone were able to develop a process of synthesis and storage of this miracle, Rockefeller would be a beggar with him. Don't tell me it can happen by itself, just inside a living body!"

"For a paranormal investigator, you stand on the ground amazingly hard," Never laughed.

"You'll be surprised, but it's indispensable when you want to study the inexplicable," said Octavio. "Sit down, now we'll talk seriously."

The guests, obeying his words, sat around the laboratory table and looked at the host expectantly.

"As you know, we have our limits," the Spaniard began. "We are a reluctant people to travel, which is not always good. Of course, we correspond with the whole world, but nothing can replace, so to speak, an operational group in the field. You are more open and that is why I want to offer you a reconsideration of a permanent job for the Institute."

"Go on," Never said, with a glint in his eye.

"You would gather information about strange events for us, and also solve puzzles that require a personal look at everything. It's all for a fair remuneration."

"Money will be useful. We're broke," said Theo sadly.

"Let's say we agree," Never silenced him with a wave of his hand and stared at Octavio.

"To start with, I will give you what we have prepared a long time ago," di Mauro took a few boxes out of the cabinet. They contained a variety of items, including vials with colored liquids and, which surprised everyone, jewelry. They stared at it with stupid faces.

"These are detectors and a set of antidotes, a camera with additional film rolls plus a contact address to which you will send exposed film." The Spaniard showed his friends a card resembling a business card. "And various useful little things. Of course, it's all free."

Theo was primarily interested in a camera of the size and shape of a pocket watch. He never ignored the spy gadget, but instead picked up one of the detectors and began to watch it. It looked like a bracelet made of a piece of flattened chain and an engraved plaque. It was slightly thicker than standard jewelry of this type, and a miniature microphone grid was on the side of the tablet.

"Near chemically pure silver, it will start to squeak," Octavio said in a tone of explanation.

"Useful," Indian admitted meekly. "Free, you say... Experience has taught me that what you get for free is usually very expensive."

"Don't be so distrustful, Rajah."

"Better put the cards on the table, redheads. It's hard to fool me. Something is happening here, something you can't handle."

They measured their eyes for a moment, then a sad smile appeared on the Spaniard's lips.

"I'd rather you were wrong. But yes, we have a problem. And I admit it openly, that's why I brought you here instead of giving you this whole stuff somewhere on the surface, in an agreed place."

Friends abandoned the gadgets they were watching and came closer to not miss a single word.

"A spy is hiding at the station. I am sure of it, although at the same time I know that he has not forwarded any messages to principals yet."

"How do you know?" Gerard asked, paling.

"I know because I closed the station and blocked all contact with the surface," Octavio replied calmly.

Never scratched his back of his head and frowned.

"Okay, so how do you know you have a spy here? Because, as I understand it, it's just circumstantial evidence, otherwise you would catch the bastard."

"It's not so simple. See, I know everyone here personally. I'm not objective, because I can't believe that one of them was a traitor."

"So how...?"

"Have you seen the aviary? I accidentally caught one of the parakeets while I was outside. She had a microfilm capsule on her paw. Even if she left herself, which is impossible, she would not attach anything. Understand? Someone smuggled in a trained bird to carry messages."

That did not sound good.

"What's on the microfilm?" Never asked after a moment.

"Patents. Documentation of several of our inventions."

"So, industrial espionage is at stake, not Van Helsing. Good for that."

"Yes, but that's not good." Simon said. "Someone of "ours" is selling the test results we are all working on. We need to know who."

Oggy grunted, which sounded like a muffled bark. They looked at her.

"There shouldn't be a problem with that," she said. "Show me this microfilm and this parrot."

"For what?"

"Great idea!" Never immediately understood what the girl meant. "Her sense of smell is worth all the money of the world. Come on!"

Di Mauro did not look particularly convinced, but he left and after a moment brought a cage with a screeching cockatiel and a transparent microfilm box. He put both on the table.

Everyone stared at Oggy. The girl first opened the microfilm box and, with closed eyes, checked the smell of its contents for a long time. Then she brought her nose closer to the cage, almost sliding it between the rods and avoiding the pecking. She inhaled loudly several times, like a sniffing hound.

"I think I already know which smell it is," she finally said, raising her head. "Come on. We have to make a round at the station again. But first..."

She came over to Octavio and sniffed him thoroughly. Then she did the same with Simon and Tygier, who protested violently.

"Relax, I just had to be sure," she answered his words. "Now I know it's none of you and I can keep looking."

"Let's go then. I am coming with you, I want to know who this treacherous slut is. He won't live long enough to enjoy his money."

Oggy snorted in disgust.

"Eh, this Polish viciousness... It's enough to banish him."

"No, it is not enough." Octavio unexpectedly supported Tygier. "If he sold our patents for money, he would bring hunters here for a correspondingly larger amount. Weeds must be exterminated, not out of the door."

Gerard wanted to say something but remained silent. He was still against killing, and his humanistic soul rebelled against the killing of anyone. Never had to feel his dilemma because he turned to him.

"Stay with Simon. Until we return, no one can enter this studio, no matter what they say."

Gerard nodded and immediately asked:

"And if someone wants to come in?"

This is a simple question, do not know why, unexpectedly disturbed the Indian.

"Oh mother, you blow him with something heavy! Do I have to tell you everything? A little imagination, artist!"

"Calm down, Rajah, I'll lock the door." Simon thought it's appropriate to break the nascent row. "Nobody will enter here, not even on his dead body. You have my word."

Moving away, they heard the clink of a key in the lock, indicating that the alchemist had taken his declaration seriously. Nobody said it out loud, but everyone was relieved. They liked Gerard, but they knew well that if he had to fight he would be the least effective member of the team. He did not like bloodshed and refused to use violence, even when it turned out to be absolutely necessary.

Even if the staff of the institute were surprised at the return visits, they did not show it. They seemed completely absorbed in their work. Certainly their commitment would surprise anyone who has a standard idea of vampires and their habits.

"Over time, commitment to work, which is a passion for life, increases." Said Octavio. "Especially among those of us who become more and more agoraphobic with age. They must have a purpose in life, and with time it gets harder and harder."

"You don't like traveling too?" Oggy asked, without interrupting the air smell test."

"I? No, it's not a problem for me. But for example Mercedes hates leaving the underground. She only does this, when she really has to."

"Where is she now?" Fronda asked vividly, looking around slightly.

Octavio poked him under the shoulder blade.

"Paws and teeth from my sister from afar," he warned playfully. "She is invulnerable. Anyway, she would break your bones if you tried something. I warn you, several have already found out that it is better not to pick her up."

"Well, but where is she now?" Theo persisted.

"She's probably working on a new picture at home. She doesn't like company. She's a loner. If you had any hopes, you'd better let it go."

Fronda murmured something incomprehensible. No difficulty had ever deterred him from the woman he had chosen, and it was obvious that he was already thinking about how to meet Mercedes in private.

Oggy, sniffing around the corners, thankfully did not hear this exchange. Focused on her task, she entered the studio, sniffed the walls of corridors, sometimes turned back and made a circle, at times she almost stood on all fours. Nobody paid special attention to her. Octavio's words suggested that they did not see such things here and probably take her behavior as another behavioral department experiment.

They went down and down. At each subsequent level, the girl shook her head after completing the tour of the studio and utility rooms. They followed her without losing hope, though there was less and less chance of finding something. Finally, she stopped helplessly.

"Nothing," she whispered. "Several times I caught the olfactory trace, but weak," she broke off for a moment, then hit her forehead with her open hand. "Idiot!"

"What?" Octavio was surprised.

"And you aren't better, hotshots! What are you waiting for? Lead to the housing department! Do you have access to all accommodation units?"

The conclusion was so obvious that everyone groaned with one voice. How could they not figure out where to start searching?

"We'll use the elevator, it'll be faster," di Mauro decided.

The residential department was slightly above the first level of the laboratories, just above the recreational department. The smell in the corridor was so pronounced that Oggy would have no hesitation in bringing friends to the right room.

The sign on the door read "Nick Harmon".

"Without a doubt. Here lived the man who dealt with the parrot and put the microfilm into the capsule." She said categorically.

"Holy shit," Octavio muttered, looking around the spartan room. "That's our supply man. I sent him..." he paled violently. "...I sent him a few days ago to the Vito Ricci colony!"

"Can he be dangerous to them?" Never frowned. Only he was not disturbed.

"Who knows? If he is so greedy that he has robbed the station, anything is possible."

"We must go there. I hope nobody snatched a car in the meantime. It stayed where your sister took us."

"No worries. I sent my best sidekick to watch over it."

"Sidekick?"

"That's what we call, so to speak, internal protection. Come on? Not everyone has a solid brain, some work here as security guards or staff, and they are also needed."

"Well, they didn't show off," Theo said sarcastically.

"What you want, first of all, I failed. Come, I will give you a picture of Nick and lead you to the surface, we will only take your friend along the way. I do not know what will be useful for you, but ultimately..."

An hour later, friends were already sitting in their camper and rushing at the highest speed toward the Sierra Nevada. The commune in which Vito and his clan lived was on the slope of Puntal Caldera. Getting there was very difficult, but they already knew a convenient shortcut, which is a secret for most people.

"And how do we find him?" Gerard finally dared to break the silence in the car. "What must we do? You said yourself that we are not killers hired."

"Because we're not," Never accelerated, "but it looks like we won't have much choice. Fanfan, noble soul, artist of God, so always full of ideals... The world is not what you think."

"You mean what?"

"Like black and white. Sometimes, to prevent something nasty, you have to reach for the decks of evil in our interior. There is no other way. Believe me, I have experience."

The actor winced and said nothing more. He snuggled into the corner of the camper and pulled his knees up to his chin, falling into silence. He understood well that sometimes you need to reach for radical solutions, but he still shuddered at the thought of them. He hated violence. Besides, it's different to fight for your life, and different to go somewhere to shoot someone on the spot. He could not come to terms with such a thing and did not want to participate.

They passed the first "gate", i.e. the place where the inhabitants of the community hid the alarm sensor. Then another one. They were surprised that nobody tried to stop the car and see where it was going. Vito told them that if they received a signal from one of the "gates" they immediately send two of their dressed up as police officers. They control passers-by, issue a ticket and direct them to a different route under some pretext. Meanwhile, no one was visible. The stony road, overgrown with tree roots, was empty and calm, so to speak, too calm.

"I have a bad feeling." Never muttered under his breath. "Maybe this is not the way?"

"I'm afraid, however, this the right one." Theo spread a map on his lap and tried to understand something from it. "If Vito did not lead us up the garden path, then two more turns, and we will be there."

"Leave it and check your guns. You two too." The Indian looked at Oggy and Gerard. "Have you heard? Keep your guns ready, and I don't want to hear any nonsense like someone here doesn't like bloodshed."

"Oh, come off," Gerard reluctantly took his magnum from the storage under the armchair, examined it carefully, and reloaded it just in case. Just because he didn't feel like shooting, it didn't mean he wanted to be surprising without a gun. He knew how it would end.

The camper made two more turns and drove to the rising diagonally behind the tree line. In the distance there were three single-family houses, stylized in the style of cottages of Old Spanish highlanders.

"I think it's here," Theo said uncertainly.

"I think so," Never agreed with him. "Don't you think there's something wrong here?"

It wasn't just him, who think like that. There was no light in any of the houses, the windows were dark and still. Nobody went out to check what was happening, and there was no indication that the defenders were lurking somewhere in the dark.

"That's not good," Fronda muttered.

Oggy growled in yes. Her hair bristled slightly on the parietal and occiput, her nails gripping the handle of the hand magnum darkened, thickened and lengthened into claws.

Taking all precautions they got off the camper. There something weird about the silence, and it certainly wasn't natural for a settlement inhabited by twenty-five people of both sexes.

Oggy sniffed and growled again, this time with a fear she couldn't hide.

"It smells of death here," she whispered. "Blood, lots of blood."

"Someone alive?" Never asked after a moment.

"Yes. Man. The woman." She sniffed for a while longer. "It's Gina! She is here..."

"Gina?" Fronda raised his eyebrows high. Oggy nodded, looking around alertly.

"We're searching everything. Don't split up." Never ordered harshly. "And silence until I say otherwise."

Already the first apartment discovered four bodies - all stretched out on the floor, with pegs embedded in the chest. The house looked like a cyclone. Oggy growled, sniffing the dangerous smells, and trembled all over her body. She knew that in the dog form she would have realized the situation faster, but she preferred to remain human and be able to use the pistol in her hand.

"What a butchery," Never murmured, making sure everyone found was dead. "We're going on. Keep peace and quiet."

Another house, more dead bodies. And everything was ruined. It wasn't until the third that Gina's fragrance became clear enough for Oggy to say without hesitation:

"It's here. In the basement."

They quickly searched all the rooms and only then headed for the stairs from the basement. If it weren't for the werewolf, they wouldn't even find them. The entrance was perfectly camouflaged in the floor and locked from the inside with a latch. Never tapped the staves and, after tapping out the place of mounting the latch, put a magnum barrel on it.

"I'm shooting, against the wall!" He shouted, waited a second and pressed the trigger.

A single bullet smashed the staple, the flap dropped to reveal the stairs. Gerard turned on the flashlight - everyone could see quite well in the dark, but not so much. Almost immediately there was a muffled sound of a shot, and the bullet dangled dangerously close to the light source.

"Stop!" Cried Fronda. "Gina, it's us! We won't do anything bad to you!"

A beam of light swept the underground shelter. At the bottom of the stairs was a man from the photo. Thanks to his snow white hairs was obvious that he is dead. The blood-flooded shirt with a hole blackening at the height of the heart left no doubt as to how he died. Then the light came out of the darkness huddled against the wall, a shivering girl and another man in whom they met Vito. He lived, although at first glance one could become convinced that it would not last long.

Oggy approached Gina, and drew a small browning pistol from her fingers.

"It's okay," she said reassuringly. "We're here."

"Careful," Never warned her. "She certainly has silver bullets. They'll burn you if you touch them."

He crossed Nick's body and walked over to Vito. Crouched beside him, he began to examine his injuries and makeshift dressings, which the daughter had put on.

"I... I killed him," Gina moaned desperately. "And probably one of those... Father was wounded... There were too many... We tried to hide, but he found us... He knew about the hideout... Shoot... I shot at him and locked the lid..."

Fronda embraced her and hugged her tightly.

"You must have, *cherie*," he said reassuringly. "Sometimes it is that there is no other way. You saved your father. You were very brave."

"Don't trouble yourself, she is shocked." Rajah raised his head. "We take them to the cart. Vito requires quick surgery and Gina requires strong sedatives."

"How did it even happen? How were they surprised?" Gerard helped him raise half-conscious Ricci from the floor.

"Undoubtedly Nick's work. Octavio was right in saying that whoever loves money too will not only sell patents. Support him more strongly and do not release the second hand. It is not known if anyone is lurking on us."

Together, they led Vito outside. The rest followed them. Gina was still shaking so much that she almost fell, and Fronda finally had to take her in his arms. Contrary to fear, no one was waiting for them. The attackers had to recognize that they had done their part and left in the unknown, satisfied with the liquidation of another vampire commune. Probably not the first in their career and perhaps not the last.

"Rajah, I don't want to bring you down, but lightly counting, the Hunters are already leading ten to the egg with us," Theo said, placing the still hysterical Gina on the mattress at the back of the camper. "We have serious problems."

"Talk to me yet," Never helped Vito lie down on the second mattress. "As if I didn't know. Gina, stop roaring at last because I can't collect my thoughts! Oggy, give me a first aid kit."

"Your or human?"

"Give both of them!"

He broke the neck of one of the ampules, took a transparent liquid into the syringe and stuck the needle into the sobbing girl's shoulder. She didn't even notice it in annoyance. After a short moment she was quiet and Never could take care of her father alone.

"He should survive," he said, examining him carefully. "He was very lucky."

"And has a good daughter," said Vito barely audible. He opened his eyelids slightly. "If it wasn't for her, they would stick a stake in my heart like others."

He hissed in pain as he never adjusted the pressure dressing.

"This baby so fighting?" Fronda asked, trying say it in lightly tone.

"I don't know. But when the time of trial came, she knew how to behave," he caught the air with short, shallow breaths. "She hit one of them with a stool on the head and took his weapon. And when Nick ran after us to the basement, before she could close it, she shot him like a dog."

"He had a pistol for silver bullets."

"It is clear. He was a hunter. Like all of them. Nick brought them in. A bastard."

"You'd better not say anything anymore. You have a damaged lung," the Indian poured a few drops of strengthening tincture into his mouth, tried and tested many times. "We're taking you to Octavio."

"And Gina?"

"She sleeps. I gave her a barbiturate. Just in case, she would not know the way to the institute yet."

"She won't betray."

"I told you to keep quiet. You probably are right, but we won't risk it. Gerard, sit behind the wheel. I have to stay with them. They both need a doctor."

*****

Mercedes smiled at Fronda, looking at her paintings as if he were admiring the greatest treasures of the Louvre.

"I didn't know you knew art."

"Because I do not know." He answered her honestly. "I divide paintings into two categories: those that I do not like and those that I like. I find yours beautiful."

"You speak honestly?"

"Of course. If I didn't like them, I would say that I know nothing about art."

They both laughed. It was obvious that maybe Fronda's personal charm won here by defeating the coldness of the beautiful Spaniard.

"Okay, enough of these romances," Octavio said, peeking into his sister's room. "Come, Theo. Rajah is impatient. I have a well-paid job for you, but it will require a long journey."

"China?"

"No, but you're close. Russia."

"Oh, that sounds interesting."

He followed di Mauro to the well-known Simon Mage studio in the Recognized-Supernatural Affairs department. Everyone was sitting there. Gerard was reading the newspaper, Oggy was playing with a parrot whose cage still occupied a place on the table, and Never talked to Simon. He paused at the sight of Fronda.

"You are finally here, you provincial Casanova," he said sourly. "Haven't you ever stayed away from Mercedes?"

"Come on? I just watched her paintings. What's wrong with that?" Fronda put his hands in his pockets and looked at his friend defiantly.

The Indian waved a hand in discouragement.

"You will never change," he said and turned to Octavio. "Is that all?"

"Yes, I gave you a set of documents. Do you have any questions?"

"I have," said Gerard. "What will happen to Gina?"

"We'll see. For now, she must rest and recover. It is not your concern anymore."

"Indeed," Never agreed with him. "Okay, so let's go. If anything bad happened it wasn't our fault and watch out for hunters."

"And you watch out for Gusto Vanderbelt." Octavio threw it right back. "He is still alive and tracking."

"Let's not judge him too harshly," Simon sighed. "Let's not forget that in the film and literature the Vampire Hunter is always a positive hero, so after proper brainwashing someone like this traitor could simply believe in his mission."

"Oh, shut up," Fronda and Oggy called almost simultaneously.

"Come on?"

"A good hunter is a dead hunter," Never said grimly. "Although our "Ge-ge"[10] probably will protest soon."

Everyone looked at the actor, who shrugged reluctantly and said nothing. Despite so many corpses seen on his way, he still didn't believe that violence could be a cure for anything.

Never waved his hand.

"Does not matter. Let's go. I don't know what is with you, but I'm getting claustrophobic. I don't like being locked up, especially underground, like in a grave."

"A matter of taste. We don't understand here how you can roam the world the way you do it." Octavio smiled, wrinkling his freckled nose. "Good luck and remember about the documentation and where to send it. You work for us again.

Fronda touched the watch hung on the jeans belt, inside which a tiny camera hid, and raised his thumb up.

"Address Meyerbeer 28, Brussels. I remember."

"Well then, Vaya con dios."[11]

"Merci, mon vieux."[12]

Oggy suppressed a laugh.

"No offense, Fronda, but I really would like to know what your God would say about what you do now and who you have become," she said maliciously as she followed a friend into the elevator.

---

[10] In France, **Gege** is a diminutive of Gerard, just like Nana is of Anna.

[11] *(spanish)* Go with God.

[12] *(fr.)* Thanks, buddy.

"We'll both find out someday," he replied seriously, putting his arm around her. "Unfortunately, sometimes you can't live the way you want. I hope He understands this."

# Part 2 - When Demons Awake

"If you accept this assignment, you'll get one hundred thousand of green. In advance."

Fronda whistled through his teeth, clearly stunned by the amount of the sum. Never silenced him with a short glance.

"Go on," he encouraged the red-haired Spaniard.

"I won't hide it, the job is disgusting," Octavio continued. "But you may still accept them. You have to kill someone."

"Wait, we just had to find someone! We're not paid killers... I think...?" Gerard protested.

Octavio ran his fingers through the red head. He caught up with four friends at the airport and was glad that he managed to catch them. Two hours left to take off, so he managed to persuade them to visit the airport café. He knew, however, that he would face a difficult task of convincing them to listen to him.

"I know this. However, listen to me to the end, before you make your final decision."

"I spoke on the phone with the leader of the Russian subculture. He speaks English poorly, by the way. They've always been isolated, more than any other vampires. They didn't want to have anything to do with capitalists, so we know very little about them. After the collapse of the USSR, their stabilized situation changed radically. Now it is very dangerous there and it looks like our Russian colleagues have stopped doing well. The thing is that Russia is currently ruled by mafia structures, fuel barons, having their own army and their own small kingdoms, which the official police or army will not even approach."

"As you make your bed so you must lie on it" Fronda muttered sarcastically.

"One of such barons, Genadij Osipowich Rolskij, is a great lover of illegal fights, modeled on gladiator fights. As rumor has it, he kidnaps strong men and forces them to fight."

"What do we have to do with it?" Never interrupted sharply, frowning in dissatisfaction.

"Trouble began when he discovered the existence of vampires. As you know, we are not as strong as they say about us, but nevertheless it is difficult to defeat one of us in combat. We are more agile, we have predator reflexes and much more resistance to blows than ordinary people. This makes us perfect recruits. So Rolskij started looking for vampires and quickly learned how to do it. The result of his search was that someone from our blood began to help him. He is responsible for at least ten dead, and many others are trapped in his estate."

"That's terrible," Fronda frowned, and his eyes began to cast lightning.

Octavio nodded.

"In addition, if he ever thinks about say what he knows... understand? Even today, Russians are quite primitive, they believe in what seems impossible to people here more easily. Think of the mass hunt, not a relatively small group of Hunters, who have no support from official services, but entire villages. So it was in the deep Middle Ages, and even later and how many of us survived?"

"Do you think this Russians can start something like that?" Oggy asked dubiously.

"You really have to stop him. But where does this idea come from that we can succeed?" Never, apparently, had a different kind of doubt.

"I think Rolskij's mysterious helper is Gusto Vanderbelt," Octavio said, looking at the table where the coffee cups were intact. "From what my informant said, it's possible. Russians don't know him. You, yes. The conclusions are obvious."

There was a heavy silence. It has still not been officially confirmed that Gusto was helping the IVH Hunters for some reason, but all the evidence clearly pointed to him. Former friends of the sympathetic Austrian found it difficult to come to terms with it and still hoped that the circumstances had just conspired against him.

"There is one problem," Gerard said after a moment. "Let's even say that we agree to serve our cause as killers, although I announce in advance that regardless of the case I will not kill anyone. It's just that none of us knows Russian. How are we going to talk there?"

It had never occurred to anyone before, although the matter was elementary. Intoxicated by the fact that they succeed, they took it for sure thing that they would manage somehow.

"I've thought about that before. I will send a Tygier with you. He is Polish, but almost everyone there knows Russian," said Octavio. "Irka Kralova or Tamara would be better, but Irka did not hate traveling, and Tamara once told me that she would never, at any price, return to the Soviet Union, whether it was former or not. She has her reasons, and we should not be persuaded her. So, Lambdon will go."

"Then we'll have fun. Lambdon does not recognize sovereignty, and he always acts according to his own vision." Theo snorted.

Octavio shrugged.

"It's your problem how you master him. Nobody else will go with you and you need a translator. Russians rarely know foreign languages, and even less often want to use them. So, what is your decision?"

Never looked at his friends. Gerard sat pale and terrified, Oggy snuggled into Fronda's hand. As usual, she didn't care what would happen, as long as she was with Theo, whose eyes were now shining with suspect. It has already been said that he needs dangerous adventures to live. Never even had a name for what troubled him -

adrenalineholia. He needed powerful stimuli so that the concentration of adrenaline in his blood would reach the level that satisfied him. It was known in advance that he would agree to everything.

And Gerard? He was completely different from them, and one could not be sure that he could handle this task.

"Don't look like that," the actor said, as if he had guessed his thoughts. "I will not desert, although I must admit that I am not delighted. I'd rather not get to some mine or to a lumberjack camp in Siberia."

"We've all read 'The Gulag Archipelago'," Octavio interrupted tartly. "Your fear may help you not to get into trouble. There you will really be like in a hostile zone during the war."

"Honey alone," Theo chuckled.

Gerard gave him a look of anguish. Sometimes he wanted to leave this crazy company and hide in some quiet place, but he was aware that he would not live long. He needed them, so he had to accept that the life he leads with them would always be far from comfortable.

*****

They did not prepare the plan. It would be a tactical mistake if they didn't know all the data yet. The commander of the operation was of course Never, and Lambdon Tygier subordinated quite easily as for his rebellious nature.

"You're so crazy, since you agreed to this mission," he said openly as they waited for customs. "But since you are agreed for this, nobody will say that I, a Pole of flesh and blood, are a coward in comparison with you. Never can be a commander, but don't try to talk to anyone. I will be a liaison officer."

"Is Lambdon Tygier a Polish surname?" Oggy asked curiously.

"Not at all. This is the name of the character from the Polish playwright Witkacy," replied Tygier. "I had to name myself after emigration, because no one outside the country could pronounce my name."

"I can try. What is your name?" Gerard looked at him questioningly.

"Mścisław Strzegborski." Replied Tygier and laughed with satisfaction seeing that the actor's eyes became big.

"Can you name in that way?" He asked in obvious disbelief.

Theo patted him on the back with a laugh.

"Give a break, Fanfan. Nobody has ever repeated it.

Gerard shook his head and, silently moving his mouth, tried to pronounce what he heard, but it proved beyond his strength. He tried again. His desperate efforts were interrupted by a call to customs.

After passing through the chamber, he finally gave up on diction exercises and, looking at his friends, he noticed that Fronda had lost his humor.

"Keep your head up, it won't be so bad," he comforted him.

"Back off. I hate planes. If God wanted people to fly, he would give them wings," Theo growled reluctantly.

"And if he wanted them to swim, he would give those fins," replied the actor, "do not be such a backward, because it badly affects the beauty. I would even go to a space rocket if they suggested it to me."

"There is no such thing."

Theo insisted that the entire NASA and USSR space program was a cleverly faked fraud, and no physical evidence would have convinced him otherwise. In general, progressing in this case showed remarkable stubbornness. While he was very interested in all UFO reports, he couldn't understand that with so many financial problems of Earthlings, famines, wars and tornadoes, someone was wasting billions of dollars a year to "allow a few crazy walkers on the moon," as he said in short and bluntly space program. Pictures? Fabricated. Transmission? Filmed in a better studio. Rocks? There are a lot of stones on Earth. There was no way for him to change his attitude.

"Sit down and don't whine," Never ordered. "Oggy, control yourself. Theo, take a chill if you wash out and don't say too much, because you can blurt something out. Hey miss, cognac for this man!"

"After the start, sir. Now fasten your seat belts," the flight attendant answered politely.

Fronda, as pale as death, closed his eyes and dug his nails into the arms of the chair. His aversion to flying was not entirely unfounded - during the Second War he was supposed to be parachuted onto the enemy and literally the moment he jumped, his plane was hit from the ground. The force of the explosion threw Fronda so far away from the drop point that he had to break through to his unit all night, barely avoiding hostile positions. As a result of a bang, he lost his hearing for over ten days, and his tanned hair only grew after a month. Until now, it was not known how he did not suffer any serious injuries.

Oggy, who, as always, took her seat next to Fronda, took his hand. It was freezing, so she squeezed it lightly as if to say:

"I'm with you."

Hearing the thunder of running engines, Theo clenched his teeth tightly. When the plane took off safely and the beautiful stewardess finally handed him the glass of cognac ordered by Never, he drank it in one gulp and asked for a second one in a choked whisper. Only then he dared to open his eyes.

Gerard shook his head slightly at his friend. He had no idea how he could drink pure alcohol. Exceptionally a vampire weighed on such a thing without diluting the drink with plasma.

"The flight will be long," Never said. "Let's ask for a menu card."

"I think it's a passenger list," giggled Tygier.

"Do not be stupid. We have to order this to camouflage, otherwise we are dripping that something is wrong with us." The Indian spat.

This was their main problem when they had to be between people. While they could drink any liquid if they need, they were unable to swallow anything that would be solid body. The narrowed and extremely sensitive vampire esophagus excludes such a thing.

"Let's order anything and hide it slightly," Gerard suggested. With his acting skills, he never had trouble pretending to be eating something.

"I think we'll have to," Never said grimly. "It's a long flight, they'd be surprised we don't eat anything. Fronda, just don't drink anymore because you may lose your temper."

"Don't lecture me," Theo snapped.

When he was afraid of something real, he was always grim and aggressive. Even the best friends found it difficult to bear with him then, but Never got used to it long ago. Others had to adapt somehow, as landing could not be expected soon.

"Indeed, we'd better order something and then pretend we're asleep," said Tygier, who didn't like planes either, for reasons other than Fronda.

The flight was supposed to take a long time, but due to the change of time zones along the way they flew in a continuous night and were to land in such part of a day. Their happiness was the existence of such lines, created for lovers of night flights. For vampires forced to interstate or intercontinental travel, this was a great solution. After all, few of them are "martens", most are "moths", allergic to sunlight. This is also the main reason why vampires rarely and reluctantly travel.

When the plane landed at Magadan airport, it was still a deep night. Behind the barrier surrounding the landing strip, a crowd of people waited. Five friends underwent customs clearance and then went out among the people. They were on the spot. Their plan ended in landing because, as Octavio said, "someone is supposed to pick them up there." Meanwhile, they had no idea how to see someone they did not know about whom they did not know anything, among those who talked with languages unknown to them. Many of men lifted large pieces of white cardboard with Cyrillic inscriptions, of which they obviously didn't understand anything. It couldn't help them. They were in a foreign country that they knew nothing about.

Lambdon looking around suddenly squeezed Never's arm.

"There he is," he said. "That dull cyclist guy. The tablet has the words "Octavian Group". It's about us. I think so."

Friends pushed to a small, poorly dressed man with a furrowed face. Lambdon talked to him and for a moment they exchanged comments, of which the others could not understand a word.

"He's supposed to take us to a certain address. He was paid for it and knows nothing more," said Tygier finally, turning to his friends.

"Let's go then," Theo, delighted at the fact that he was no longer on the plane, he was ready to agree on everything.

Friends, lingering a bit, somehow packed themselves in a shabby taxi. The thought that someone they don't know was supposed to take them to a place they had never even heard of was a bit depressing. It seemed, however, that the taxi driver did not know who they were, and he did not care. He drove them through the city for some time, until he finally stopped the car on some dimly lit, almost empty street and spoke a few words.

"Here," said Tygier. "Don't ask anything, this cabby won't say anything. He was paid, he brought us here and the rest doesn't care him. He's right. In this country, it is really, better to know too little than too much."

"Okay, but what shall we do here?" Oggy asked miserably, looking around the hostile surroundings. She felt like a duck put out to shoot and would have sworn that more than one pair of eyes were watching them.

The rest did not feel well here either. The houses, usually made of bricks, with falling off plaster and faded paint, gave a ghostly impression in the dim light of the few active lanterns. Almost all windows were dark. They barely saw people, except for a militia patrol that had passed in the distance, a few drunks and a derailed man sleeping under a wall. This dark street was dominated by an indefinite threat atmosphere, as if it lived its own life, independent of the human race.

Friends looked around, unsure what to do next, and fought the urge to hide somewhere immediately.

"*Pajdziom na maju kwartiru, galubczik.*"[13] A drunken prostitute who show out of nowhere, pulled Never by the sleeve, not discouraged by his lack of interest.

"Where did she come from? Lambdon, tell her I am not interested in her services," the Indian finally got impatient when she repeated her babbling invitation for the fourth or fifth time.

Tygier got into a conversation with the girl, trying to convince her to leave them alone, but he was doing poorly. Finally, he turned to his friends:

"Look, she's a liaison officer. We are to follow her."

"Are you sure?" Gerard wondered.

"She gave the password, I know that much. Do we have a choice? If the militia takes us, we can end badly."

"Tygier is right," Oggy interrupted. "Russian prison is easy to get to, but it is harder to get out of it than from any other prison. I do not feel like it."

"Who want to?" Never looked at colleagues.

Both were as uncertain as he, even Fronda, usually very sensitive to female charms, gazed at the Russian with distrustful eyes.

"Well, as you said "A"…" he finally muttered.

---

[13] *(russian)* Let's go to my apartment, love bird.

They followed their guide, looking around. The girl walked without looking back, as if she didn't care much whether they followed her or not. She was fast and no longer looked drunk. They could hardly follow her. After marching, completely dark alleys, not lit by even one lantern, they entered a basement. Through the rusted hatch they went down to the stinking canals, where a small boat was waiting for them. The girl stopped and said something to Lambdon.

"She tells us to get off around the fifth turn and come to the surface," he translated. "A van will be waiting for us there. What kind of the van?"

He looked at the guide questioningly, but she was already leaving the way they came. For a moment they saw her slender legs on the ladder, then she got out through the hatch and closed the hatch.

"My word," Theo sighed as he entered the boat wobbling on the city's sewage.

Others followed his example, though the fragile "vehicle" filled them with some fear.

The boat looked as if it were about to sink or fall to pieces, but somehow it remained on the surface. Theo, as the strongest of the five, grabbed the double paddle and moved forward. They did not even try to guess how deep this stinking river was, and they did not want to think what would happen if they overturn. Just in case, they sat stiffly, not even trying to move.

Around the fifth turn, Theo skillfully guided the boat towards the canal casing. He pressed the oar on the edge of the casing and jumped out of the boat. Before she could drift again into the center of the canal, he grabbed the moor and tied it to a ring fixed in the wall.

"There's a hatch," he said. "We're going upstairs. We don't have much time because it will be dawn soon. You don't care, but Lambdon and I really need to beware of sunlight."

"Then stop talking and move on," Never urged him impatiently.

The smell of sewage made him nauseous, and the darkness in the canal choked. His deeply hidden Achilles heel was that he was basically afraid of the dark, which for a vampire was a feature so unexpected that it was almost ridiculous. He was not afraid of dark nights, caves or dark forests, but he was frightened by dark rooms built by people, no matter how big. And he knew why this was happening, though he never told anyone about it.

A van was parked on the street. The man leaning against its side was very much like a taxi driver - he had similar pants and a shirt, except that instead of a cyclist he wore a beret with an antenna, and a smoking cigarette hung from his mouth. Seeing the newcomers coming out from under the ground, he threw it on the sidewalk, stomped it and muttered

"Nu, Amierikancy, pajechali."[14]

He opened the side door of the van and showed them the interior.

"What does he mean?" Gerard asked helplessly, looking at Lambdon.

"He takes us for Americans." The Pole explained to him. "He invites you inside. Do not be lazy, faith! We get in."

"All right, but under your responsibility," Oggy said, on which the Russian made the worst impression. From the beginning, moreover, she felt bad in this city and barely maintained a human figure. Once, in times of danger, her transformation took place almost automatically, but since contact with Vandis Winger, she knew how to control it quite well.

The interior of the van smelled of cheap alcohol, but someone made sure there was a flashlight and a few blankets. They were useful because the night was cold and windy. Vampires are not very sensitive to temperature changes, but they also feel what scientists describe as

---

[14] *(russian)* Well, Americans, let's go.

thermal discomfort, although to a much lesser extent than humans. Plus, Oggy wasn't a vampire.

"I don't like it," she said angrily, wrapping herself in one of the rugs.

"Me either, but if we want to do the job, we have to play for now as if everything was in perfect order." Never opened his briefcase and took out what looked like a flat suitcase.

"What is it?" Fronda asked, pointing the flashlight at him.

"A Laptop. The computer in a nutshell." Said Never. "A new type of prototype, miniaturized. People don't use them yet, although they are being worked on. I got it from Octavio, although I don't know if we will be able to use its possibilities. It is hard to expect IT genius after centuries-old vampires."

"I took the course," Fronda said proudly.

"A two-week study you didn't understand much of," Never snorted. "Oggy, and you?"

The girl thoughtfully touched the laptop. She also completed the same course as Theo, but being younger than him, she had a more flexible mind. She also had a technical sense and mathematical skills, which she did not realize until the course.

"Do you want me to handle this thing?" She asked, touching the computer.

"Someone has to."

She took the suitcase by the handle. The laptop was amazingly heavy for its size.

"Good," she said. "I'll watch it when we're safe. If Octavio has given you such a miracle, it means that we may really need it."

"He probably thinks that anyone who has grown out of diapers must be able to handle it," Gerard muttered reluctantly. Computers overwhelmed him, though he admired their capabilities. He would gladly take care of operating a compact device, but to his great shame he did not even finish the course that Theo passed as such. He lacked abilities, which - as it turned out - was concealed in a rudimentary form even in a medieval knight.

The van rode for a long time, turning from time to time and turning back before it came to a standstill. Someone jerked the door from the outside. Theo and Tygier instinctively huddled in anticipation of the sun's rays, but the vehicle stood in a large, dark hangar, not in the parking lot. The man who brought them here was just saying something to Lambdon, who was nodding his head.

"We're to go upstairs," he said to his friends. "There are stairs."

The unimpressed Russian slammed the van shut and went somewhere, no longer interested in his peculiar "load." They watched him for a moment.

"So, are we going, or stand here?" Gerard finally asked.

"We're going, sure we are going... I wonder what this place is." Never murmured as he headed for the stairs. "Get ready to fight, just in case."

This caution was justified, but fortunately it proved superfluous. The hangar was not actually a hangar, but a very large garage, over which a multi-story residential house was built. A spiral staircase led friends to the corridor. At its end, they noticed a half-open door through which a streak of electric light fell - unusual since it was daytime. It seemed that the light was an invitation addressed specifically to them and proclaimed without the words "Blinded windows, here you will be safe". Still looking slightly and trying to walk relatively quietly they came to the door.

They almost leaped back as they suddenly opened to their full width. A real giant stood at the threshold, almost filling the entire door frame. It looked a bit like a roughly hewn block, though it was probably not a gram of fat on it. He was not stout, rather massive, very tall and muscular, a real strong man. His head seemed too small for this large body. Still, he didn't look threatening. A broad, good-looking face, short-cut, soft polished bronze hair and small eyes aroused trust at first sight. Added to this was an almost childish smile that immediately captured everyone, even skeptical Never.

"I am Wissarion Igorowich Orlov, for friends Wisha," said the Russian in correct English, shaking their hands in turn. "I am to be your liaison and guardian during the action. Nice to meet you.

"We too," said Lambdon, without giving up his role as 'liaison officer' - "Won't we meet the others?"

"You will know, they will come after dark. For now, I am looking after you. Make yourself comfortable for now. Miss... also a vampire? Somehow, a young lady smells like perfumes..."

One of the features that distinguished vampires from ordinary people was that they not only did not emit any smell, but also effectively neutralized any which could remain on their skin after contact with something fragrant. Only the tobacco aroma clung to them for some time.

"You have a good sense of smell," Oggy said (she had to look high up to look at his face). "No, I'm not a vampire."

"Neither do I, but I work for Gayane. Well, for organization. I am very useful. Do you also working like that?"

Oggy smiled at him. This Russian, built like a tank, seemed immensely sympathetic to her, and she noticed with pleasure that he was looking at her as if he liked her.

"Call me Oggy," she said. "It's a diminutive. My name is Augusta Monteloupi."

"Oh, you are Italian? Come va, signorina? Lasciami perdere che sarò la guida per la signorina..."[15]

"No such talks in company, okay?" Lambdon interrupted him with dissatisfaction. "You will flirt with Oggy at other times, if she is so willing that her eyes shine. For now, we have other things to talk about."

---

[15] *(it.)* How you doing, Miss? Let me be your guide.

Indeed, having heard the family speech, the girl forgot about the action and listened to Wisha with brightened eyes. Rarely had the opportunity to talk to someone in Italian, and even if someone spent decades in exile, native speech will always be the most beautiful for him.

Wisha seemed very nice to friends. They seemed that he likes them too, but he didn't want to say anything about the mission that awaited them. They had to be patient. Therefore, Never took from his bag the crime story of his favorite Agatha Christie and plunged into reading. Gerard and Lambdon, tired of traveling, went to sleep. Oggy, delighted with the beautiful bathroom found behind the apartment, prepared a hot foam bath for herself. And Theo was happy to discover that Wisha can play chess and convinced him to play. He always did that when he found a chess player on his way, and rarely lost.

When the sun stopped looking into the gaps between the blinds and window frames, the apartment door opened with a slam. A young girl came in, accompanied by two big men who would be best suited to the term "gloomy bully boys." They looked like thugs ready for anything, but to tell the truth the girl looked just a little better. A tall, well-built blonde might seem very attractive if it wasn't marred by sharp makeup, provocative clothing, a hard look and constantly contemptuous expression on her lips. They were also bright red as her tight, leather pants and that was the most conspicuous.

"Which one of you is the leader here?" She asked sharply.

"What is this, an interrogation?" Gerard replied, angry that he had been lifted out of sleep.

She looked at him as if she were looking at a lizard.

"If you are not a leader, keep quiet."

"Slowly," Never stepped forward and raised his hands slightly. "We're not your subordinates. You will not command us. If you want help, say what and how. If not, that's fine: we'll leave like we arrived."

"Not so hard. Since we're hiring you, I'm the boss and you are the subordinates, okay?"

Never paled in anger but remained silent. The reasoning of the girl was impossible to refuse logic, and he respected people who could logically raise their arguments.

The Russian looked at him and softened a little. She sat down on one of the chairs, folded her foot, and lit a cigarette.

"I know your names," she said. "I don't know which one is, but it doesn't matter. I am Lena Platonovna and call me like that. Next: since you are here, I understand that you agree to help us."

"In fact," Never said cautiously. "But tell me exactly what you expect from our five."

Lena shrugged and threw a slogan to one of her companions. He pulled several litre bottles of blood, vodka and glasses from his briefcase. He set it all on the table, then with his companion backed out the door.

"The matter is very difficult," the Russian began, pouring vodka generously with each drink. "Rolskij bonds of a dozen or so of ours, forcing them to fight in his parody of the Gladiator Games. Many have already died in these battles, both vampires and humans. You will say for a long time that we should deal with this matter on our own."

"Well, kind of," Never nodded politely. He drank from his glass and coughed violently. Russian vodka turned out to be... a spirit in the company's bottle.

"The problem is that Rolskij's estate cannot be reached unnoticed. It is literally packed with electronic sensors and traps, and in many respects self-sufficient. It has its own mini-power plant and even a drinking water intake with its own water tower. As far as we know, neither Rolskij's guests nor his private soldiers are aware of the unusual nature of some bloody party players. The only initiate is Rolskij himself and his evil spirit, who we know nothing about. The saddest thing is that he is probably a vampire, too, but possessed with the idea of destroying his own species.

"Gusto, for sure," Gerard muttered.

"Don't say anything," said Fronda, who still couldn't believe this revelation about his old friend.

"I can't understand it either," growled the Indian angrily. "Finally, maybe it's not him. More than once, all the evidence against someone testified, and in the end, proved to be innocent. Lena, do you guarantee us to help when we know what to do?"

She nodded, blowing a large cloud of smoke out of her lips.

"If you only knew... We've tried to approach him several times, but for nothing."

"Do you even have a map of his estate?"

"Just a rough sketch. That's it. One of ours made it out from the air when he flew on an agricultural flight, during spraying... You know, he works for the pest control departments of fields and forests... It won't help you much, but there's always something."

She opened her purse and took out a folded piece of paper. Someone who drew a map on it had to be familiar with this work because it resembled professional maps available for sale. All lines and contours were drawn with a firm hand, inked and even key was there. Unfortunately, in Russian.

"Relax, I will translate it as needed." Said Tygier cheerfully, seeing Never's anxiety at the sight of Cyrillic characters. "I know Russian almost as well as Polish. Eight years of elementary school, four of high school."

"We hire you so that you can cope with the preparation of the plan and its implementation," continued Lena Platonovna. You will keep in touch with us via Wisha. The fewer bystanders know our quarters, the better."

"We need a photo of Rolskij," Gerard pointed out soberly.

"Nobody has a picture of him. Only his family and close associates see him directly, and they don't take pictures. We don't even know what the bastard looks like. Maybe you will have more luck?"

"How to not love the Russians, they always like to do everything with other people's hands." Tygier chuckled happily. He poured himself blood and alcohol and took a big sip.

"How is that? Are we supposed to do the dirty work for you and you won't even give us a contact address? Thanks for the trust, lady." Fronda was clearly offended.

"He's right," Gerard unexpectedly supported Lena. "We were too trusting, and what came of it? How many of us lost their heads in Paris?"

The Russian did not even look at him. She smokes a second cigarette from the cigarette butt which she crushed directly on the table-top.

"You don't know what you don't know," she said firmly. "If you don't know our addresses, even the devil won't get anything out of you."

"That's right. Okay, we already have a general vision of the situation, we can develop a plan. As for your support, we thank you humbly, but we can do it without it." Never finished his drink with an impenetrable expression on his face and stood up. "Is that all?"

Lena also stood up, adjusted her tight pants, and walked to the door, swinging on her ridiculously high heels.

"Oh, and don't walk around the city," she added, turning slightly in the doorway. "You are too different from ordinary residents."

"We would never know without you," Fronda said ironically, swinging rhythmically in his chair.

"According to the Russians, only they are smart, the rest are knuckleheads," Tygier explained to him sweetly.

Lena shrugged and left, closing the door behind her.

"And "thank you" and "goodbye" where?!" A Pole shouted for her.

"Be quiet, Lambdon," Gerard waved a hand at him. "After all, you don't like Germans, and they are the Russians, something wrong with them?"

"Who knows what's worse, German or Russian."

"Enough. Don't make him tick, Fanfan. On this subject, he can talk even all day. Let's advice how to lead them out of this stupid situation. They have real problems here since they decided to ask us for help with all their aversion to the world outside the Iron Curtain." Never uncapped another bottle. His movements became slightly nervous under the influence of strong alcohol, but no one paid attention to it.

"How do you like Lena?" Wish asked with a smile on his chubby, bushy face.

"Pretty," Fronda admitted. "Very pretty, but..."

"Vulgar," Gerard replied for him. "Obnoxious to me."

"She is what she is, but it is her merit that the local organization somehow holds up to this day," Orlov explained to him.

He poured himself a vodka and drank it undiluted in one sip.

"Maybe you would stop talking about crap, we have a serious case," Never reminded them, but no one paid him any attention.

Theo threw himself on the couch until the springs groaned and humped the song. After a moment, he paused and looked up, looking around alertly.

"Where's Oggy?" He asked.

"In the next room. She took this ridiculous item in a suitcase and is trying to guess how it works," answered Wisha.

"We're in so much trouble, and she had toys in the head," Gerard snorted.

"This toy can be damn useful."

"That's true," Never backed Wisha. "I don't know if you know, but Oggy is a great, self-generated talent in the field of computer science. You'll see what she can do."

"And Octavio said why we needed this lactok or what?" asked Theo. He put both hands under his head and stared at the ceiling, whistling through his teeth.

"Laptop." Corrected his friend. "He said it would definitely be useful."

"For what? To play hearts?"

"No, hotshot." Oggy tilted her tousled head from behind the door. "With such a device you can paralyze the work of even the largest institution, if it is computerized and find out what anyone wants."

"State secret too?" Gerard opened his eyes wide and looked at Lambdon for confirmation. He was not sexist, but he was brought up in the belief that men are not only more talented in science than women, but also wiser in general. He couldn't get rid of that approach.

Tygier nodded affirmatively. As a fluent technician, he knew the latest equipment, especially since Octavio regularly organized training courses for station employees.

Theo shrugged impatiently.

"All these modern inventions are worth the devil," he said. "In my time, you worked with a quill pen and an abacus and I would like to see some lady that would use the button suitcase to confuse the institution of that time."

"Goddamn it, times are changing!" Never got on him, nervous about the tense situation.

When he was in this mood, it was better not to annoy him, but Theo did not pay attention as usual.

"They change, it's true," he nodded warily. "But why worse, huh?" Now people are not ruling things, but things are ruling the people, exemplar these computers."

"You'd better shut up!" Shouted the Indian.

"You are saying stupid things," Gerard said. "You would like it, Fronda that people would still shine their muzzles and ride on horse-drawn carriages."

"And why not?" His friend replied. "A horse is a wonderful animal! Cars stink, make noise, and are extremely dangerous, and non-contact. You will not stroke the car, do not weave his ribbons in his mane or feed him with sugar after the ride, and he will not whinny..."

Never punched the table.

"Fronda, I will call an ambulance for you and tell them to take you to the madhouse!" He bellowed furiously. "I swear to the court that you're a freak because it's true!"

"And what language do you get along with the local catchers?" exclaimed Theo, who loved arguing with him. The Indian rarely went berserk, but when it came to that, thoroughly, and the arguments were such that they were talked about for a long time.

"Once one of yours was taken to the madhouse," Wisha interfered. "I had to pretend there a paramedic for a week before I could pull him out."

Never, who was already preparing to throw Fronda all the insults he knew and summon each of the three million Indian deities separately against him, frozen with a half-open mouth.

"I have an idea," he muttered after a moment. "Man, how good... Let no one bother me now."

He dug a notebook with a pen out of his bag and locked himself in one of the rooms.

His friends knew that asking him would not work now, so they had to be patient and wait for him to explain the details of his plan to them. Wisha didn't know him, but he didn't care.

"Won't you help him? After all, every two heads are better than one." He pulled a chessboard out of the drawer and started placing pawns.

"There is no such need, and Never is the brains of our team. It has an IQ well above two hundred points. If he doesn't come up with something reasonable, then we certainly won't. And besides, he does not like to disturb him." Theo jumped off the couch and with brightened eyes sat in front of him.

"Don't you have anything better to do but play?" Gerard grimaced. He sometimes played a game with Fronda himself, but seldom. He wasn't a big chess fan, although he played quite well and sometimes even won.

"Give them a break, let them have fun. Let's play too. The checker board is busy, but there are cards here. Do you like canasta?" Tygier pulled a deck of greasy cards from the drawer and began shuffling them.

Gerard nodded, though without too much enthusiasm. He didn't want to hurt Lambdon. He had already liked this Slav vampire with a cheeky face and an annoying tendency to change from one mood to another. He was never known how he would react to something, he was capricious and uneven, but he was absolutely loyal to his friends and always honorable. In addition, there was truly Slavic fantasy, a volatile mind and personal charm, with which he gained general sympathy.

"You all don't like Russians?" He asked, looking through the cards he had received.

"We have nothing to like them for," replied Lambdon. "They're less mean than Germans, but it's actually like choosing between a herd of hyenas and a swarm of hornets. Whoever prefers."

"They helped you after the war."

"They helped... You know the proverb 'They come to rescue and save by stealing'? What the Germans didn't take from us, then the Red

Army took. And for them to stop at robbery, it wouldn't be bad yet. England and America sold us in Yalta to Stalin by the hands of Roosevelt and Churchill, and they didn't care what would happen to us. Anyway, let's not talk about it, okay?"

"Theo said that better not talk with you about certain subjects at all."

"Is it possible with him? There are matters that can only be understood by those who fought in the fields of the Hundred Years' War... and there are matters that only the Pole of flesh understands. Let's play, brother, instead of talking."

They played eagerly until the door of the next room boomed open and Never feverishly popped out.

"Listen, I have a plan," he called. "Infernally dangerous to Fronda, but probably the only one who can succeed."

"Talk, then," Theo left the chessboard and walked to the windowsill where his friend had laid out a chart. Others followed him.

After a while, five heads bent over the map received from Lena.

"Nobody will break into Rolskij's estate, so it's a shame to waste time on idle considerations," Never began. "And since you can't sneak in there, you have to do something to invite one of us there. We already know that Rolskij's helper is hunting wrestlers for his games, so Fronda will let to catch him."

"Wait, why Fronda?" Tygier interrupted him. "He doesn't speak the language. I will go."

The Indian shook his head negatively.

"Maybe we need you here because of your language skills. You will go with Wisha to Lena and ask for things from the list I will give you. Gerard is not suitable, because he is weak, and I have to conduct external action. Theo is perfect for this role: strong as a buffalo, agile like a monkey and knows how to use any type of weapon."

"Sure," Theo muttered with satisfaction.

"Don't be prematurely happy," he choked coldly. "You can easily die, because if the traitor is actually Gusto, he will want to liquidate you even before the official competition. Rolskij probably does not know that his adviser is a vampire, and even if he knows, his other people certainly do not know. He will not risk exposure."

"This is definitely not Gusto... and I can do it myself without your advice," Theo grumbled, as always, when someone tried to spoil his fun.

"We will see. I'm the boss here, so say right away: will you be in a team or not? Because if not, I throw my plan in the trash and arrange another."

"Okay... I will submit" Fronda sighed and his handsome face was deeply disappointed. He was very disliked to act on whose instructions and he was the boss himself.

"I still think I would be better," Lambdon said. "After all, Wisha is the link and I am no worse than Fronda when it comes to melee combat and physical resistance.

It was pure truth, but never just shook his head. He could not say to Wisha that he preferred to have his own translator, because he did not trust any of the locals, but there was one more reason. And about which he could tell.

"Theo has one more advantage over all of us: he can kill, and without a second's hesitation. He was trained like that since he was a child and it is in his blood. None of us will match him in these game." He explained reluctantly.

"Even you?"

"Even me."

"Well, give me your plan."

Never's idea was seemingly crazy, but when he spoke about it, it began to seem more and more sensible. As he explained more details to his friends, it became clear that he thought of everything and each weak point was fortified with additional options. Everyone had a designated role, even Wisha, who was extremely happy to include him in the action. He treated it as an unexpected distinction and was really grateful, especially since Never's plan did not provide for the participation of either Lena or her subordinates. The Indian preferred that the "locals" not interfere until it was actually necessary. Still, he did not trust them. Orlov was supposed to be an exception, although he decided to observe him very closely.

*****

For several nights in a row, Theo hunted near Rolskij's estate. All this time he did not contact his friends, wanting to avoid being exposed, which was not too emotional for him - he could handle any situation. He knew loneliness better than anyone, because he hadn't talked to people for over sixty years, merely being with the wolf pack. Wolves taught him a lot, including avoiding dangers. And now he had to force himself to be careless.

The plus was that he could finally eat his fill. Bottled blood does not meet all the needs of a vampire. It allows him to survive, but leaves him feeling unsaturated, both in a physical and mental sense. Never and Fronda never touched it, except occasionally. Everything has changed since Gerard began to accompany them. Sensitive than others, reluctant to violence, a poet in his soul, an idealist to the bone, he refused to attack people, and new friends did not intend to force him. Even they switched to "canning" themselves, just to avoid a full look of green eyes. They liked him too much, they didn't want to hurt him. They saw that every time hunger forced him to attack like the vampire, he experienced it for weeks.

Fronda had no such dilemmas. At the time when it was preserve, only blood drunk directly was available, and he himself lived in the forest like an animal. He saw no reason to change his habits now, especially since he only hunted for social outcasts. Almost everyone like him did it - not because of moral scruples, but of reason. Since they needed live "donors", it was better to choose them from among people whom no one would claim. Although it is said so anyway, no authority in the world wastes time or resources on investigating a littered lout or beaten offender with a rich file. Such matters are willingly swept under the rug and you forget about them as soon as possible.

Gerard did not accept this. Whoever he dealt with, he never forgot that he was a man, and even if he drank "live blood", always be careful not to harm him. He couldn't do otherwise. Without judging new friends, he didn't want to become like them completely. They respected this imbued humanism and childish naive view of the world, even if it sometimes irritated them. Although he was a valuable companion during combat or travel and had brilliant ideas, he was definitely not suited to such missions as the one that Fronda was performing now.

He didn't have much to do now. He slept in the bottom of the dugout serving as a storage room, and wandered around at night looking for victims. The town, from which the oligarch's estate was relatively closest, was a model example of a miserable town, full of derailments and drunks. Most of the inhabitants worked in a nearby sawmill belonging to Rolskij, as did the workshops surrounding him. Fortunately, there was no shortage of employment for men as well as women. They worked equally with men, excluding housewives and surprisingly numerous prostitutes for such a small town.

People living here probably got used to it, and they probably didn't have anywhere to go. So they lived, worked and lived the life they could afford. After work, they had a choice of one of the many bars, one of two cinemas with a repertoire of at least twenty years or sitting at home in front of the TV. The river that smelled through the city and smelled of sewage, littered to the limit of impossibility, the park resembled an illegal dump, from which half-dead trees protruded sadly. Nobody cared about anything here. A dream fishery for a lone bloodsucker.

His efforts were successful only after a week, when he went out hunting and sensed rather than saw a group of armed men lurking in the dark. The wrist detector slightly vibrated. This meant that chemically pure silver was nearby. Theo smiled slightly to himself. This was the beginning of the game in which his life was at stake, and he loved such challenges. He was far more reckless than he was told and usually did not think about anything but adventures, although he carefully concealed this weakness from friends. Fortunately, he knew that it was not only dangerous to him, and that is why he usually kept his risk in check.

If he wanted, he could have escaped these people. This awareness gave him a perverse pleasure when he allowed himself to chase between buildings, until he finally allowed him to be surrounded somewhere off the beaten path. The pursuit was rather small - just a few people armed with silver bullets and small crossbows, but Theo sensed the presence of someone else. He was informed by a psycho-locator, that famous sixth vampire sense, akin to, as some said, the bat echo. He reacted only to representatives of their species and was very useful.

He tried to locate the "bloodhound" at once, but people's flashlights blinded him, emitting some length of light unpleasant to the eyes of the vampire. It wasn't until they were dimmed that he saw the figure behind men dressed in masking suits. His heart tightened painfully before he saw him clearly. He also met him and stepped forward.

"What are you doing here, Fronda?" Are you looking for death?" He asked, almost friendly.

He looked different than when they had last seen each other. He wore a military camouflage suit, hair cut almost to the skin and reflex glasses that gave an absurd impression in the middle of the night.

"So it's you. I was hoping someone else was a traitor about who everyone is talking about," Theo sighed, succumbing to the hands binding him.

He still felt pain in his heart, the more so because Gusto was his friend for many years and he always trusted him - he, who in principle did not trust anyone at that time.

The Austrian winced slightly. For his part, he liked Fronda more than the rest of his kinsmen, but he did not hesitate to sacrifice anyone in the name of his projects.

"I'm sorry, Theo," he said. "This is war, and in war, you know, don't have mercy. Who like who, but you should understand this best. By the way, I expected your buddies here too. Well, they put you aside?"

"They've been dead for over a year," he replied briefly. "They hunted us. I thought I would be safer here."

"I'm sorry, man."

Theo tossed his bangs aside.

"But why? Because who else killed them, not those you work for?"

"Error." Gusto grinned sarcastically. "I work only for myself. As you can see, now for Rolskij."

"No difference."

"You're wrong. He doesn't kill blindly. He has other plans for all of us. Perhaps your great career begins today."

"What do you want? Absolution from a guy that you get money and deliver other for almost certain death?" Snorted Fronda. "I'll tell you something. You are a traitor and a rat, Vanderbelt, and if I somehow get out of it, I will devote all my strength to chasing you, even if I were to do it to the end of the world."

Gusto didn't answer. He just turned and walked away. Perhaps the words of his old friend caused him something like shame, or maybe he just decided that he did not have to answer.

People in military overalls pushed the bound Fronda into the small jeep, which hit the road sharply. Thanks to the map he received from Lena, he knew that they had to first pass through two solid gates, each of which was under strong guard and independently equipped with electronic sensors. A small sensor hidden under his hair was to register a code combination opening both gates. He felt it, a tiny spider, clung to the skin behind his ear with the help of thin needles, felt a slight tingling of electrical impulses when animated by the proximity of the defense system began to work.

It wasn't the only gadget he had with him - it was mainly Never's plan that was based on it. Theo did not have much confidence in the technique, but he tried to remember all the instructions he received. Rolskij's men did not search him very well, and they only sought weapons. The "toys" that Octavio gave them were miniaturized to the limit and it was easy to overlook them. Theo did not know what a microprocessor or integrated circuit was, but he could use any device as long as he was explained.

"If only they didn't start suspecting something and it would be good," he thought, snuggling into the corner of the car.

Where he was sitting, the blackout window was slightly torn, and through the resulting translucent he could observe the way with one eye. In his mind he noted everything that could prove to be important: the terrain, the number and armament of the people seen along the way, buildings... Something from it could soon save his life.

He was not afraid, it was not his nature, but he understood his position and danger well. He was a prisoner of an unknown enemy, very powerful and having many ruthless killers on his services. He was alone here and had to manage somehow until he managed to do his part of the plan and give a signal to friends, and at no time would he be sure of his life. This awareness pleasantly excited his adventurous, twisted self.

Absorbed in his observations, he did not pay attention to Gusto, who was sitting with his back to him and struggling with his own thoughts. He did not want the deaths of those he cheated on - he just wanted people to be safe from them. The brainwashing he went through at the Van Helsing Institute did not make him a slave of the Hunters, as was planned, but changed the way he judged the world. He now believed that their persecutors were right, at least to some extent, and sometimes he really helped them. Usually, however, he acted alone. He did not have to explain to anyone, and, which was important, he was safe from the Hunters.

Neither Theo nor anyone else knew what Vanderbelt's motives were, though it must be admit that nobody cared. He was now the enemy of his kinsmen, and that was enough for everything. Even worse, he served the Hunters, so he became a traitor, and that would not be forgiven by anyone who remembered knightly ideals. Especially Fronda, perceiving the world in a simple and unequivocal way.

After a long drive, the jeep stood in front of the gate of a huge, brightly lit mansion. Guards armed to the teeth walked along the fence. They scrupulously inspected the car, then opened the gate and let it in. Jeep drove up a winding road between low-rise buildings to a three-story villa, surrounded by a carefully maintained garden. In the background you could see a huge pool over which there was a party. An orchestra was playing in tuxedos, well-groomed butlers distributed drinks and snacks, laughing women in evening dresses walked along the banks of the pool in the company of sophisticated men.

Theo didn't have time to look at this fun. He was dragged out of the jeep and, ignoring the resistance put on the show, he was taken to the back entrance of the villa. There he was brought down the stairs, to what had to be a kind of prison, but arranged like a high-class gym. A powerful Russian in a paramilitary uniform looked at the "new", exchanged a few words with those who brought him and pointed down the corridor.

If it was a prison, Fronda had to admit that it was quite luxurious. There were already a dozen other prisoners in the cells they passed, only men, and undoubtedly his kinsmen. He couldn't be wrong. All well-built, undoubtedly strong and well-fed. They were certainly not missing anything.

The last few cells were empty. He was introduced to one of them, or rather pushed.

"This will be your home now," Gusto said, removing his handcuffs. "From today you are a gladiator, Fronda. I hope you haven't lost your abilities. If you are the way you used to be, you have the chance to become a champion, and I really enjoy it. I like you, and I would prefer you to live for some time."

"So these are real life and death fights?" Theo rubbed his wrists and looked around the small room. It looked comfortable and even pleasant.

"Yes, but in the meantime you can live quite well... if you don't rebel against all this. I assure you, it's not worth it. The wayward get there."

Gusto pointed to the glass wall of the great oceanarium behind the cells. Behind the glass, the sea rippled, corals and sea anemones grew at the bottom of the tank, and above them some creatures danced in blue-green water, beautiful and pure in their innocence, resembling crystal bells.

"What the devil?" asked Theo with calm interest.

"Jellyfish," Gusto explained to him. "Gena Rolskij likes them very much. They are very young and therefore can stay together. In this tank there is a lion's mane jellyfish, this is the yellow-brown one, and the Portuguese man o' war is the cream-blue one with red accents. Those gray-green at the bottom are Cassiopeia that like sunlight, so they illuminate it with ultraviolet light. Do you see the bright red? Sea wasp. Baby, right? But it is deadly already. Once it will catch you and you will remember it for a long time... if you survive it."

"Oh, I'm shaking now."

Theo turned his eyes away from the giant aquarium and looked at the equipment. Comfortable bed, table, bookcase. There was even a color TV in the corner.

"Make yourself comfortable for now," Gusto said, and went out with armed guards.

Several prisoners from neighboring cells talked to the "new" almost simultaneously, but he shrugged helplessly. The Russians realized that he did not understand and began to call someone named Lonia. Fronda thought for a moment that she was a woman, but the summoned one also turned out to be a man. He slept in one of the cells, and so hard that it only woke him several times. He stretched and yawned loudly, showing sharp fangs. He must have been old, from the era when you were still "biting". For a long time, no vampire has used teeth to get on someone's blood, except occasionally. They no longer sharpened and lengthened as much as in the older generation.

"What language do you speak, fresh meat?" He asked first in English, then in French, sitting on his couch.

"Both," Theo replied, eyeing him with restrained curiosity.

The Russian was terribly thin, and his head was covered by a huge shed of curly, almost white hair. He looked a little funny, but when he stood up, his movements showed strength and resilience.

"Leonid Rodionowich Korolev." He introduced himself. "What are you doing here? I didn't know that some foreigners had infiltrated our community here."

"I didn't infiltrate anywhere. I came here for a vacation."

He preferred not to disclose the real reasons for his presence in Russia, at least for now.

"Holidays," Lonia snorted, amused. "Then you will have a vacation, let my enemies have such ones..."

"Are we fighting among ourselves?" The Frenchman asked him.

"No. With people. Rolskij brings them here from some forbidden places, choosing such that nobody would look for them and nobody would miss them."

"And... are we have to kill?"

"Yes. For us it's a chance for an additional meal. You see, when you inflict a lethal blow, from the ramp around the arena segments of the dome slide out, which closes over the players. Then you can drink blood without fear, you have about fifteen minutes before they come for you. Such a bonus."

"Charming," Theo muttered in disgust. Like any vampire, he loved blood drunk directly from the source, but this form of obtaining a meal seemed morally disgusting to him.

"Have you ever seen this guy?" He asked after a moment. "Well, Rolskij."

"Neither I nor anyone else." Lonia fell on his shaggy head and yawned again. Apparently he sits in the middle of this property like a spider in his web, he sees everything and hears everything. And it controls everything.

"Pretty," Fronda sighed. He took one of the books and flipped through casually. Having said that it was printed in Cyrillic, he put it back. "And I am to be his next toy, right?"

"You have no choice anyway. All right, I'm going to bed. I advise you too, because when they wake us up, you will have to practice until you fall down. You'd better recharge your batteries while you have the opportunity."

Fronda did not answer. He had already created a fairly coherent picture of what was happening here and did not think he needed more explanation, at least for now. He did not intend to initiate anyone into the real reasons for his arrival in these parts. He waited until the light in the strange barracks turned off and carefully detached the spider receiver from the skin behind his right ear. He broke off the thin latches from him and slipped the device into the open watch case. Now he could be sure that he would not lose the information it contained.

The clock was not taken from him. Just in case, he was given one that no one would be afraid of. The large, terribly ugly, heavy Soviet "onion" was perfect for its intended purposes. Of course, someone could suspect something, but here with the help of the conspirators... spy cinema and the gadgets shown there. Filling the seemingly ordinary watch with additional functions seemed to be so trivial, and shown in so many films that no one would think about it seriously. Robbing something so worthless was also for no reason. So no attention was paid to the ragged "rocket"[16], drowsily tickling on the prisoner's wrist.

Having done what Never told him when they discussed the details of the action, Theo took the advice of Lonia and simply went to sleep. There was no point in watching, and though there were no windows in the underground, he could sense through the skin that dawn was approaching.

He was awakened by the sound of cheerful military music from the radio station. Imitating others, he left his cell whose door opened automatically and followed them to the shared bathhouse. He took a cold shower and wiped himself with a rough towel. He felt strange and insecure among those foreign men talking in language he didn't speak, but he tried not to show it. They didn't pay much attention to him.

After putting on new and clean clothes, similar to a judo kimono, he went to the next room, which - as it turned out - was the dining room. Following the example of others, he took a tall glass full of

---

[16] A popular brand of hand watches in the USSR.

green, opaque liquid from a large tray. He sniffed it distrustfully. The smell left no doubt. Yes, it was blood, and when he overbear and he tried it, he concluded that it was very tasty despite the coloring additive.

He looked for Lonia.

"Why is this product green?" He asked quietly.

"It's so that people don't know what they are giving us," the fair-haired Russian answered him equally quietly. He pointed his eyes at the guards. "They think it's a special, experimental nutritional blend, and that's good. How do you think they would react after learning that half the players are vampires?"

"Smart," Theo admitted. "Really nobody knows anything?"

Lonia shrugged his powerful shoulders.

"Not nobody. Rolskij and his grandchildren know. Our trainer as well as some of the guests know. The most important ones."

"You mean who?"

"For example, those Japanese who bought back Andriusha, your predecessor in this cell."

"Is that good or bad?"

"Good. They offer better conditions and employment opportunities in yakuza structures, after trying, of course. Many of our employees work for this organization, but it is not easy to get involved. It's even harder to the Chinese triad, but there are also a few apparently caught up there."

That sounded interesting. Theo looked back at the guards, then asked quietly:

"Japanese don't mind our, well, otherness?"

"Not at all," Lonia smiled indulgently. "Asians generally have a different approach to certain things. They are less fearful of what goes beyond everyday life, and much less sensitive. I assure you that they are not afraid of vampires."

"Well, well. Good to know."

After drinking the last drops from a glass, he went to the gym, where after a short warm-up he began to practice how others did it. He had never dealt with such devices for increasing muscle strength like these before, but after a while he found them interesting and functional. The trainer, a short, wiry man with a head cut in half matches, briefly explained to him the principles of machine operation. According to his instructions, he set the indicators to maximize the load and began testing the machines one by one.

It was like fun, and although the price could be very high, for now Fronda had a great time. It was his special skill - he could capture every moment of pleasure on the fly, even when the situation was not favorable at all. It was to this that he owed the youthful joy of life despite the terrible experiences and several centuries of nightlife.

Exercises, interspersed with recreational breaks, continued until the evening. As far as he knew, everyone had to practice, and the trainer had an eye on everyone. Obedience guaranteed not only regular meals, but the ability to sleep in a comfortably furnished, single cell. The rebels were reportedly threatened with severe punishments, but Fronda did not see any of his companions in misery trying to rebel. They've been in this place too long to hope to get out of here.

The guards might not have been initiated into everything, but they were well armed and strictly obedient to orders. The electronic surveillance system prevented prisoners from taking any action to free themselves from these strange catacombs. However, within the designated space, they had as much freedom as possible.

Lonia, eager to help, explained to Fronda that in the past escapes and guards had been tried, but it always ended badly. Electronic sensors detected everything, while the resistant went to the oceanarium. Armed with rifles for chemically pure silver and silver knives, the guards were ubiquitous. The jellyfish, if they didn't kill, were able to effectively take away any desire for any rebellion. Their venom even for vampires can be fatal, and certainly caused very painful burns and persistent neurological problems.

Theo listened to all this and slowly composed a clear picture of this place in his mind. The guards were obviously not their own masters. Orders were given to them by personal transmitters from the headquarters, where the controllers sat. And they watched on dozens of screens everything that was happening on the property. He did not yet know how to use this information, but he felt it was important and noted it in his memory. He could only connect with Never once, so the messages had to be precisely worded and as short as possible.

The transmitter in the watch had to transmit primarily the code combinations captured by the sensor, and the verbal message only in the second place. He couldn't hurry up. Everything he was about to broadcast had to be released only after he had collected the most important data. He also had to give friends time to prepare the action. He knew they were going to hurry up with everything, but it had to take some time.

Being impatient by nature, he had to control himself well all days and nights spent in the "gladiator's barracks", as Lonia called it with humor. He was cheerful and friendly by nature. They liked each other and talked often when they had the opportunity. The cages were usually not closed, so they could visit each other. "Gladiators", except for Lonia, rarely used it.

He noted that they were very introverted, slow to make friends, and they and the French shared a language barrier. Theo did not know Russian, and they did not speak other languages. Besides, they did not look for any closer contacts with each other. Sometimes they exchanged a few casual words, but as if casually. Vanderbelt didn't appear again, and it was even better. He didn't want to see him or talk to him anymore.

*****

The guard in camo suddenly appeared and threw something leather, studded with metal studs to Fronda.

"You have to put it on tonight," he said shortly, in poor English. "I'm waiting at the end of the corridor. Hurry up."

Theo unrolled the package and looked at the black leather shorts, the tight cut vest, and the shoulder straps with amazement.

"What is this? I should dress it?" He asked helplessly.

"Correction. You fight in it," Lonia told him from his cell. "It means they signed you up tonight. They must have a good opinion of your possibilities, since today... It's kind of..."

"Honorable mention, do you want to say? I don't like such distinctions, but ok. Let it be."

Fronda changed into a gladiator outfit and, looking in the mirror, could not control his laughter.

"I look like a porn-shop dancer," he said. "What about armaments?"

"You'll get a knife before entering the arena," said the Russian. "Your opponent will have a similar, but silver, so be careful. Those they train to fight us are real killing machines, and in addition, before entering the arena, everyone gets a plot of amphetamine. Do not be too self-confident, because you end badly."

Theo entered his cell and patted him on the back with a cheerful smile.

"How old are you?" He asked.

"Sixty-nine, why?"

"And I have over six hundred. I can handle every situation."

"Over six hundred! We don't have anyone older than one hundred and fifty! Geez, you are old fart..."

The Russian stared at him with his round eyes, reminiscent of light blue colored glass balls. He now looked like a zoologist who unexpectedly discovered something completely unexpected in a long-studied ecological niche.

"What a term..." Theo wasn't sure if he supposed to be offended or laughing.

He had never thought of himself as someone old before, and he didn't like it much, but logically he was old and there was no point in denying it. He looked in the mirror again. The polished surface showed him the graceful figure of a twenty-year-old boy with a smooth face and shiny black hair, combed to his forehead.

"Possible," he finally decided, "but I'm not bad for my age, do I? Hell, I'm hungry."

He drank from the glass the guard gave him. The coloring additive did not spoil the taste, but it was palpable - a light, chalky aftertaste, neither unpleasant nor pleasant. If not for the prospect of death in the arena, he could treat this place as a resort. Comfortable cells with access to mass media, a gym, regular meals and a beautiful view of the oceanarium. But Fronda did not take into account the possibility of losing anyway. He knew well that his skills and strength gave him an advantage over each individual opponent, so that the only problem remained the silver weapon of his opponent. If he pierced his heart or neck with a silver blade, he would probably die within a few minutes, and he didn't feel like it. He always thought life was very pleasant and he had no intention of giving it up prematurely.

The guards led him to the "arena". It turned out to be a perfect circle about ten meters in diameter, surrounded by an automated ramp high enough and slippery enough to not be able to climb it. The center was poured with golden sand, and the ramp was crowned by a single grandstand, where there were about thirty, maybe a little more people of both sexes. Apart from them, the arena was also watched by the electronic eyes of cameras and sensors, which transmitted the image directly to Rolskij's residence, and maybe somewhere else. He didn't know that.

Rolskij himself did not honor the Games with his presence. Fronda could not understand the use of being the head of a criminal organization, of having fabulous wealth and power over people, even if you do not leave your home, but postponed these considerations for later. It was not the best time to philosophize.

Opposite him, a giant wrestler dressed in light brown leather emerged from a small door in the ramp. His bare shoulders were covered in blue tattoos, as was his shaved bald head. On the chest was a snake-wrapped heart, and on the right forearm an anchor and a word written in Cyrillic that the Frenchman could not read. The man moved confidently, and his deep-set eyes measured the scornfully thin boyish-faced opponent. He clearly told himself it would be an easy victory.

Theo smiled slightly. He didn't even have to draw a knife to feel confident in this new role, so far the swagger was harmless to him. People like him put all their trust in their mass and strength, most often not letting them think about losing. Fronda, agile like a weasel, smart and much stronger than one would think of his appearance, he could fight such. He bent slightly, not taking his eyes off the tattooed giant.

The fight began at the sound of trumpets. The Russian competitor fell on the Frenchman with such impetus that if he got to him, he would break his bones with his very weight. Theo moved away smoothly from the attack, and when the Russian, unable to stop, lost his balance, he kicked his knees from behind. The giant fell on the sand and immediately jumped up again, clearly enraged. Certainly, composure was not one of its advantages.

He threw himself at Fronda again, who let him close as soon as possible. Then he grabbed the man's wrist and twisted his hand in such a violent motion that the bones popped like dry wood. The giant howled in pain. He could not know that such exploits were a spectacular issue of Fronda, which was trained by the greatest masters of six centuries and was not prepared for it. It was actually the best time to end the fight, but there was enough knightly spirit left at Fronda not to take advantage of this opportunity. And knightly ideals demanded that give the opponent a second chance.

Pushed back to the ramp, the Russian fell. He rose to his feet, hatred burning in his eyes. The broken arm must have hurt a lot, and yet he had no intention of giving up the fight. He reached for the knife with his left hand. In a split second, Theo noticed that his opponent's hand was passing a silver dagger and was wandering around the pistol handle barely visible behind the wide belt. So someone was cheating here, not at all knightly.

"Bad manners, Captain Hook," he growled through his teeth.

In a quick motion, he grabbed his knife and threw it. That one was also fast - he managed to bring out the shiny browning and aim before the knife hit his throat below Adam's apple. The roar of joy that came from the grandstand surprised Fronda so much that he froze. He knew these people were here for sick entertainment, and yet he was surprised by such overt contempt for human life. He wanted to shout something to the viewers, but there was no time for that. Black glass dome segments shot out of the ramp, closing over him and a riled Russian in the sand.

"Fifteen minutes," he muttered to himself.

He leaned down and stuck his lips to the blood-spitting wound on the neck of the tattooed wrestler. He didn't feel hungry, and he hated such tattooed thugs. They were usually dirty and smelled of digested alcohol, and their skin had a nasty, sour taste. He would gladly refuse this meal, if only out of spite, but he just wanted to shorten the agony of the Russian. The blood turned out to be much better than he thought, and it turned out he was hungry, though he hadn't felt it before. He stopped drinking when the giant's heart froze and sat on his heels, wiping his lips mechanically.

The viewers' reaction to what happened not only surprised him, but also filled him with disgust for the distinguished guests of this beautiful residence. He began to understand why the local community considers the killing of Rolskij as the only way out of this confusing situation, and he was right in their spirit. For this man, someone's death was just entertainment, as for other regulars of the residence, and they were supposed to be "better" than the vampires hunted by the hunters? They protected them?

Fronda, although he could be ruthless, did not like to kill. It wasn't a problem for him, but he didn't like it. He was a vampire, a bloodthirsty creature by definition, he was once a knight, a medieval fighting machine. Still, Never was wrong in saying that his friend could kill without hesitation or remorse. Of course, it would be an exaggeration to say that victory in the duel lay a stone on his heart, but he was not proud of himself. He would have preferred to win without killing this tattooed derelict about the body of a mammoth and a hummingbird's brain, if only because he was furious at acting according to the will of the post-Soviet chieftain, who thought he had him in his hand. However, until the time came, he couldn't get him out of error.

After the prescribed fifteen minutes, guards arrived, carrying Fronda back to the barracks. From the expressions on their faces it was obvious that they had respected him and preferred to be careful. The companions of misery greeted him enthusiastically, and although he did not understand what they were saying, he understood his admirable tone of expression perfectly.

"You did very well," Lonia said when he finally pushed to him. "You're really great. This bastard you killed has already killed two of us and just thinking that I would fight him... You'll be a star here, man! But I need you..."

"I don't care to be a star in a circus of executioners, without Burt Lancaster," Theo interrupted, taking off his bloodied uniform in disgust. "I need a good shower, I'm sorry."

He had never felt such an urgent need to wash the spilled blood before. His unspeakable disgust was filled with the thought that he would be forced to perform similar "performances" until the time was right to start the action, but there was nothing he could do about it. He knew it, but his desire for rebellion was growing, which was difficult to tame.

He left the bathroom, wiping himself with a rough towel, and froze at the sight of the three guards who were waiting for him.

"You come with us," one of them said briefly.

"Again? Well, ok..." Theo glanced at Lonia, who just shrugged helplessly. Now he could explain nothing.

The guards led Fronda to a gloomy room behind the barracks, where two similar young men in expensive suits waited.

"Hello, new master," one of them said. "We haven't met yet. I am Luka Porfiriowich Rolskij, and this is my brother Platon, the grandsons of your host. We want to congratulate you on your victory."

"Thank you," said Theo, looking both of them reluctantly. "Although I admit that I would rather be completely dressed, not in my pants, and see an old dog here, not a few puppies."

The young men laughed as if it were some great joke.

"Good joke," said Luka. "Grandpa doesn't receive visits, although he sees and controls everything. But we didn't have to bring you here just for congratulations. It's about letting you know that you're just a slave and our grandfather is your master."

The guards pushed Fronda into the center of the room and fastened chains hanging from the ceiling on his wrists.

"It's something new," Fronda murmured sarcastically, though he felt a cold chill.

One of the guards took a short handle from the wall, wrapped in a braid of silver, hair-thin wires. Theo clenched his teeth tightly. He did not scream, but every whimper pulled a deafening grunt from his chest, for the chemically pure silver around the thong made every vampire's body unbearable, and Fronda was no exception.

When the guard finally finished and the other two took the chains off the vampire's hands, he failed to stand on his feet and fell down, gasping for air with his mouth parted. One of the twins came over and put a foot on his nape in the expensive shoe on him.

"Always remember who the master is here," he said emphatically and turned to the waiting guards. "Take him."

"You will make it?" asked Wisha.

Oggy raised her warm eyes at him and smiled. She had already known for several days that the Russian strongman who looked like a log liked her and she was flattered by it. She was aware that she was not pretty and usually men overlooked her. It was different now. Wisha could not "make advances", but eventually she understood his clumsy attitude and had to admit to herself that she enjoyed this expression of admiration.

She had to gain more self-control than ever. She could have liked Wisha too, who finally knew nothing about her, and let on something. She couldn't afford to talk to him honestly, and whenever he was close, she pretended to be very busy exploring the capabilities of the laptop. Now, however, when it was time to start the action, this excuse was no longer good.

"I should," she said, trying indifferently. "If the information provided by Fronda is accurate, it won't be difficult for me to get into the system. The only danger is that we must first get to the property and find electrical contact there. I must have something to connect this marvel.

Wisha shook his head, too small on the thick neck. He couldn't figure this girl out, and he liked her more and more. He admired her brilliant mind and sense of humor, and above all those beautiful brown eyes. He just didn't know why she was helping vampires, though she wasn't a vampire herself. He couldn't find it out, and Oggy didn't want to tell him anything despite the talks.

"Can I go with you?" He asked.

"It depends on Never, not me. He's the boss," she told him.

Wisha looked pleadingly at the Indian, but he shook his head in the negative. He did not want his presence during the attack on Rolskij's estate. He didn't trust him. Wisha was not preserved and they have not yet found out what he is doing in the clan commanded by Lena. Perhaps he was an "acolyte", that is, someone who had just been promised fixation, but they did not know it either. Nobody wanted to talk to them - strangers in this area - about the life of their group.

The Russians were secretive, and in a rude manner, as if contemptuous. Never didn't want to waste time fighting prejudices, but he also did not show confidence in them. While he could finally accept the help of those who were vampires, he wasn't going to trust an ordinary man. Life taught him that when working in teams, it is dangerous to introduce new elements into an already developed system just before the action. It could end badly, so it was better not to risk it.

"I already have a signal on the emitter," Lamdon Tygier looked up from the device being tuned. "Let's hope that Fronda gave us the right codes, because if not, everything will fail."

"Fronda is a weirdo, but in some respects amazingly solid. I bet my life the codes are right," Never said carelessly, buttoning up his shirt.

Tygier nodded and began to examine each weapon carefully, then placing it on the table. Although military was not his hobby, he knew the weapon well enough to take care of it.

"If only Fronda didn't pay his life of sending this message," he murmured after a moment.

"Caw, caw, caw. You can only crow," Never yelled. "Get together, because it will get dark soon, and when it gets dark, we must be there."

He also thought with care about the comrade-in-arms who was alone in this hornet's nest, but tried to push such thoughts away. They could not help but rather disrupt his combat performance. Once he has finished refining the plan, he should not reconsider it and deal with implementation.

The van delivered by Lena, similar to their old van, gave them a lift near Rolskij's estate. They had to sneak away on foot until they took a pre-selected position. From this place, the sentries could not see them, but they could sneak up to the gate, using the shield of viburnum bushes. Once in close proximity, Never and Lambdon aimed carefully and fired arrows filled with sleeping pills, aiming at the sentries.

The arrows were small and so sharp that their hits resembled a bite sting. It was prepared by Ivan Bury, armored officer of Gaiane, a small man with a gray, sunken face. Nobody would accuse him of being a vampire, and he was one of the most dangerous in this area. His skills, however, surpassed anything he could do as a warrior, so he constructed weapons such as flashlights resembling shooting tubes. They were windbreakers, and their cartridges were filled with a numbing agent, acting too fast to raise the alarm.

At first, the sentries did not realize what had actually happened. Then it was too late. Slowly, like on a slow motion, they lay on the ground and stood still, falling asleep almost immediately.

"Now," Never whispered.

Lambdon ran to the gate and started his device. He felt a soul on his shoulder, because if Fronda or he were wrong, the whole mission would end here. Fortunately, the codes were correct. Both gates opened silently. Rolskij's estate was open to friends. They still had to get to the buildings where they expected to find the electrical outlet necessary for Oggy and her laptop. Since this place was packed with electronics, you could control it and turn its power against the owner. Now it was a good time - Rolskij celebrated his birthday, to which he invited all the important notables from the circle of his influence. There was a chance that among so many guests the security could be deceived. A small chance.

Thanks to their extremely sharp senses, they managed to avoid confrontation with one of the patrols at first, but the sensors detected them almost immediately. Alert guards managed to surround them only at the building marked as A, but it was too fast. By the time they could repel their attack, alarm bells were howling all over the property, and halogen headlights were sweeping the beam of strong light.

"Oggy, let's get to work, we cover you!" Cried Never, breaking the building door with Lambdon. "You know what to do!"

The girl ran into the building and looked around for any electrical outlet. A great man lunged at her, brandishing Kalashnikov like a club. Without losing time for a full change, she opened the wolf's mouth with a terrifying roar, in which her face suddenly changed for the Russian. He jerked back, literally stuffing on Never's knife.

"Not bad," Oggy said, kneeling down in electrical outlet and plugging a laptop into it.

"Faster." The Indian urged her, fending off the next attackers with Tygier and at the same time calculating in spirit the amount of time left before all of Rolskij's forces would collapse behind them to this place.

"One moment, it is on fire or something... although it actually does..."

Oggy's nimble fingers ran along the keys at lightning speed and after less than a minute in Rolskij's entire estate the lights went out.

At the same time, Fronda was active from a good moment. He quickly picked up a piece of wire and opened the door of his cell and the door of the other vampire cells.

"Are you crazy? We'll all get to the jellyfish!" Lonia exclaimed in alarm, but Theo ignored him.

"What do you want to do?!" The Russian grabbed his arm.

"What you should do, much earlier," the Frenchman shouted in his face. "My friends are sticking their neck out, out there. If you want, you can help them, and if not, get the hell out of here!"

He opened the last cell, then with the barbell from the rack overturned the two guards who had fled down to the barracks. After a moment of numbness, caused by surprise, Russian vampires rushed to fight against their tormentors. Fronda, without looking at them, fell out of the underground into the fresh air. Finally, he did not have to pretend submission and was in his element. He broke the heads of the next two guards with a bar and ran to the pool, where a great party was taking place.

He did not forget the flogging received after the first victory and did not intend to go on this. He had to find Rolskij, though he couldn't answer the question of how he wanted to meet him, since he had never even seen a picture of him. Lena promised to deliver them, but she did not. Still waving a metal pole, he broke through the crowd of muddle-headed people, knocking everyone down who stood in his way. If his guesses were correct, Rolskij was in the mansion in the center of the property, and it was there that Fronda had to get.

Guests wandered sideways in panic. Their bodyguards lost their heads. They could not use side weapons, there were too many people around, and they had no chance with the raging Fronda. There was confusion, because no one knew who the enemy was. The very fact that mercenaries infiltrated the residence questioned the safety of all of them, for everyone could be the enemy. Mafia oligarchs were only seemingly here on good terms, no one really trusted anyone. The soap bubble of champagne fun and jovial patting on the back burst immediately.

Theo fought, smashing the heads and necks of those who got in his way and praying that the panic would not stop too soon. He had a chance to break home until a firearm was used against him. The situation could change in a moment, as soon as someone had mastered the panic and took over the command. He knew very well that these people were only seemingly a partying aristocracy, in fact they were tough, unscrupulous gangsters, only temporarily surprised by something they did not expect.

They pulled themselves together quickly. Those who did not want or could not fight fell to the ground, the rest began to organize and the air came from the shots. Theo hid behind a pedestal of one of the statues decorating the garden. Bullets cracked at pieces of marble, but none reached him. Then the shots stopped and he could look out carefully. Armed men looked around in panic. Two lay motionless on the grass, one writhing with its leg shot through.

"What the hell?" Fronda muttered to himself, trying to spot the mysterious allies.

"Here he is!" Lambdon's triumphant cry sounded behind him and it was good that the impulsive Pole, as always, could not refrain from him. Otherwise, Theo might have smashed one of his friends' heads before he recognized him.

"You made a nice mess," he said appreciatively when they were with him, headed by a stubbornly Oggy tail. Along the way, she shifted into the dog, not quite out of goodwill, rather instinctively, as always when too much adrenaline got into her blood.

And it was thanks to her dog's smell that they found a friend so quickly.

"This mess, as you have graciously put it, is thanks to our little one," Never said wryly.

The screams of confused people rang around. Confusion was rising, armed guards turned against each other, unsure who was attacking them now. The man with the bar from which they were hunting couldn't shoot them in the back, so who did?

"Do we have an ally?" Asked Theo in an undertone.

"You'd be surprised," Never chuckled, pointing to one of the guests.

Fronda stared at the gray-haired old man in a black suit. He had a bandage on his half face and mouth, but he didn't seem to mind. Together with a lady in dress standing at his side, who had to cost a fortune, they made their way through the roundabout road, pushing other guests away. They were both armed, but security did not pay attention to them. Never chuckled again.

"Aleksij Konstantynowich Pawlowski." He said. "Drugs and weapons. Property valued at over $ 1 billion. He was recently injured in a jaw attack, so he can't speak, poor man, and hears badly... But his latest kept woman is very talkative."

"Holy shit..." Theo recognized Lena. "And he..."

"Take a good look."

"Impossible!"

"And yet. We accepted the invitation addressed to Pawlowski. Our spy made sure that the old man did not leave the bed and did not accept anyone. And then..."

The strange couple finally reached them and stopped, panting.

"What's next?" Gerard pulled off the bandage with his gray wig and threw it down in disgust. The sleeve of the suit wiped sweat off his face and some makeup.

"What's next? Inside, the star of the stage, the screen and hematology!" Fronda patted him on the back with a flourish, almost knocking him over. "Damn you, I wouldn't recognize you, even if they paid me in gold!"

"Lena's idea."

"Why not talk later?" Russian interrupted them.

"Right," Gerard took a small object from his pocket. "Rajah, now?"

"Now."

The actor pressed a red button protruding from the side of the object. There were muffled explosions from all sides.

"What's up?" Fronda instinctively covered his head with his shoulder.

"We've been here since yesterday," Lena explained. "We managed to mine the area. I took care of the guards, and he placed the device."

"Well done."

"The water tower has gone and they are flooding now. As I know the laws of physics, the Niagara Falls are now gushing out there."

Indeed, at a certain distance, a plume of water was shooting up. Judging by the fearful calls in the air, the defense of the residence broke down to the rest. The guests went to all directions, their bodyguards stopped caring about anything and sought only in the confusion of their employers. The rest clearly ceased to interest them.

Lena looked at Fronda and looked him up and down.

"They martyred you much?" She asked roughly.

"Huh, fair to middling. I was a gladiator. I fought a few fights, practiced a lot in the gym and got flogged at the very beginning. All in all a banality." He replied cheerfully.

"In a word, it was, as always, you had fun and others worked," Never murmured. "The end of talking, this isn't the end of our mission. We still have to find Rolskij."

"Woof!" Oggy nodded, her ears merrily. She could not control her emotions and the transformation took place automatically, but it was even good for her friends. Oggy, a pacifist by nature, as a dog she was a formidable opponent and she bit like furious.

Theo scratched her ears and, bent to the ground, headed for the villa. She stood before them. The electronically controlled locks stopped working when the power supply stopped. The auxiliary aggregate, which was to supply them in the event of a power plant failure, was flooded with water and damaged as a result of a short circuit. Nobody looked after her either. Not anymore.

The guards, remaining on Rolskij's service, scattered in search of an invisible enemy, not understanding anything that was happening. Everyone believed in a security system invented by scientists on their boss's payroll. So far, no one has managed to break the codes, and when someone tried to break through a gate or fence without them, the alarm bells not only filled the air with their shrill sound, but also turned on high voltage on all fences. The metal wires attached to them were everywhere, and their arrangement was known only to the most trusted colleagues. The rest knew that when the alarm sounded, they were not to move from their seats and tear from the semi-automatic weapons to everything that moves, until further notice. However, nobody predicted such a situation like this.

The interior of the residence was covered with darkness, not obstructing the vampire's eyes, but certainly very embarrassing for people. Oggy growled, sniffing dozens of dangerous smells.

"Look, baby, look," Never encouraged her. "We have to find this bastard."

She ran down the corridor, lined with soft carpets, and as if she were being led by an invisible rope and her friends followed her.

The corridor ended in a huge hall, from which a suspended staircase led to the first floor.

"If he's still here, he must be somewhere at home, but exactly where? Too many doors here, and they must lead somewhere." Tiger looked around the hall, trying to guess where to search.

"He never leaves the mansion at least that was what those guardians said about him..." Theo wanted to say something else, but suddenly a light shone from the ceiling - pale, but still.

"What a hell? Lambdon wondered.

"Probably some extra emergency power supply," Never murmured uncertainly.

"You guessed it," said a calm voice from above.

On the mezzanine surrounding the hall stood two twin young men with Uzi pointed at them.

"I advise you not to charge now," one of them said. "These guns have clips of chemically pure silver. Special order, unique weapon on a global scale. One move and we will stuff you so that nothing will help you."

"What are these strange guys?" Never was surprised.

"Rolskij's grandchildren, twins from hell," Fronda replied grimly. "I've already seen them."

He did not forget the flogging he was given at their order, nor the fact that they forced him to kill against his will.

"Grandchildren and our grandfather's last line of defense," said the second of the twins. "You thought we would let you finish him off? His brain is worth millions. Without him, the whole organization would have been a subordinate band of gourmands."

"It's nice to hear that, but we don't care." Never looked slightly, calculating the possibility of escape. Unfortunately, they were not great. They were lower than their persecutors, and that alone put them in a losing position.

"We know that you blocked the power plant and destroyed the auxiliary unit. Unlock the power plant computer and we'll let you go.

"None of this," Theo said firmly. "And mainly because we can't. Our IT specialist is now a dog, and it is not known when she will be human again. And we are not computer experts."

"Why don't you do it yourself?" Gerard added.

The twins looked at each other and at the same time enabled their Uzi.

"At the moment you have to run the power plant, or tell us the code that will run it." One of them demanded sharply, with an incomprehensible to the friends, barely perceptible note of panic in the voice.

"You have half a minute," added the other with increasing nervousness. They still didn't know which is which, but it didn't matter at the moment.

Oggy twirled, whimpering and growling, but because of her nervousness she couldn't turn back into a human. The rest of the friends tried to think of something when an unexpectedly huge, dark brown bear appeared around the corner of the corridor upstairs. The animal threw a deafening roar at the twins, who released their pistols in surprise. They could do nothing more. The bear's bass voice fused into one of their terrible screams. In the blink of an eye, the air was saturated with the metallic smell of fresh blood.

"Mother," Gerard whispered, motionless in terror. The stage on the mezzanine resembled a live horror movie or a picture from Nero's circus. Lena standing behind him squeezed his arm.

"I knew there was an oceanarium here, but I didn't know it was a zoo. Someone must have opened the cage..." Theo squeezed his barbell grip desperately.

"Gee, it'll pounce on us now," Never moaned, while Lambdon standing next to him muttered something in Polish, teeth chattering.

The bear jumped over the jagged, bloody bodies and found himself on the stairs leading to the hall. Theo took a step forward, covering his friends and raising his weapon menacingly, laughable in comparison with the furious colossus. Oggy, tangling under her feet, shook herself and, with an effort calming the nerves, took on a human shape.

"Wisha…" she said in a soft voice. She knelt down and extended her hand to the big animal.

She touched his bloody muzzle and curled ears. The animal rocked its head, looking at her and responded with a sad guttural burr. Then the petrified friends passed and hurried through the door outside.

"Are you kidding…? Was it Wisha?!" Theo looked at Lena in amazement.

She shrugged.

"You didn't know?"

"What's so strange about that? You can change into a dog, you can change into a bear. Dress better, Oggy, instead of showing boobs to everyone," Never grumbled, throwing his shirt to the naked girl.

"Are we still looking?" Gerard asked helplessly. He couldn't get over the days when he was an actor and knew nothing about similar events.

"Of course it is," Tygier ran up the stairs, past the jagged corpse, and began to open all doors one after another, trying to guess which of them lead to the hideout of old Rolskij.

"He's over there," Oggy said, putting on the Indian's shirt. "Wherever the most electricity is. Some battery is working there. I felt this smell before I became human again."

She pointed to the first floor, to one of the branches of the corridor there.

"Well, we go there," Never grumbled without enthusiasm, remembering that he was the leader here.

Friends moved in the direction indicated, uncertainly glancing sideways. Nothing happened, however, only the pale emergency light under the ceiling shone faint and weaker.

Following Oggy, they peered into all the rooms until they stood before a large forged steel door, armed with three electric self-locking locks. In theory, after disconnecting the voltage should therefore lock the door, but someone had to open it earlier, because they were slightly ajar. There was a slight noise from inside.

"Are we coming in?" Lambdon asked, biting his nails nervously.

"We're coming in," Theo said and pushed a heavy door that opened silently on lubricated ball bearings.

Everyone held their breath, and Oggy moaned loudly and looked away.

They were in a huge hall, reminiscent of the interior of a futuristic spaceship. Almost the entire room was occupied by modern apparatus, blinking lights of emergency power LEDs. In the very center, a huge sphere hovered between transparent pneumatic cushions, filled with some transparent, slightly opalescent liquid. Inside was the human brain, with myriads of gold and platinum electrodes penetrating into its tissue. An intact spinal cord and large blood vessels departing from the brain, disappearing in the tangle of tubes, pumps and cables. The electrodes connected with the apparatus resembling an extremely complicated, multi-functional control board.

Apparatus gurgled under the transparent ball, supplying and draining blood, or something very similar to it.

"Mother of God..." Gerard muttered, forgetting that he is an atheist.

"What a machinery... It is ahead of ours by at least half a century. It is the technology of tomorrow, maybe even the day after tomorrow." Lambdon Tygier watched the elements of equipment piously, photographing every fragment with his tiny camera. The rest did not pay attention to the technique, they were more interested in the brain.

"Genadij Osipowich Rolskij." Said Lena slowly. "Who would have thought...?"

"Rather, who could be so mentally ill to be able to agree to such an existence?" Never asked with a shiver of disgust.

"The rich..." The Russian spat with contempt. "They even trying to cheat death. They think everything can be bought. I heard that Rockefellers exchange organs like worn shoes, but such things..."

"It's not as bad as it seems. These electrodes control everything. The guy has an audiovisual connection with the entire property, he sees and hears everything," said Lambdon, still looking at the apparatus. "He can probably also feel bodily pleasures if we consider that everything ultimately depends on stimulation in the right brain region. Someone had an idea. If the truth is what those two shits said about his genius, it is not surprising that his organization did not want to give up such a leader. After all, a powerful mind at the forefront of a criminal organization is three-quarters of its success."

"Let's get out of here, because I'll vomit," moaned Theo, whose face turned dangerously green.

Friends left the villa, completely stunned by what they saw. They did not expect such a view and still had the impression that they just dreamed about the interior of the residence.

Outside the door, they came across a freed group of Russian vampires who had already armed the weapons they had taken from the guards. They immediately flooded them with questions that they didn't understand.

Lambdon talked to them for a moment, then turned to his team:

"Two died in a clash with the guards, but victory is theirs. They ask about Rolskij. What should I tell them?"

"Tell them to go home and not worry about that damn old man again," Never told him.

"I'll take care of them. You come back to the lodging." Lena interrupted vigorously. "We'll talk soon."

"She's right, let's go back. I'm sick of this place. Besides, it will be dawn soon," said Gerard tiredly.

Theo patted him on his skinny back.

"We all deserve a rest," he said. "It was damn difficult and unpleasant action."

They walked slowly through the ruined property to the van left in the bushes.

"Lambdon, do you think this brain will last long?" asked Never after a long moment, still unable to forget what they had seen.

"Until the auxiliary power source is exhausted," replied Tygier. "According to my calculations, still an hour."

"Terrible. To be the king of life and end this way..." Gerard shook his head, still unable to recover.

"He deserved it," Theo said wearily, settling in the car. "Although, to tell you the truth, I'd personally prefer a scaffold."

"Then such a death?"

"Then such a life."

*****

"When was the first time you got it?" Oggy asked quietly.

She sat under the birches, leaning her back against the trunk of one of them. Beside her, Wisha sat, and thoughtfully broke the dry branches whose piles covered the ground. He raised his head at the girl's voice.

"I was twelve," he replied, "we lived with the whole family in a small village south of Novosibirsk. We had our own hut, we did not starve, and we enjoyed the sympathy and respect of our neighbors... I think we were happy. Until one day, I suddenly grew a coat and ripped the pig. When I came to my senses, I was terrified, I didn't know what was happening and why it happened to me."

"What happened next?"

"At night my father took me to the forest and left me there, commanding me never to return to my homeland. He said that I was a Vourdalak, like my great grandfather, and there is no place for me

155

among people. He had a reason to get rid of me, if the neighbors found out about everything, they would kill me and who knows if the rest of the family, just in case. However, it did not comfort me at all, I was desperate, and I cried all the time that I wanted to see my mother. Imagine the middle of winter, snowstorms and frost that you have no idea about. And in all this an abandoned teen, having no idea what to do."

"Terrible," Oggy whispered. "How do you deal with that?"

"I was lucky. Murman Dumbadze found me and took me to the then Gaiane headquarters. Nikita Karamozov, who managed the association at the time, was convinced that vampires would need someone like me, so they took care of me. It can be said that Murman and Nikita taught me everything I know, even how to control change. And how was it with you?"

Oggy briefly told him her story. Wisha listened to her emergence, not taking his small yellow-brown eyes from her. Since he became convinced that this girl was similar to him, he had wanted to ask her to stay with him, but he was aware of the futility of such requests. He didn't miss how Oggy looked at Fronda and how three foreigners were attached to her. He had nothing to dream of leaving them to stay with him in his hostile country.

His bitter thoughts were interrupted by the appearance of Never and Fronda.

"Do you know anything about Gusto?" Oggy asked, rising from the ground.

"He disappeared." Never said angrily, throwing his pistol on the table. "Theo is even happy about it, but I am not. Gusto will continue to hurt us all, and worse, it is not known where he will show up again."

"So? Our mission is completed, what now?"

"Nothing. We will wander a bit before Octavio comes up with something for us again," Theo said cheerfully. "Lena gave us an additional set of fake papers and she additionally paid ten thousand greens in exchange for a successful action, we have money to revel."

"Successful is a fact, but if it wasn't for Wisha, it would end badly for us."

"Am I saying that not? Wishka, you never listen to orders, do you?"

He looked questioningly at the Russian. He smiled without enthusiasm.

"Rarely, anyway," he admitted. "You didn't want to take me, I followed you on a motorcycle and intervened in due time. Although I admit that it was not easy for me to climb to the upper floor window, and if it was not ajar, I would not enter. They are made of armored glass. Post-Soviet bonzes install such in the whole house, even in the restrooms, because it's quite easy to get hit and you can buy the bazooka on almost every corner."

"It's called the free market," Never laughed.

Gerard appeared in the garden.

"Ready!" He called out.

Recently, he took over the role of a supplier and prepared the crew for the road, doing the necessary shopping. The supply in Russian stores was rather poor, but at the "black market" you could get everything that wanted. Lambdon Tygier, for whom the Russian language had no secrets, was able to get along with Russian obedient traders without problems, but flew to Spain immediately after the end of the action at Rolskij's estate. For this reason, Gerard was accompanied by Ivan, who spoke French well and knew all technical needs.

Together they traveled around stores and bazaars. In addition to the items on the list, they also bought additional pistol clips and parts that could be needed for the van, including a spare battery. Lena agreed to give them a car as an additional salary. It wasn't true their camper, it was also old, but they could have used it for some time in their planned travel around Europe.

Now they could hit the road. Russian vampires were reluctant to make close acquaintances with those who had done a black job for them, and their behavior could rather be interpreted as:

"It's nice that you helped us and now go down."

Never's group did not intend to impose themselves on them in any way, so they decided to leave as soon as possible.

They said goodbye only to Wisha, who was the only one of the Russians who apparently regretted their leaving - though probably only because of Oggy. Gerard even suspected how he was asking her for something, and the girl shakes her head refusing, although at the same time tears run down her face. He withdrew on his toes so they wouldn't see him and kept the matter to himself. He didn't want to get into love life of someone, especially since nothing could help.

They were getting ready for the road when Lena, panting from the fast run, caught up with them.

"Phone call for you," she announced. "From Spain."

"Why someone would not come up with portable telephones," Never sighed, resigning from the cab.

"Apparently they are already working on it, but for now we have what we have. Hurry up, he'll pay the fortune for this call."

\*\*\*\*\*

Octavio di Mauro was waiting at the airport. This alone was significant, for he was more careful than others and did not show up in public places. This caution was somewhat exaggerated, because Octavio, a redhead and freckled, did not match the vampire's stereotype and was unlikely to be recognized by the Hunter's spy. Nevertheless, he kept his stubbornness and gave up caution today.

Therefore, Never, spotted him behind the barrier, whistled slightly through his teeth.

"I think the case is serious," he muttered to his friends.

"May it be worth the hell of a journey," Theo looked at himself in a pocket mirror and with a few moves of his comb brought his tousled hair to a relative order.

He hated planes and was terrified of them, but he did not object when necessary. He only reserved the night flight. As a "moth" he did not want to come into contact with sunlight.

"I don't like flying either," Oggy sighed wearily. She literally fell from fatigue despite two coffees drunk just before landing.

Octavio didn't say much on the phone, but it was enough for Never to force everyone to give up their original plans and re-use the airlines.

Red Spaniard joined four friends as soon as they left the customs chamber.

"Let's go straight to the institute," he offered without admission. "I will tell you everything as much as I can tell along the way."

He led them to a blue Chrysler standing in the parking lot. Behind the wheel sat Mercedes, dressed the same as when they saw her for the last time, as if she didn't recognize any other outfits except this old-fashioned dress. She nodded seriously in response to their greeting, then shifted into first gear and carefully maneuvered the car from among the hundreds of cars parked there.

"So talk," Never demanded as Chrysler safely got out onto the highway.

He did not answer immediately. First, he took a heat-insulating bag from under the chair and gave everyone a bottle of dark red liquid, and Oggy handed a nice piece of sirloin in foil. She grabbed it with badly masked greed and began to devour, murmuring with contentment.

"The case is dark," he said finally. "We don't know what happened, and none of us can explain it. It started barely a month ago. Some of us began to mumble that they felt somehow bad and that malaise quickly spread to others, like an infectious disease. Then those who worked at lower levels suddenly demanded earlier rotation. They explained this quite vaguely revealed claustrophobia and stubborn nightmares, which we tried to alleviate by collective psychotherapy, but it was not better."

"Psychotherapy is one big scam," Fronda murmured indistinctly, without taking the bottle from his mouth.

Octavio continued, ignoring him.

"We all began to feel some horror, so strong that soon we could no longer work or, oddly enough, relax. And the worst was yet to come. Maybe if it happened to someone else, I would put it on the edge of weak nerves, and later events would be explained by collective hysteria... but Irinka Kralova, a geneticist, the coldest and most balanced mind at the institute was the first to see something! She jumped out of her studio with such a scream that she got everyone on their feet, and in addition she did not want to say what scared her, just took her things and went to the surface, refusing to return."

Never frowned.

"Aren't you rocking?" He asked in obvious disbelief. "From what Tygier said, your Irka would not be afraid even a devil itself."

"I'm telling the truth. Of course, we searched her studio thoroughly but found nothing. Then such cases began to recur, and their participants, literally paralyzed by fear, could not accurately describe what they saw. You probably understand that almost one hundred and fifty well-established scientists, hardened in battle, with an average age of four hundred years, probably could not go crazy at the same time!"

"I don't know... Stranger things have happened." Never was clearly convinced.

"Initially, we thought that maybe we were hit by a mascara, related to that of Stonehenge, which Fronda wrote about her, but what the individual witnesses said did not coincide with your discovery. The image that emerged when I passed the data through the computer was terrifying and I thought it was a mistake, until one day when I went down to the isotope lab, I was knocked over by... Look, I am over a thousand years old and I fainted with fear."

He fell silent and breathed deeply for a moment.

"But what was it finally?" Gerard reminded him gently as the silence began to lengthen.

"Were any of you saw the movie "Eighth Passenger Nostromo"?"

"Sure," Theo beamed. "I saw it several times. Great movie!"

"Yes? Well, you know more or less what attacked me." Said Octavio.

After this statement, silence fell again. Fronda interrupted it.

"Well, you don't want to make believe us that after your research station some creature flies, which has acid instead of blood and folds embryos in human bodies... You would already look like chopped meat and you are in one piece."

Octavio shrugged.

"I don't want to make believe anything," he said grimly. "Because it would be so unambiguous... One would expect that something like this would tear a man to shreds, but it does little in the physical sense. It didn't even scratch me and disappeared without a trace. And that's how it is. Actually, everything we deal with is inexplicable phenomena and uncontrollable feelings."

"What did you do?" Oggy asked, her mouth full.

"We retreated to the corridors below the surface and tried to work out a plan of action, but it overwhelmed us. Finally, our two geologists, Sven Barthold and Kaori Yamato, decided to visit the station and document everything they see on film. If we analyzed it later, we could learn more. We found them two days later, when we were worried about the prolonged silence in the ether, we organized a rescue trip. They were dead, despite no injuries."

"Did you do the postmortem examination?" Never asked while others were digesting this information.

"Yes. An autopsy showed swelling of most internal organs, especially the lungs and brain, something like cockroaches subjected to strong solux exposure for a long time."

"Nice comparison."

"In addition, both hearts had clear signs of infarction, the adrenal glands were damaged, and tissue cortisol levels were beyond imagination. Understand?"

"Aha..." Never rubbed his hand thoughtfully.

"What does it mean?" Fronda asked him angrily. "From these medical terms, the devil himself will not understand anything. What about me?"

"Theo... They died of fear," his friend explained to him with gentle pity.

"What about tape?" Oggy wanted to know.

"Overexposed. Trash. After this story, I could do nothing but contact you." Octavio lowered his head in resignation, as if to say that he did not believe in this help either.

"I understand, a drowning man catches at a straw," murmured the Indian grimly. "I have no idea what we will find there, but you can be sure that we will search well. We don't believe in ghosts, ghouls or monsters from horror movies.

"Speak for yourself," Theo said, who wholly believed in all apparitions, though he had never seen one. He also believed in monsters, although he had some basis here.

Never didn't listened to him, however. He was clearly annoyed.

"I thought you scientists were smarter," he said. "How far can stupidity go, huh? You should know that there is nothing supernatural in this world."

Octavio looked at him with a heavy, deadly eyesight. He wasn't even offended.

"Do you think we don't know that? We know, or rather we knew. Now we are not sure of anything. What attacked me defies description, because it is not like anything that can be seen on this earth. When it roared in my face, it was as if I would go back to prehistoric times in a heartbeat. I felt the fear of the caveman who saw something deadly something he did not know. Whatever it is, it affects the part of our brain that we inherited from animal ancestors, and it becomes dominant."

Theo snorted angrily.

"Maybe you come from a monkey, but I don't and I don't like similar comparisons," he said proudly.

"Shut up, medieval man," Never nudged him with disgust.

Although Fronda attended Darwin's lectures in his time and tried to be "up to date" with modern science, he still suffered from medieval prejudices. The theory of evolution did not appeal to him at all. Not only to him. Never also didn't fully believed in it and in the silence of the spirit that evolution on Earth was initiated by some other intelligent species of unspecified beings, called gods in the Indian Vedas.

"We arrive." Said Mercedes briefly.

Until now, she has not interfered in the conversation, considering that there is nothing to say in these matters. Friends already knew from their previous visit to Spain that this girl says little, and only when absolutely necessary, they were not surprised by her silence.

At the entrance to the underground maze, they saw a lonely figure. It was only up close that they met Trelawny, an employee of the research station engineering department. She was sitting on an overturned barrel and, with her hands supporting her round chin, was clearly waiting for them. At her legs lay a caracal outstretched and she plowed her ears like a hunting dog...

"It's good that you are here," she said standing up. "The crew agreed that if you don't come, they'll leave the station. They are deadly terrified."

"And you don't?" Never asked, kissing her on the turned cheek.

"I have a house nearby, I don't care. Besides, Octavio entrusted me with commanding in his absence. But there is something else."

"What?" Octavio worried.

Trelawny looked at him guiltily.

"Tygier went to the institute," she muttered softly.

"What?! I forbid exploring the danger site until I came back!" Roared Octavio.

"Don't yell, it's not my fault! Nobody would listen to me!" Cried the girl pathetically. "People are afraid, you don't understand? And Tygier is not guilty either, that idiot Klaus egged him on!"

"How is that?" Oggy asked, remembering Klaus Guttenberg, a small, fat German, an extremely talented biophysicist, with some difficulty. He didn't look like he was bothering anyone."

"A German with Pole are irreconcilable," explained a dark-skinned engineer. "They'll always argue. As they began to recollect the sins of their ancestors, Malbork, some Grunwald, partitions, the first and the second war, I immediately knew that there would be nothing good about it. And it turned out to be like that. At one point Klaus said that Tygier probably did not inherit courage from his ancestors, because he fucked up the institute as much as we all did. As Lambdon heard it, he drank a half-liter bottle of 'Smirnoff' vodka in one breath and went! Inside. Then we have not seen him."

Octavio waved a hand hopelessly. He now looked as if he regretted getting involved in the organization of the research station in this post-Frankist bunker that was supposed to be an underground factory. He was clearly at the end of his strength and even Never felt compassion.

"Keep your head up, we'll get him out of there," he said comfortingly.

"It's my fault. I should take him with me. I forgot, damn it, that Lambdon is Polish," said Octavio, rubbing his face with his hands with the motion of a weary man.

"What the hell does this have to do with it?" Gerard was surprised, who had some Polish blood in himself, after his mother, but he knew little about Poles.

"And it has something. It is said that if you want to do something unfeasible, then you should bring a few Poles and strictly prohibit them from interfering with it in any way." Trelawny explained to him.

Octavio nodded with steady movements on his red head.

"Exactly. And I know them well because I was at Somosierra. You have no idea what was going on there. I know that a Pole, when good, is good, but by the time. Discipline is not a penny, but a fantasy so that it could export it. He can't listen to orders, but he can drink. And then he always asks him misfortunes. Every normal person, when he is upset, gets into the pellet and sleeps, and the Pole catches what he has at hand, and goes banging, and who it didn't matter. I should have predicted that Tygier would not stand..."

He gritted his teeth and opened the hatch.

This time he did not go to the center and his friends followed him to one of the branches of the main corridor of the old canals. As it turned out, at the very end it branched into a whole network of rooms, which were once bunkers, built for war purposes, and forgotten after the war. Now these primitive shelters were full of vampires of both sexes, trying to arrange them somehow in cold, uncomfortable rooms.

"There's no time left" Never decided. "We're going straight away. Oggy, you stay. In case we don't come back long, you will lead a rescue trip. Your sense of smell can be an invaluable treasure in such an eventuality."

"Okay, okay," the girl grunted. "You know, I'm a woman, so you just think I'm not fit. There should be a paragraph on people like you."

Never waved a hand at her.

"Octavio, watch over the suffragette so that she doesn't do something stupid," he said. "We're going to have enough trouble with ourselves and the drunk lab technician, which he got there on his own, I don't want to worry about that little one."

"Sure. You can be calm. Sister, lead them to the elevators," Octavio said, eyeing Oggy with a stern look.

Mercedes moved without a word, leading three friends through the electronically opened and closed airlocks. The research station was now strangely quiet and empty, even here on the administrative floor, which was entered directly from the corridor. And even here, there was an atmosphere of terror that seemed to fill this place to the last corner.

"Here you have a map of the workshop and all the sensitive points of the station." Said Mercedes, pointing to a large, framed diagram, hung on the wall near one of the elevators. "Remember it because you won't have a guide down there."

"Very interesting," Fronda said appreciatively, diligently studying colored drawings.

"Are we going down?" Gerard asked uncertainly when Mercedes left them alone in this sterile, shiny white and metal room.

"It's hard for us to go up," Never snorted, programming the elevator. "We're sticking together, okay? And no insubordination."

"Yawohl, Herr Lieutenant," Theo pushed him away from the programmer and touched a few buttons. "Better go by the stairs from the minus first floor. We will be able to check everything more closely. I opened the stairwell shaft."

The stairs in the station were secured by automatic doors on every level up to minus six, considered safe. From each elevator it was possible to program the main machine so that all doors were open at once. It remained a mystery how Fronda, a technical anti-talent in his own judgment, remembered all the codes. Perhaps he was simply not such an anti-talent at all, or maybe the secret was in his phenomenal memory of numbers.

"You are right," said the Indian appreciatively. "We wouldn't see much from such a canister. Come on, boys."

The prospect of checking several underground floors for wraiths was not very joyful, but the three felt stronger and none of them had betrayed their fears. They already had some skill in searching suspicious places and making documentation, but they did not know what to document here. Everywhere there was disorder, as if the scientists working here were in a hurry with moving out, in several places the interior equipment was completely destroyed.

"It's like somebody's crazy here," Never said, looking at the damage.

As they descended to lower levels, friends felt choking fear more and more. Darkness, lying in the corners, thickened imperceptibly, extending its spectral tentacles toward the center of the room and they did not immediately notice that this darkness seemed to drain light from everywhere. The station was brightly lit, and yet they saw it getting worse. This was even more remarkable when one considers that vampires usually don't mind light. Flashlights didn't help. This thickening darkness seemed to be blessed with their own lives, almost felt it as hostile, incomprehensible intelligence, watching their actions in silence. For now in silence. The ceiling lamps were still shining with the same light, but it was still getting darker. They still couldn't find anything that could be called tangible proof, no matter what.

The darkness suddenly played with different sounds, at first barely audible. Fronda described these sounds as something intermediate between a whistle and a bass howl from the depth of the metal pipe. There were also other ones, reminiscent of wheezing. They were coming in from different directions, appearing here and there, giving a ghostly impression as if it were an exchange of opinions or perceptions. Almost simultaneously with the sounds, cold and hot breeze appeared, their faces or neck suddenly brushing, shadows began to take ominous shapes.

Gerard, still calm, began to tremble so that he could barely hold the camera.

"I will probably have to go to a psychiatrist," he muttered through his throat.

"Oh, shut up," Never said angrily, without admitting that he was barely able to keep his imagination under control.

"Forgive me, Rajah, I'm getting off," the actor excused himself. "I won't make it. I haven't felt anything like this in my life. I do not know what is sitting there and I would rather not find out, because I feel that I will never sleep peace..."

He paused because he tripped over something big and shouted terribly as he released the camera from his hand.

"Stop it, it's Tygier!" Fronda grabbed Gerard by the shoulders and shook him hard. "Calm down, mollusk"

"I think we're late..." Never knelt and examined the still body for a moment, shining a flashlight in his teeth. They looked at him, holding their breath.

"Luckily alive," he said finally. "He is healthy, and he thinks something has fallen on his drunken head because he has a tumor like a watermelon, but he's alive."

He took an ampoule of ammonia from his handbag and after a moment Tygier groaned, letting him know that he was coming back to consciousness.

"What a mess," he muttered. "What is going on here?"

"You tell us that." Gerard gave him a careful support and helped him sit down.

"Me? Yes, I went here... I lost my flashlight... then I tripped over something and I hit my head into the wall..." Tiger shook his head while touching the bump on his forehead It seemed that even if he saw something, he was too drunk, to remember anything. He spoke incoherently, rather mumbled and, despite repeated attempts, he could not get up.

"Just what we needed." Never murmured.

He took a clear liquid from some ampoule into the syringe and gave the Pole an injection in his arm. Soon Tygier sobered up enough to be able to regain coordination of movements, though not enough to be useful. Vampires get drunk very easily, much easier than people, and Lambdon drank almost half a liter of pure alcohol, so of course there was no use of him. Friends took him only because they were afraid to leave him alone.

Unfortunately, a large dose of pure alcohol also deprived Lambdon of control over his nerves and quickly became horrifying. Normally, you could support him spiritually, but it would be difficult now. The three friends themselves kept their nerves in check very tightly in check. Admittedly, they still kept up well, although what took the station followed them step by step. For now, they didn't see anything out of the ordinary, but they felt - and that was enough.

The reality has changed from the minus seventh floor. Nothing was what it seemed to be, the contours of the objects blurred, and the darkness began to take on tangible shapes. Still, they could not find anything that could be blamed for strange phenomena. Well, if only phenomena... Actually, it was not the worst that they could see or hear. Much more monstrous was the fear that paralyzed them and did not allow logical reasoning, the fear that grew in their brains like a parasite from the SF horror film and tried to take control over them.

Even Never, not susceptible to this kind of emotions, with an increasing difficulty refrained from chattering teeth. Still, he bravely pushed ahead until at one point two rows of small, but very sharp teeth suddenly bit into his darkness. He grabbed the bitten place and felt that blood was pouring down his arm. However, raising it to his eyes, he did not see any traces of blood, but at the same time he felt another bite, this time in the neck.

"Awww!" He shouted, losing his temper. "What is this? No, I'm not going any further."

"Thank God," Gerard sighed.

"The atheist said... What, are we turning back?" Asked Tygier uncertainly.

They turned around, trying to look through the darkness that rippled around like a sea of pitch. It seemed impossible for them to return through all these scary corridors, but not for external reasons - as if the barrier lay within them, impossible to remove. Helplessness overwhelmed them.

"We can't give up now," Theo whispered, afraid to raise his voice.

"I don't know what is with you, I will give up even on my knees," Gerard huddled on the floor, clasped his fists to his ears to suppress the sound of foreign sounds.

"I would have gone, but damn my legs won't listen to me," moaned Tygier, shivering so that it was hard to understand his words.

There was silence for a moment. The prospects seemed miserable, since they couldn't force themselves to move forward or backward. This helpless silence finally made Fronda angry. He one of them wholly believed in the wraiths and, paradoxically, tamed with fear of them for centuries, somehow managed to tame his terror. Anyway, he didn't let him paralyze like the others.

"Sit here like wet hens!" He screamed, stop counting anything, until his voice echoed around. "I keep looking! This maggot must be here somewhere and I will find it, even though I would die!"

"Will you go there alone?" Groaned Gerard, but Theo ignored him.

With desperate courage, he turned and entered the darkness that covered the stairs to the minus eighth level. He felt as though the thick, slimy black snake was running down from under his feet, curling up the steps. It was even worse than the experience at Stonehenge, because at least he saw it, and here... He looked up. The ceiling lamps were still shining strong, and he couldn't see anything beyond a step. He thought he was now in the office, because staples, pens and piles of paper were cluttered on their desks. He barely saw them, and only when he blinked.

Something caught his hand, which he stretched out in a blind man's motion - a shaggy toothed muzzle, hot as lava. He pulled a hand from his teeth with a cry of terror. Did he think he was indeed a six-legged shape, as large as a wardrobe, but with strangely blurred contours, brushed against him and disappeared into the corridor? Theo hissed barely audibly, his back to the wall. He felt that what was rubbing against him left sticky mucus on his skin, but touching his clothes with his hands he sensed with amazement that it was dry. It all looked like a compilation of the worst nightmares, just like a nightmare that you can't wake up from.

Shivering all over his body, he took a step forward and jumped back against the wall again. A pair of red blinds were clearly looking at him from the corner, and... Did he think he heard a deaf growl? He backed away, knocking back the hanging cabinet on the wall, behind which a device fell with a clink. He raised it automatically. It vibrated in his hand, and when he lifted it to his face he felt a faint smell. Something leaked through the tiny holes from the inside, stimulated by a working motor. He searched for a piece of a thick branch, wrapped it carefully and secured it with an office tape. Only then he put them in a haversack over his shoulder.

Low sounds drilled into his poor, bemused brain, as if directly, bypassing the organs of hearing. Perhaps this statement in Fronda's distracted subconscious mind made a vague association, like a sense of deja vu, which he did not immediately notice. However, the association returned stubbornly, like the phrase of a melody played from a cracked disc, and, unwittingly, he listened to it with the last of his strength. The answer exploded under his skull like fireworks at Disneyland.

"Hell, I am such a girl!" He screamed furiously. "I believed in ghosts as if I wasn't six centuries old!"

He knew everything already, as if the chaotically scattered pieces of some puzzle suddenly matched themselves. If so logic could suppress his feelings... Fear has not diminished, but its quality has changed. He could already separate it from other feelings and ignore.

Gathering all his strength, he remembered the station diagram. What he had to reach was at the very bottom, close to its heart - the nuclear reactor. Theo knew that the scientists working here built it themselves, although he had no idea where they got uranium from, and this question was nobody wanted to answer. What he was looking for was next to this dangerous and beneficial device. Normally he wouldn't even get close to it, but he had to.

As he descended, he stopped seeing anything, except for the short flares during which he tried to remember as much as possible of the topography of the place where he was. These flares seemed to confirm his theory and he was grateful for that. He had to hang on to the certainty that he was right, because the atmosphere around him was thickening and he saw more and more indescribably terrible shapes in these inconceivable darkness.

Minus tenth, minus eleven, minus twelfth... He felt like Alice in Wonderland when he finally reached minus sixteenth level, where the reactor continued to rumble. The braiding atomic stack apparatus was in constant motion, and its stopping threatened with an uncontrolled chain reaction. Nobody risked it.

Theo wet his dry lips with the tip of his tongue, then walked over to the computer controlling the entire station centrally. Fortunately, they forgot to close it, so he didn't need a password to access the program. He did not know much about computers and did not want to know them, but he had to "take" a short course and now blessed Never's persistence, which forced him to do so.

He quickly found the right option on the list. He hesitated for a moment, calculating suspected damages in his mind. He could not judge them properly, he only knew that one must not be turned off under any circumstances - the reactor cooling system. He had to finagle it. He chose quickly from the list to order down the blind window, all of them just in case. He knew from what Maryon Humphrey, the head of elementary particle department, had explained to him that when the option was turned on, the reactor would automatically go into a sterile state, but it didn't tell him anything. He could only hope it would be good for him.

Making sure that the cooling was secured against switching off, he pressed the "Enter" button while moving the cursor after subsequent commands. When the command flashed on the screen to activate or cancel the process, his nerves again refused to obey him and he hit the keyboard so hard that his hand ached.

First the sounds died down, then the darkness disappeared. The station was again filled with steady, bright light, everywhere there was peace and quiet. The fear tormenting Fronda's mind also disappeared, as if it were never there. Theo leaned against the wall, feeling sweat trickling down his back and face. The sudden relief he felt caused him not to gather his thoughts for a long time, but only stared blankly at the broken keyboard. The electrical impulse caused by its damage had to affect the computer somehow, because endless strings of mathematical symbols flew through the screen, quite incomprehensible to Fronda.

He forced himself to set out on the return journey. Actually, he would prefer to sit against the wall and sleep off all this nervousness, but there was no time. Returning, he had the opportunity to better assess the extent of damage. They were really big, as if the scientists working here turned into a herd of cattle escaping a fire under the influence of what was happening. Even the conservatory was destroyed. Disoriented birds flew here and there, hiding as much as they could. Poor creatures were clearly frightened, although in the physical sense nothing serious happened to them. The panic they succumbed to was clearly gone.

When Theo reached his friends, he immediately noticed that they were in a much better condition.

"How did you do it?" Never asked reluctantly.

Whenever Theo turned out to be better than him, the Indian vampire would get jealous. He didn't like to feel worse."

"I just turned off the reactor and everything I could," Fronda explained to him. "There is a lot of it here! These cyber brains are constantly adding new ones, and you have the effect."

"What effect?" Gerard's voice trembled a little longer, and the remnants of terror flickered in his green eyes.

Theo sat next to Lambdon, who was still staring at him unconsciously.

"To tell you the truth, I wouldn't have guessed my life if it wasn't for chance," he confessed. "You know that I read science publications eagerly, even if I didn't understand it. In one of them, a cranky professor described the experience with a magnetic chamber. At a given field strength and frequency of air vibrations, people locked in a chamber individually felt strongly that someone was there except them. I was interested so I read it twice. And now I remembered."

They looked at him with wide eyes, so he added:

"And I found it."

He took a found object from the haversack. Tiger carefully unwrapped it and turned it off immediately.

"Where did you find this?"

"It was hidden behind the cupboard I came across. What is this?"

"Type of diffuser. Was spraying something. Perhaps there are more of them here. What about the reactor?"

"I turned it all off. It became calmer at once. You know, I've read that infrasound causes delusions and..."

"Did you turn everything off?" Tygier interrupted him.

"Yes. In addition to cooling the reactor, of course, I did not want it to dissolve after all."

"Fronda, you're an idiot," said Lambdon with resignation. "Go back there and turn on the central system. When deactivating, it closes the staircase windows, how do we get out of here? The elevators don't work without electricity."

"But... the electricity seems to work..." Gerard looked around uncertainly.

Tygier waved a hand.

"It's emergency lighting," he explained.

Theo scratched his back, not even offended.

"I'm afraid I've made a short circuit," he said remorsefully. "I hit the keyboard a little too hard and the computer broke a bit... Maybe from some other?"

"They're online. If you damaged the program of one, they all broke." The Pole finally stood up and looked around. "We have to find a way to get out of here. The reactor cooling has three types of functions, one is associated with accelerated air circulation around the core, which is then discharged outside through a filter system to avoid contamination. The station is hermetic, and at the moment the cooling apparatus sucks air out of it. We are threatened with anoxia before we die from the vacuum created in this way.

For someone who had drunk half a liter of vodka on an empty stomach a few hours ago, he was amazingly sober. He reasoned logically, though his conclusions were not comforting. They had to get out of the station, which now resembled a soldered casket more than anything.

"What's crawling there?" Gerard asked weakly, breaking the heavy silence.

Friends looked instinctively in the indicated direction. A huge bird-eating tarantula spider was slowly marching on the floor, in which they met Dr. Kawrechkina's favorite. The monstrous creature was clearly lost and did not know what to do.

"Fronda, don't you dare," Tygier warned his friend.

The arachnophobia of a medieval knight was no stranger to him, as was everyone who met him closer.

"What?" Theo shrugged. "After what I have recently experienced, would I still be afraid of spiders? I'm over it. Come on, Chikita, don't be afraid of Uncle Fronda."

He crouched down and reached out. The bird-eating tarantula walked without hesitation on his sleeve and curled up there. Spiders do not have expressive facial expressions, they do not communicate with representatives of other species, but everyone understood her feelings. It was clear to them that the female was clearly relieved to find herself on the shoulder of a man. She was used to people and felt safe under their protection.

Now that the light was clear, the road became much easier, but it ended quickly. The shaft of the stairs was slammed shut, the elevators were obviously not working, and as for air, you could already feel the difference in oxygen content. The attempt to open one of the shafts turned out to be beyond the strength of friends trapped in the station, so you had to look for another way out. There were elevators that could, however, effectively block the exits, and it was known in advance that they would not move without the help of electrical apparatus.

"Elevator number four is under renovation," said Tygier. "It's on level sixteen. If we open its shaft, we will be able to climb the safety net to the very top, and there only the main lock will remain to open."

"Yeah... but how do you open the door?" Never said skeptically.

If the current were still flowing in the crane circuits, it would be easy to make a short circuit, but in this situation Never's all technical knowledge was useless. Fronda's methods proved to be more useful - straight from the Middle Ages. Theo looked for a crowbar somewhere and, putting all his strength into it, slid its flattened end between both halves of the door. Friends pushed to the other end together. They thought that none of it came when there was a faint grinding sound and the door slid open slowly. The dark shaft was open for them.

"The emergency light dims and we have less and less oxygen. It's time to get away from here," said Tygier, wiping sweat from his brow.

"We seem to have to fall up. This is probably the only such accident in history," Theo chuckled.

"Hide this sarcasm for a better opportunity." Advised the Pole. "We have to climb the safety net to the very top, and we don't have ropes to tie them together, so everyone is on their own. Fronda, watch out for Chiquita. Tarantulas have a fairly delicate armor, and are relatively heavy, so falling from a small height can kill them."

Theo stroked the spider in his shirt. Her fur resembled the feel of a mouse or a hamster, and was not at all disgusting, as he once thought. He was surprised himself that he felt some tender concern, instead of the revulsion and fear that usually overwhelmed him at the sight of spiders and most insects. This hairy bird-eating tarantula, clung to him confidently, was now under his protection - and he took the knight's duties very seriously.

"Don't worry," he said.

Climbing the vertical walls of the shaft in complete darkness and heavier air was not easy. The metal mesh was uncomfortably sticking to the fingers and toes, which could hardly be pressed between the wall and the thick wire links. The lungs worked less and less efficiently in the air, which was becoming less and less frequent. Friends did not know if there really was so little oxygen or just how they felt. However, they were aware that they had to get to the top quickly if they wanted to survive.

A fall into the shaft would end tragically for all of them under these conditions. Vampires are very resistant, and their nervous tissue, unlike typically human, easily regenerates. However, when the brain is damaged too deeply, the matter is very difficult, and when there is a stroke in the medulla oblongata, the breathing center of someone fixed can be paralyzed as effectively as the center of any man. For a vampire, this is a tragedy - an infected respiratory compress usually means death, because 'in order to regenerate its tissues they need oxygen, and in large quantities. The ability to fall into lethargy is then priceless, as it reduces the demand by 90% - but few of them possess this skill sufficiently to fall into trance quickly enough.

When they finally reached their destination, all four already had a concentration disorder and they were overwhelmed by the more and more difficult to overcome their drowsiness. The situation became very dangerous. The pressure decreasing with a constant value was severe, though it did not yet exceed the critical value. In addition, there was another nasty surprise waiting for them. The exit was closed by an armored flap that could not move.

"How to open this hatch?" He is sucked in deafly," Gerard whispered, his hand touching the symmetrical flaps of solid metal fitted into the wall. They fit so well that you couldn't squeeze your fingernail between them, and the internal emergency levers couldn't move. They tugged at them with all their strength remaining, but with no effect.

"What now? Never asked helplessly.

"Let's pray and say goodbye," Theo suggested with unusual resignation.

He was already struggling to stay on the metal mesh. In the silence that fell, his breath mixed with the equally heavy breaths of his friends. It was becoming clear that they only had a few minutes left before they passed out and fell down.

"Wait... do you hear?" Gerard suddenly held his breath, listening to some sounds outside the elevator door.

Indeed, there were some grinding, metallic noises from outside that they could not correctly identify.

"Someone is tinkering around..." whispered Never after a moment with new hope.

He was right. A dozen or so endless seconds and hermetic door slammed open, letting the light of flashlights enter the elevator shaft and, what was more important, a violent stream of fresh air. They really needed it badly. Drawing the last strength, they crawled out of the shaft, grabbing the helpful hands of those who opened their way to freedom. They lay on the rough floor for a long time, greedily catching their breath.

"It's called at the last minute," groaned Gerard, staggering to his feet and barely straightening his sore cross. "How did you guess where we are?"

"When the light went out and the ventilation stopped working, we realized that you would have no other way than this shaft," Trelawny explained, putting away the crowbar she no longer needed. "We didn't have the right tools, which is why it took us so long to open the stile for you. Everything that is most effective works after all on electricity, and there is no electricity here... Why? These demons turned it off? What exactly was there?"

"A whole army of Christian hells and Greek Tartarus," said Lambdon, with superiority to Klaus Guttenberg. "I'm not going to shred my mouth, but there is someone here who will tell you everything. Fronda, go on."

Theo explained, in the most concise words possible, what measures he had taken to free the station from the tormenting demons, and a group of scientists listened intently to him. It was obvious that they were very relieved and at the same time a bit of shame. They liked Fronda, but at the same time they considered him an ignorant and superstitious weenie. And here it turned out that this superstitious ignorant dealt with their problems in a way that they should come up with.

"I didn't even know you could operate a computer," said Simon Mage, looking at Fronda with involuntary respect.

"He knows a lot, he doesn't admit it," Oggy said proudly, hugging her friend's side.

"It's Never's merit," Theo admitted honestly, scratching her head in spite of his will, as when she turned into a dog. "I have never even learned to use typewriter. Never forced me to take an evening course where I got the lowest score, but I learned to distinguish a mouse from a joystick and enter from escape. And that was enough for me, as you can see."

"We have something else," Tygier gave Octavio a diffuser. He looked at it intently, opened it and took out an ampoule with a greenish liquid. He looked at it against the light for a moment.

"Either I'm wrong or someone has planned a diversion here," he said finally. "Give it to chemists. I want to have the result of the analysis as soon as possible. Fronda, what do you have on your shirt?"

"Ah, I forgot. Where is Dr. Kawrechkina? Tamara Siemionowna!" Theo took Chiquita from his shoulder and looked around.

Doctor Kawrechkina pushed through her colleagues and gratefully took her favorite from him.

"I was so worried about her... Thank you, you're so sweet, that you took her," she said, hugging the spider lightly to her cheek.

"There are still birds down there. They fly around the remains of your conservatory and are probably nervous."

"We'll take care of them. And I invite you for a good meal."

The corridors separating the station from the ground bunker were once thought of as warehouses. Finding spare equipment in them was not difficult, and on the same day, before Never's team slept off its action, analysts from the chemical department could present the results of the study.

"I don't believe it," Octavio said, reviewing the document presented to him. "Impossible! After all... it was in the theoretical phase!"

"Unfortunately, man. It looks like someone has gone beyond this phase." Replied Tygier, who brought the results of the analysis.

"I forbid it... We don't make weapons!"

The Pole shrugged.

"It is not yet known if psych ran would work as a war gas. Rather average, I think. The question is why he put the atomizer in the offices next to the reactor. We should investigate this as soon as possible."

Octavio was of the same opinion. He quickly called the physicists and the reactor's technical staff, selected the best of them, and sent them down to be sure in suits and closed-loop oxygen suites. The second team came to save the animals left at the station. Everyone was calmer and began to consider what to do next. In the endless discussions, the prevailing view was that the institute must be moved, and the farther the better. It meant crazy work, but there seemed to be no other way. They stopped feeling safe here.

"Where are you going with all this stall?" Fronda asked when he and others had attended one of these meetings.

"We'll make it," Octavio told him. "We've always made, and it won't be any different now."

"If you say so..."

They haven't left yet. Not because they were needed here, but because they simply wanted to help. The situation did not look good at all. On the one hand, it was necessary to deal with the disassembly and packaging of equipment, on the other, the type of collective psychosis that affected almost all permanent residents of the station was no less a problem. They could not shake off what happened to them, even though it was behind them, and what is worse, they stopped trusting each other. If one turned out to be a traitor, it could also be someone else, the only question is who.

Symptoms of the disease were primarily disorders of coordination of movements and depressed mood, sometimes overwhelming weakness, which could hardly be overcome. Everyone wanted to work and did it well, but their eyes were dark and as if absent, and their reactions slowed down.

"Severe depression, probably caused by recent events," said Jorge Pescado, institute physician. "The trouble is, an antidepressants don't work on our bodies. We have to stop at psychotherapy and occupational therapy, which they have already ordained themselves."

"Psychotherapy is a bullshit. Tell them to smoke a little weed, their mood will improve soon," proposed Fronda, who recognized only simple solutions.

"You nuts? If a vampire gets addicted to drugs, the matter is almost hopeless. He will not stop taking. It will be better when they cry a little." Never tapped his forehead confidently, looking eloquently at his friend.

Theo shrugged and left whistling one of Edith Piaf's songs.

Pescado and Never continued, alone, to discuss appropriate therapy for emotionally exhausted scientists. Jorge, who actually called himself a factory doctor at this futuristic institute, has not yet had to deal with more serious cases. Vampires are phenomenally resistant to all diseases, and their wounds heal instantly. The role of their doctor was basically to treat burns (not uncommon in laboratories) and to adjust sprained joints or broken bones. Jorge didn't know anything about psychiatry - he was only now catching up, sitting up to his ears in specialist literature.

Never was a doctor, but he practically did not practice. Perhaps this did not allow him to a peculiar, self-ironic sense of humor, due to which he did not consider the vampire to be the appropriate continuator of the teachings of Avicenna or Galen. He rarely had the opportunity to chat with a representative of his profession, so now he did it all the more willingly. The discussion between the two medics was only interrupted by Octavio, who entered the medical point ruined like other rooms with a cloudy face.

"We already know what happened," he said.

"What?" Asked the Indian, putting away the file of sick cards. Pescado also looked up from the psychiatry textbook and looked at him questioningly.

Di Mauro did not answer immediately. First he poured himself a huge portion of whiskey mixed with plasma, which stood in a carafe on the table, drank and sat down heavily on the couch.

"Luis Zoltan and Trelawny examined the reactor," he said grimly. "Fronda was right about this infrasound, but it's more interesting where they came from. Well, from the reactor turbines."

"Is this how it should be?" Oggy asked, who, along with Gerard, came to the office behind Octavio and was now standing in the doorway, listening intently to what was being said.

"Not at all. It is said that these turbines are a bit dilapidated. They were overclocked and repaired several times because performance was falling and new ones are not available. Not in our situation. Despite all efforts of Trelawny and her team, the performance was getting worse... and now we know why."

"So?" Gerard urged him.

"Nick was not only stealing the results of our work. A thorough examination of the reactor parameters showed that someone was systematically taking enriched uranium from there. What is its market value, I don't have to say."

Never whistled in admiration.

"Not bad! He had to earn a lot from it. But how...?"

"Exactly. Hence the diffusers with psych ran. When he had the order, he started it and after a while the employees were in such a mental state that they escaped from there. And Nick could act as he wanted until they returned."

"What exactly is this psych ran?" The actor asked.

Octavio drank again before answering.

"In general, depressed gas. A type of chemical weapon, invented during the Great War, but never synthesized. At least not officially. Simon Mage had a formula, but put it down *ad acta*. We didn't want to work on combat gases. Someone got to it."

"Nick Harmon."

"It looks like. Who will guarantee us that he acted alone?"

Pescado dropped the book.

"You must be kidding..." he objected in a weak voice.

"I would like. Unfortunately, I've known Nick for eighty years and I'd be sure of him, so since he turned out to be a traitor, I don't know who to believe anymore."

"Not good," Gerard admitted. "Can we help?"

Octavio shook his head.

"Bring Fronda and Tygier," he said. "I need to talk to all of you."

"Since when does this Pole belong to our group?!"

"He shouldn't be, but I want to send him with you again. I have reasons, I will explain everything."

Gerard found Theo and Tygier in the recreation room, the least ruined by recent events. An old-fashioned, wind-up turntable, brought by someone from the museum of the technical department, played a lively Latin melody, and Theo and Lambdon danced folk Mexican dance. The women gathered in the hall clapped their hands to the tact and shouted like a feast.

"Are you crazy?" Gerard asked in shock.

"No. We wanted to tear our friends a bit, they were so sad..." Fronda explained innocently, shooting his eyes at the really amused audience.

"Yes, I can fool around with you."

He joined his friends and they danced in three for a while. Then women joined them, imitating their movements. The party went on, until Never entered the room.

"Are you crazy?" He shouted angrily. "We are waiting for you, and you do nonsense here!"

He rushed to the gramophone and stopped it. The music stopped.

"What do you want, gloomy?" Theo asked.

"Octavio has another job for us. Or rather a request."

"Still work and work, I fuck this life," Fronda grunted, but obediently followed his friends to the medical department.

*****

"Wow... what a cluster. I haven't seen so many trucks and passenger cars in such a small space in my life," Never said, leaning out of the cab.

The string of cars stretched as far as the eye could see. Drivers played cards in the light of car headlights, sipped or quarreled in a language incomprehensible to the Indian, but they rather thought this situation was perfectly normal. Defiantly dressed younger and older girls hung around the cars, no doubt engaged in a well-known profession.

"That's weird," Gerard scratched his head.

"Why weird now? This is just another border crossing." Said Lambdon Tygier sleepily. "It's just a little clogged. Get used to it because we'll stand here for four days."

"Seriously?" Never winced, but after a while decided to accept the facts.

At Octavia's request, they took Vito Ricci and his daughter to Andorra, where they both were received by the head of the local clan. This was almost their last task - they were given one more, not urgent. For now, they were in no hurry and could treat everything that was happening as another instructive adventure. They have already crossed many borders, using false documents with such freedom as if they were the most authentic under the sun.

"Tygier, don't sleep. Go and find out what a borderline is," said the Indian.

"Why me?" Lambdon yawned miserably.

"Because I say so. Come on, go," he rushed him, then unraveled the braid and began combing his long hair with a sandalwood comb. He didn't use others, it was his slight weakness.

"It's already dusk. Let's at least stretch our legs," Theo got relieved from the van with Oggy jumping happily after him. She liked to be crazy in the dog's form when she had the opportunity.

"Where exactly did this crazy Pole go?" Gerard asked after a moment, blowing his head out the window and looking around. After a while he got out and joined Fronda.

"He wants to speak with people, of course. In my day, for this purpose, a forayer from a hostile camp was caught and his soles burned," a friend answered and threw a stick to Oggy. He did it only when they were among people, so that no one would doubt that he was carrying an ordinary dog.

"Fortunately, those days are over and we are not at war."

"Don't go away!" Never called to them without interrupting his comb operation.

By the time he finished combing and tied his hair with a ruby clamp to his ponytail, Lambdon was back. His eyes were round and shining suspiciously.

"It's a queue to cross in Kolbaskowo." He said. "Do you understand what that means?"

"What does that mean?" Kol... Kol... baskowo? Is that something to tell us?" Asked Gerard, stroking mechanically Oggy's head, who was fawning over him.

Lambdon leaned on the cab and looked at his friends for a moment, eyes shining like two suns.

"Behind that barrier is Poland," he said. "You understand? This is Poland."

...It sounded like he pronounced the name of a beloved girl.

# Part 3 - Polish Vacation

*A huge ball, decorated with shimmering gems, shone ominously deep in the cave.*

*"Gallum's heart can only be destroyed by those whose heart is pure and noble," Marianna read slowly, lighting the inscription on the wall with a torch. "Let one of you press the Heart into the air before sunrise and let the other pierce it with an arrow. If the Heart falls to the ground, it will condemn everything within a thousand miles. Those who destroy the heart of Gallum will save the world from Satan's rule, but they will fall ashes themselves when the heart is destroyed."*

*Robin squeezed his bow tighter in his hands.*

*"Marianna..." he whispered in a choked voice.*

*The girl looked at him, slowly brushing her copper-gold hair from her forehead.*

*"We must do it. Remember what the Priestess said: only the two can destroy the Gallum Heart, and there are the two of us. We must do it. It has already taken over the minds of too many people, and this is only the beginning."*

*She removed the ball from the pedestal and went outside with it into the cave. Robin followed her. He wanted to say a lot, but there was no time for that, so he was silent, looking at Marianna with unhappy eyes. The girl caught his eye and smiled sadly. She knew what the young man whom she had learned to love and respect only for being like he was wanted to tell her.*

*"That's the way it should be," she whispered, looking at the sky*

*where the rising sun was already reddish.*

*Robin pulled her to him and gave her a kiss, short and hot. There was no need to say anything - it was all clear.*

*"Push it," he commanded, raising his bow.*

*Marianna threw a Gallum Heart into the air with a broad swing. Robin tensed his bow in a flash. A slender arrow flashed like lightning and hit the center of a flickering ball that splattered into a rain of shimmering debris. At that moment the sun rose. It illuminated the grass, covered with golden dust, and on it two patches of gray ash. At each of them lay a quiver with arrows and a bow split in two.*

Oggy finished reading and closed the book with a quiet sigh. She read aloud to her friends for many days before bedtime. Never had eyesight lately, and Fronda was fluent in French only. In other languages he only managed for scientific publications, and fiction tired him too much. Oggy was a great reader because she read, translating English or Italian into French. They listened to her with pleasure.

"Awful nonsense," Fronda said from his bed. "What did Robin Hood have to do with magic? This fashion is mixed with various types of literary genres. An indigestible melt is formed."

For several weeks, friends lived in Warsaw, a city that was supposedly the safest shelter for vampires. There was no cure for hunters here, and Poles were able to deal with all sorts of external threats. Lambdon Tygier, before he took the girl he had just met and went to the sea with her, explained everything to them. He said that Poland is a country of all miracles and that one should not be surprised at anything. That no Hunters can handle it here, because public, suburban and interurban transport is always late and the only unknown is, if. Therefore, it is not possible to rip actions within a specified time. Traffic jams and endless road works on the streets are destroying the effectiveness of using private vehicles, and like the world (apparently) no Pole has ever helped a lost foreigner, showing the worst malice or the wrong direction.

In addition, the administrative provisions and countless paragraphs of both codes made impossible every hunter activity in this country, as long as they wanted to operate under the guise of law. If they tried to circumvent the law, they would run the risk of an organization that Lambdon described as "the Pruszkow mafia." These people apparently were not joking and did not even try to understand what the intruders meant. The vampires themselves from this strange country were also unusual, and certainly much more belligerent than any other. Oddly enough, they seemed less xenophobic. They received the "Rajah team" kindly, perhaps thanks to Lambdon's guarantee, and accommodated them in one of their "apartments" situated under a huge building in the city center.

"It's called the Palace of Culture," Lambdon explained to them. "The most hated building in the capital, and probably the most functional."

The headquarters of the Warsaw undead clan housed between the foundations of the Palace, in what was probably conceived as an atomic bunker and forgotten immediately after construction. It was arranged pleasantly and comfortably, although more than half was occupied by the host's medical laboratory. Some Polish vampires were apparently no less eager than Octavio di Mauro and his PhD students.

Stasiek Zakrzewski entered the room. They learned how to pronounce his first name after a few days of trying, the second names didn't even try. He was unpredictable and explosive, they had already quarreled with him several times, but otherwise they liked them. For a foreigner, he spoke excellent English and French and Italian, and he also knew Japanese and Greek. He was a doctor, like Never, but unlike him he had a degree and did not see the world outside his profession. Even when he was "preserve", he continued to devote his time and skills to the good of all - humans and vampires.

"What's up, Stash?" Gerard asked him, seeing that the Pole had a very serious face.

"I don't have good news," said the doctor. "I examined your blood samples using our markers. Since the result was positive in one case, I did additional research."

"And?" Oggy urged him uneasily.

The Pole sat on the window sill and stared at the night city. He didn't like the night, but only then he was active. Like few Polish vampires, he was a "moth", so he slept at day, which worried him and he was constantly looking for some way to fool nature.

"One of you is very sick," he said after a moment. "You, Never."

Everyone looked at the Indian, who was sitting motionless in the club chair and, despite his eyesight problems, tried to browse the press. "Time" made a peaceful move. He didn't seem surprised, but others did. Although they have noticed recently that their friend has gone a bit pale and his golden eyes have become tired, they have had so many adventures that everyone could feel a bit tired.

"What is this?" He asked.

"Multiple myeloma, a specific type of hematopoietic system cancer that is unique to us," said Stasiek. "It's extremely rare. Cancer cells multiply imperceptibly, attacking all tissues, and finally comes to what is called general glioma. Then the breakdown of cells is inevitable. Accelerated aging occurs and eventually the patient turns into a pile of rotting protein."

Everyone fell silent, struck by the news like lightning. They had never thought before that there was a disease capable of knocking down a vampire, whose body, after all, is characterized by the incredible possibilities of self-repair.

"How much time do I have left?" Never said calmly, showing no emotion.

"Hard to say. A few months... half a year to a year, I think. That is why I consider it my duty to inform you that a form of therapy has already been developed, which is extremely risky but gives certain opportunities."

The Indian was silent for a moment, then asked.

"How big?"

"Not very big. We have only in vitro results so far, but they are promising. The thing is that the myeloma cells are very radiosensitive. Of course, we don't have photon accelerators, but at night we can break into the oncology center and apply the right dose to you. It will also be necessary to provide cytostatics. The doses must be shock, and at the same time strictly calculated, because a little too low will not destroy all cancer cells, and a little too large will destroy you. The margin of error is really minimal and you must know that we have only used such therapy once."

"So how do you know it can work?" Called Oggy.

Stasiek looked at her sadly with gray-blue eyes.

"We don't know anything," he replied. "These are just theoretical calculations. Multiple myeloma is so rare that I have only treated this one case so far."

"The patient has recovered?"

"Yes. And that's why I say you have a chance. Do you decide to take this risk, Raja?"

Never remained silent for a long time, mechanically turning pages of the magazine. There were no emotions on his oblong face, not a single muscle under his swarthy skin, yet his friends guessed the storm that must have gone crazy in his heart. The vampire often faces the threat of sudden death, but never before the prospect of dying slowly as a result of a chronic disease process. This is one of the advantages of being a "night creature", and not the only one.

"I'll risk it," he said finally. "I think that surrendering to the disease without a fight is total stupidity. But how do you want to get to the accelerators?"

The Pole smiled widely.

"Is this a problem? We will go to the Oncology Center at night and enter it through the back entrance. They have bad locks, and Fronda is a brilliant burglar. With his innocent doll face, skillful fingers and gorilla strength, he would be a perfect criminal."

"Do you want to get hit for the doll?" Theo asked menacingly, but he returned the smile.

He liked Stasiek, just like the others, although he still made lugs for his beauty. Indeed, were it not for growth, Theo with his delicate face and slender figure could give a not male impression during the worship of big biceps and testosterone. However, the one who would judge him by his appearance would be disappointed painfully, because even as a knight of his time Fronda had extraordinary strength and dexterity in battle. The beauty and innate elegance of the movements were as if intended for a court poet - the will to fight and skills for a warrior. Such traits are extremely rare in one man, but he reconciled them all.

Never looked at friends with absent eyes.

"When we start?" He asked.

"Even today. We leave after midnight, then it will be the safest, but you have to prepare for the fact that it will not end on one trip. You must take a series of ten exposures. Chemo can be given once, but with radiation it is not so easy. Here metabolism is not decisive."

Stasiek patted him on the back and went out to work out the right doses. It was not easy when the object of treatment was to be a vampire. Although the doctor made a bad face, he was very uncertain about the effect of his efforts.

"That it must have happened to him," he thought along the way. "Maybe it has to do with Marfan syndrome? I could bet it has. The funnel-shaped chest, long fingers, an excessively long face, almond eyes and a deformed skull... everything is correct. Holy shit, if I'm right, then only myeloma is lacking to him."

Stanislaw Zakrzewski was a doctor before he became a vampire, so unlike Never he could boast a diploma or even a degree. He became "immortal" by accident, as he told them himself. His mistress, Jadwiska Lemanska, was drunk at the stocks when she offered him a blood exchange, and he, quickly calculating in his thoughts for and against, agreed. That same night they performed the ceremonial, which successfully passed without interference.

The girl, who thus became his mistress and mentor, was a highlander from around Poronin, where Stasiek also came from. Unlike most highlanders, he had honey-golden hair and light blue eyes, which with his slim form and very dark skin did not make him a typical highlander or a typical vampire. He was more like a Viking, though less so than his younger brother, whom Jadwiska preserved at his request a few days later. Janek Zakrzewski was taller and much more athletic than his brother, his face was lighter, and his hair was always tousled as if by the wind. He was commonly called Gladiator, because he was quick to fight and he was invincible on his fists. He did not follow in the footsteps of his brother. Before consolidation, he was a professional soldier in the Podhale Riflemen unit. Fronda made friends with him from the first moment, although they could not get along very well due to language deficiencies.

The exposure schedule was not ready until the next evening.

"It's best if we start right away," the doctor said, showing Never the completed card. "Just... better shave your head right away. And so you will lose your hair, if not after irradiation, then after chemo.

"Never looked at him bitterly with his golden, now dull and gray eyes.

"As you like," he said with studied indifference, stroking Oggy mechanically, putting his wolf head under his arm. Recently, somehow she was more eager to be in a dog's form, as if she was relaxed or as if for some reason she was finally reconciled with her otherness.

"Is it really necessary?" Gerard asked. Compassion fell on him, all the more that he had cancer behind him and only Never's whim saved him from death.

"Unfortunately, yes," Stasiek told him. "It will be possible to make a wig from cut hair, so that our buddy does not have to walk with his bald head..."

"No," the Indian interrupted him. "No wigs. I am neither an actress nor a model and I will not fool around. When are we going to this hospital? I would like to have it all behind me."

"In a few hours, once you know that no one will hang around there."

Theo squeezed his friend's shoulder sympathetically. He was not very good at comforting, and Never was not one who was easy to comfort. Now he also moved his arm impatiently, shaking Fronda's hand away.

"Has anyone got a razor?" He asked.

Under the crescent blade, Never's long, shiny hair fell, curling on the floor like snakes. The vampire's face deprived of this binding suddenly took on some elusive aristocratic expression, like a statue of an Egyptian ruler from millennia ago. This impression was compounded by an elongated skull like on ancient Egyptian frescoes and an unusual regularity of features.

Friends could not resist the impression that they were looking at a completely stranger to them, and the coolness in the gaze and pursed lips further strengthened this impression. It was probably the result of illness, but Never moved away from them, and every word, every move and look seemed to say:

"I don't need you. I can handle it myself."

In fact, he was deadly terrified and for the first time in his long life helpless against what happened. Once, in India, he felt omnipotent whenever he discovered his extraordinary powers, especially his ability to overpower his scream. Then, when he was forced to travel to an unknown world, he felt intoxicated with a sense of freedom and strength, thanks to which he was never afraid of anything, even when he faced death. What he encountered was, however, a purely external danger and therefore insurmountable.

However, now the attack came from within. His own body, long, flexible and strong, betrayed him - and he could not fight it anymore. He preferred not to rely on the support of his friends. He liked them very much, but he felt good only when he relied solely on himself and the help of others was not necessary to him. He helped eagerly, but he hated it when he was reciprocated. He was losing the sense of security that had been built up over the years.

His friends were eager to help him, but they understood that this was not possible. They were also tormented by a sense of powerlessness, awareness of the drama that the unquestioned leader of their group must experience.

"Life is like that. Destiny will always get you, in a certain place, on a specific day and at a specific time." Said Zakrzewski's assistant, Ola Dowgird. In addition to strictly scientific matters, she also dealt with occultism and secret knowledge, which most Polish vampires were passionate about.

They, newcomers from another country, did not quite understand the specifics of this community. She was different than those they had met so far, even different than the Russian community. Polish vampires were almost without exception 'martens', not 'moths' - they also used the terms 'cats' and 'bats'. They were not afraid of Hunters or anything at all. Seemingly reckless and unorganized, they were able to be really difficult opponents. When the VH institute opened its branch near Warsaw, at the first signal of danger, "cats" and "bats" closed their ranks and dealt with their persecutors without pardon.

The hunters did not recover from this defeat. They did not have anyway. There were hardly any recruits from these areas. The impression was that Poles, as they were said, have more important things on their minds than vampires. In general, they were not believed here, and one could risk saying that what they know does not bother with it anyway. Also the main feature of Polish vampires was that they didn't care about anything. And when you had to commit a crime to protect your incognito or for the good of the group, they didn't think.

There was one more crucial thing that distinguished the Polish community from others. Women dominated it, almost all fair-haired and so pretty that Fronda, a womanizer, was looking after them. However, he has not achieved anything yet.

"Polish women are extreme." Gerard explained to him. "I read about it. In this country there are either declared whores or monogamists. Try it anyway, try..."

There were maybe a quarter of men among "cats" and "bats" and few of them had real beauty. All of them, however, showed intelligence well above average, which again proved very well the preferences of the local girls. Apparently, those who considered beauty as a secondary matter, and given the consolidation of anyone, first of all looked at his mental qualities. This was another significant difference.

French, American or even Russian Vampire women definitely preferred hunks, which they soon abandoned. The Polish community was not divided by sex. There were hardly any affairs between them, but they lived together, played together and hunted together, usually in pairs.

Fronda and Gerard have discussed at the chessboard more than once, which can also make Poles so different, but they have not come to any conclusions worth noting. Their organizational structure was also different, freer. They loved freedom and did not recognize you over themselves. One could say that everyone made decisions, although they sometimes discussed the one final one for a long time. However, they rarely really worked together. They definitely preferred what they called the "Zorro system" - acting on their own, because then everyone was their own boss and subordinate. Even when, forced by necessity, they undertook something together, the commander elected by a simple majority could not have any certainty that temporary subordinates would abruptly obey him, caused by a temporary whim.

So the "locals" only formed a loose relation. They stayed together, because in this way life was easier for them, but none could endure someone ordering him something. So how was Stasiek's cooperation with his assistants arranged, it was difficult to comprehend. Somehow, however, they worked together, since the exposure schedule was ready on time, and the current work did not suffer.

"Fronda, you must force the locks," said Dr. Zakrzewski when his black BMW stopped in front of the Oncology Institute. "They're pretty bad, so you shouldn't have trouble with that. Did you get your lock picks?"

"I have! Sure. I never part with them." Theo took out his wallet and looked carefully at its contents. After a moment, he chose one of the lock picks and walked to the door. Oggy tinkered up at the box with the alarm wires, untangling the cables and reconnecting them in a different order.

"Ready," she finally said. "You can start."

Theo examined the door locks, shrugged dismissively, and began manipulating the selected lock pick with one of them. Friends were waiting for him to finish looking around to see if anyone was coming. The institute's surroundings seemed to them at least not encouraging. A real concrete desert, full of high-rise buildings, with a rickety birch or miserable grass growing here and there. It was ugly and sad here, although in other districts one could always find a certain charm, if not even beauty.

Polish cities had this kind of disheveled charm, old tenements and beautiful churches stood next to modern buildings, disgusting shanty and eternally disordered parks. In all this you could find something charming when you tried... but not here. It seemed strange that people suffering from such a terrible disease were cured in such an unpleasant place, where one could lose the will to live rather than regain it.

"Ready," Fronda reported cheerfully. "Oggy, stay at guard and bark twice as if."

The girl nodded and jumped gracefully out of her dress, assuming a doggy form. No one will pay attention to the sheepdog running at the institute.

Friends entered the dark, gloomy hall, with massive doors and control panels on both sides.

"This door is terribly thick," Gerard whispered, feeling the involuntary thrill of terror at the thought of the people locked up here every day.

"Yes," Stasiek answered him. "The door to the cobalt bomb bunker can still be opened manually, but those from accelerators must move the mechanism. What you want is a lead block over half a meter wide. Now, keep your fingers crossed once for me to turn everything in the right order, two, and so that the noise does not lure anyone here. So I start... Cooling first."

The doctor disappeared into the bunker and soon emerged from it. He flipped some lever in the fuse box and went back inside. Only after leaving the place he finished turning all sections on again. For vampires, creatures with sensitive senses, it seemed unlikely that the noise of the device did not stand on the whole hospital section, but no one paid any attention to what was happening in the radiotherapy department. At night, no one looked there, and the hearing of an ordinary man may not alarm what was happening here.

"Come on," he murmured to Never, who stood beside the control panel with an impenetrable expression, as if all the bustle was about someone else.

Gerard and Theo positioned themselves at strategic points from which they could observe the long, dark corridor behind the glass door. They really didn't have a definite plan in case someone unwanted appeared, but they had to watch. Outside, Oggy watched the door ajar, whining softly from time to time, as if she wanted to let them know that everything was all right.

After a time that seemed to everyone infinitely long, Dr. Zakrzewski opened the door of the bunker and carefully turned off all the apparatus.

"How are you, Nev?" Asked Theo anxiously.

The Indian gave him a short look and habitually ran his hand over his head, wincing slightly when his fingers met only bare skin.

"It's good yet," he said. "But I know it won't last long."

"How do you know that?" Gerard asked thoughtlessly.

"I'm a doctor, my green-eyed, remember? I know very well what the side effects of radiation therapy are. And when chemo comes to this..."

Stasiek looked at him with compassion. He also knew, and it was all too well, that cancer treatments can kill worse than the disease itself, but he could see no other way. The therapy he developed gave Never at least a chance. Abandoning treatment would have catastrophic consequences without any doubt.

Friends went out into the dark and empty street. In the dim light of the lanterns, from which probably only a third operated, the concrete skyscrapers looked like gloomy specters. Oggy was running around men, still not abandoning her doggy character. She liked to run as a quadruped whenever it was possible. Fronda, accustomed to her transformation for a long time, tucked her dress into his inseparable haversack. This dress was taking off like a glove - but the real trouble was when it was really cold. Oggy then had to decide at home whether she was walking as a human or a dog, and then stick to it. Winter clothes could not be removed so easily.

They made a long round between the skyscrapers, deftly dodging the few police patrols. Next to the nightclub, they ambushed drunken customers, getting dinner, and then decided to return to the car. At their sight two dark figures, trying to get to their BMWs, broke quickly into darkness.

"No thieves will break my locks," Stasiek said contentedly. "We have a talented designer in the family, he deals with them. Get in. A few more visits await us in this unpleasant place, you will have to watch out for these thieves. If they get too intrusive, we'll handle with them."

Everyone knew that coming here day by day increases the risk of mishaps, but they could not go back if they wanted to finish the treatment. And it wasn't particularly easy or nice treatment. Before the cycle of radiation and chemotherapy was over, Never looked like his own shadow. He was emaciated like a skeleton, and his face was like a skeletonized skull in which large eyes shone feverishly now. He could hardly eat and the doctor used intravenous nutrition for some time, fearing that his patient's exhausted organism would give up any moment. Indeed, it seemed that it would happen any day.

Fronda, Gerard and Oggy were left aloof now, saddened and terrified of their own uselessness when they were most needed. They could do nothing against the enemy who had now attacked one of them, so they were trying to somehow fill the waiting time for the final verdict. In this respect, the Poles could not offer them much, as they had the impression that they were not doing anything specific themselves. They did not conduct scientific work or entertainment - they simply existed. They lived a mysterious life, centered on trifles, trips to the cinema or an amusement park, reading, vagrancy... Only Stasiek and his assistants seemed to be working on something, and it was not so certain.

The newcomers had to fill their own time. Theo learned Polish enthusiastically and without major effects. Oggy wandered the city or sat for hours at her laptop. Gerard, who suddenly discovered a talent for painting, almost did not leave the tiny room, transformed into an atelier. All three, however, were thinking of Never. Some Poles wondered why they were not accompanying him in the fight against a terrible disease, but the Indian did not want their presence and expressed it categorically. He wasn't used to feeling sorry for himself and didn't suffer when others did it. He belonged to those proud natures who prefer to suffer in loneliness and silence.

"Give him a break if he wants to be alone." Advised Dr. Zakrzewski to friends, and they listened to him without protest.

Stasiek himself looked after him as best he could. He had time because his outpatient clinic was not under siege by patients. Vampires rarely need medical attention. His own scientific work did not take him all day either, and to tell the truth he rarely dealt with it. He was aware that it would be of little use, so he treated it as a way to fill time, not something important. Now that he was in Never's care, he supplemented his notes on myeloma. The second such opportunity he could not miss soon, though... From the information he gathered and his own observations it appeared that the tendency to develop this specific cancer increases in the vampire population.

The introduction of the A-503 marker, developed by a Czech scientist, revealed that about 10% of the subjects have inactive cells of this cancer in their blood. Stasiek felt that if he could detect a factor activating their development, he could develop an effective and not so destructive therapy. He still did not know where the malignant cells really come from and what they pose a real threat to the future. He explained it to new friends who listened to him, not quite understanding the medical terms.

"Death is terrible," Gerard whispered finally. "And especially death from such a disease. People know what they are afraid of.

"People are not afraid of death, they are afraid of dying," Oggy said sadly.

"There was no such thing as cancer in my day," Fronda said, shaking his hands under his head. "Anyway, who knew what killed people then? If he did not die on the battlefield and was ill, it was usually explained by bad spells or God's scolding... Life was simpler and death was simpler even though we did not have today's facilities. For example, anesthesia, antibiotics... I remember getting an arrow in my chest. The medic had to pull it out of my body and then burn the wound so that it would stop bleeding... It really hurt, but I recovered quickly. I was strong. The weaker were dying. Natural selection, right?"

"There is some kind of true in it," Stasiek agreed. "Thanks to this, the society was relatively stronger and healthier. Do you think it should still be like this?"

"Never in my life! Every human being is precious, he has a soul, an immortal soul. It's good that medicine now saves more and more lives."

"And more and more idiots," Lidka remarked wryly, a nurse at Stasiek's outpatient clinic who had just entered the room. "Thanks to the progress of medicine, a lot of mutilated premature babies lives, children with hydrocephalus and after perinatal paralysis, from which deeply handicapped beings grow up, all their lives relying on others. This is not good at all. Stasiek, there's a phone call for you."

"So what do you suggest, euthanasia? Do you know what morality is?" Theo asked warily as he sat on the bed.

The girl gave him a pitying look. She was a fairly tall, slim person with a slightly too flat figure for Fronda's taste, but nevertheless shapely. Her short-cut hair was dark copper, her oval face with regular features always had a slightly malicious expression in her eyes and the corners of her mouth. Gerard used to say about her that she was "spicy" and gladly joked with her.

"Go to the neurology department of a large children's hospital and see what I mean. In your time, knight, such children were dying.

Mother cried a little, put everything to God's will and next year she had another, with a bit of luck healthy. Today, she often remains a slave to her handicapped child for the rest of her life and never stops suffering from mental torture. Do you think this is moral and fair?" She asked.

Fronda shrugged and left the question unanswered. He has long ceased to argue with women, aware that each of them is able to talk over him whether he is right or wrong.

"Don't be angry at Lidka, Fronda. I'll bring you something to drink," Oggy offered, and jumped out into the corridor, from where a rattled squeak sounded.

"Tygier is back!" She called out.

Lambdon came in to room as cheerful as usual. His long hair was tied in a ponytail, the jeans were frayed at the bottom, and the inscription "Legia Champion!" On the white-green-red shirt. He looked rested and very happy with life.

"How are you?" He asked cheerfully.

"Howdy, Slawek," Lidka embraced him and kissed him warmly, which Tygier returned with great enthusiasm.

"Are you back?" Gerard asked not very wisely.

"No, I'm leaving soon... But I have to talk to Stasiek. I have information for him that he asked for." Tygier sat down in a rocking chair under a window dummy and began to browse magazines scattered randomly on the glass table top.

Doctor Zakrzewski returned after a few minutes, so they locked themselves in the next room and for some time talked about something in hushed voices.

"Don't you go to the festival?" Lidka asked, pouring a cocktail for everyone. "Today at the Palace there will be fun with music and fireworks. You would have fun."

"What?" Theo growled, still offended, but he did not refuse the cocktail.

Polish drinks had that, despite the sometimes shocking composition, they were very tasty and, no less important, and with a taste unlike anything that they have drank so far.

"Poles are an interesting nation. We can say talented dilettantes, also in this field," he thought, tasting a slightly sweetish liquid with satisfaction.

"I'm serious. I know you're sad of Never, but you won't help him by sitting here and worrying to death. Rather, you should look, maybe you will find help." Lidka leaned her hands on the table and looked into his eyes. "I'll tell you something, Fronda, because I really like you: Stasiek doesn't tell you everything. Never is free of cancer cells, but he doesn't know why his body is not regenerating. Stasiek is looking for medicine for him, but you should also look."

"We're not doctors," Gerard pointed out uncertainly.

The girl laughed a little bit of malice.

"If it were a matter of typical medicine, Stasiek would have it in his hand. I think that what may help Never is waiting to be discovered, but you will not make it by sitting here and pretending that you have didn't care. Maybe you will be lucky if you search well."

Theo thought, sipping his cocktail. In what Lidka said, about which Stasiek said that she was "the most insolent nurse and best friend", there was a lot of right. Anyway, it always hit the nail on the head, with its own cold intelligence and ironic cheerfulness. He had to make a decision - now that Never was out of the game temporarily, he was the boss.

"We're going to a festival," he finally decided. "Lidka, are you coming with us?"

"Sure."

The festival started at 8pm, when it was quite dark at this time of year. It was not difficult to get involved in the amused crowd and pretend to be ordinary people, although the fun itself quickly bored friends. They hadn't left the underground bunker since they'd been diagnosed with Never disease, except for the expeditions to the Oncology Center, so now they were willing to take a walk through the night streets. Admittedly, as Gerard stated, Warsaw could hardly be called a "city that never sleeps", but the streets were not quite empty yet. As they lengthened their tramp, however, they went empty and darkened, as the lanterns went out as if someone had turned them off. Of course, this couldn't bother them.

"Where is the zoo here?" Asked Theo, when they realized that they were actually alone on the streets. "I'd like to see this place in the Polish edition."

"The garden is on the other side of the Vistula," said Lidka. "We are near the Śląsko-Dąbrowski Bridge, so if we speed up the pace, we will be there in less than an hour.

Since both Oggy and Gerard did not object, they moved towards the bridge, under which the river black in the moonlight flowed. The superstition that vampires cannot cross flowing water is widespread in some cultures, but completely false. It probably came from the fact that the clear majority of vampires are unable to swim. Having lost ground in the water, the vampire usually succumbs to such powerful cramps that he sinks after a few minutes. It is not known why this is happening, but it is so and it is difficult to do anything about it. The few representatives of the species who are not subject to this rule are the object of jealousy and admiration on the part of their brothers.

"Electrolyte imbalance of unknown etiology," Octavio answered, once asked by Gerard about this mysterious property of vampires. They did not discuss this diagnosis because they did not understand anything except that it would be better for them if they give up a swimming pool. Interestingly, the Octavio's underground institute had a swimming pool, though quite shallow. It was used for both relaxation and therapy.

They walked slowly across the bridge, enjoying the night silence and the beautiful view. The night blurred what was unsightly or sad and threw a fairy tale curtain on everything around. The noise of the river merged with the sound of trees in a nearby park. The stars twinkled in the clear sky, as always calm and unshakable.

"About two thousand stars can be seen with the naked eye, and there are tens of billions of detectable galaxies alone," Theo said, looking thoughtfully at the sky.

"I wonder where you get this news from." Lidka asked, leering at him, as she usually did.

"From the scientific press and professional textbooks," answered the Frenchman, "I prefer it to fiction, at least you learn something and..."

He paused because his sensitive ear caught a nearby splash. The friends paused, looking at each other uncertainly. Everyone heard the sound, disturbing the night silence, though they could not guess its origin. Theo climbed the bridge span, despite the terrified protests by Oggy, and looked around carefully.

"Wait here!" He shouted suddenly.

He threw off his shoes in a flash and with a beautiful jumped into the Vistula currents. As one of the few vampires, Fronda knew how to swim, and he did it gladly whenever he could.

"What exactly was it?" Lidka asked, running over to the railing of the bridge.

"I don't know, but Fronda has hearing like a fox," Gerard answered her. "Maybe you, Oggy, know more than I do?"

"Somebody is drowning there," she explained with some impatience. She barely restrained the urge to jump a friend for help.

Nothing happened for a moment, then they saw something big crawling with difficulty on one of the banks of the river. They hurried down the bridge to the river beach, pebbly and littered worse than a landfill, empty at this time, except for a drunkard snoring under one of the supports.

Theo sat on the bank, gasping for breath and embracing a small shape that seemed to hysterically cry. It was a teenage girl, shaken and soaked to the skin.

"Typical for Fronda. He will always find a princess in need," said Gerard bitterly to Lidka.

"What did you want to do, baby?" Theo called, ignoring him.

Although the girl, as it turned out, knew a little French, she could not speak the language properly and Lidka had to explain her chaotic story. It took a while, because the would-be suicide woman was in such a state that it was difficult to understand her. Finally, however, the nurse pulled everything she wanted from her.

"Two months ago, this little girl was raped in a disco by her friend," she said, turning to friends. She was ashamed to tell anyone because she knew that her family would not believe her, and everyone would say that she probably wanted it. Unfortunately, she got pregnant. In addition, our law does not allow abortion, theoretically, she could apply for it, but since she did not make a formal complaint after the rape, she would have little chance. Anyway, gynecologists in state hospitals often refuse to perform such procedures.

"And rightly so!" Fronda shouted indignantly. "How can you do such a thing? This is a murder!"

"Shut up, Theo. You speak nonsense..." Oggy started on at him, which usually did not happen to her.

Gerard shook his head in disbelief.

"You have strange rights here. I can't believe you got law like in the Middle Ages..." he said.

"Get to your senses. You are talking about a human being!"

"And she is not a human being?" Lidka showed Fronda a girl sobbing in her arms. "She's only fifteen years old. If she doesn't get rid of her pregnancy, they'll throw her out of school and her family will renounce her. What will happen to her, you don't think about it?"

"Abortion will add evil to evil," Fronda insisted. In some cases, it was difficult to convince him and nobody even tried. However, Lidka did not know him from this side yet.

"This girl was raped; do you think she has suffered too little? And now, when she needs help, everyone turns away from her," she said warily. "No, I won't leave it this way."

She began to explain something in a hushed voice to the girl while Gerard tapped his forehead, looking eloquently at his friend. Even Oggy was giving him a reluctant look. Theo, usually guarding not to lag the era, sometimes showed incredible stubbornness and it was difficult to do anything about it.

"Don't do it," he asked as soon as the clearly calmed teenager moved away from them. "Don't help her with the fetus. This is a sin. It's not allowed."

"I don't like to say ambiguously," Lidka said furiously. "But if you do not stop, I will finally blow you. It's not your business, okay?!"

This whole story finally made them quit visiting the zoo. After all, it was necessary to escort the soaked girl home, and then they returned to the hideout at the Palace of Culture, having enough fun for one day.

"What did you come up with about this little girl?" Oggy asked, when Lidka had to say goodbye briefly she was about to move to her room. It occupied one of the "apartments" - a small cubicle with a bare concrete mattress, cabinet and table. There were many such rooms in the bunker, and although it could not match in terms of size with the Octavio's research station, for this group was enough. They have arranged here seemingly provisionally, but quite comfortably.

"I will borrow money from Stasiek and go with her to the doctor's," she said. "The conscience of our gynecologists is very flexible under the influence of money. But for now I will take a long bath."

However, she was not able to implement this plan. Halfway to the bathroom she came across a doctor who saw her and shouted:

"What are you doing here? Go to the infirmary! They just brought the victims of the accident at Babka roundabout, there will be something to do. Plenty of sewing, a few broken bones, and the driver came out the worst. Contusion of the heart and right-sided pneumothorax."

Dr. Zakrzewski's outpatient clinic received accident victims from all over Warsaw. His existence with such a large undead community was necessary, as transporting a battered vampire to the hospital could have ended very badly. So far such a danger has been prevented, but Stasiek, best oriented in the subject, still lived in fear. It was for this reason that he took night duty in hospitals, trying to make him known everywhere, although he risked being exposed.

Fortunately, in times of universal registration of all living things, vampires had no problem with false identity. However, one unforeseen coincidence would be enough to make their "inner world", as they call their secret world, fall into ruin. Therefore, not only in Poland, but also in other countries, vampires were bound by absolute solidarity - in response to the right slogan each of them had to hurry to help everyone. Otherwise they would become a doomed species and would be exterminated very quickly.

As soon as the doctor, Lidka and the other two nurses finished treating the lightly wounded, one more was brought.

"Lucja Sajnow, Th4 and Th5 compression fracture, large hematoma, torn dura. Help me, Lidka, I need to decompress the core."

Stasiek opened a small but well-arranged operating room and began scrubbing his hands over the sink while the nurses were preparing the patient for surgery. Although the risk of intra-operative infection is virtually zero for vampires, Dr. Zakrzewski preferred not to risk it.

There was rare real surgery here, but the doctor made sure that his operating room was always ready, and now it paid off. The procedure was long and complicated, and when they were done with it, Lidka literally fell into fatigue. Even so, she looked at Never on her way to her room. The Indian lay there, lost in his reading, but at the sound of footsteps he left the English-language magazine and looked at her. He looked amazing with a naked skull, skinny body and huge, shiny eyes. They lost their beautiful color, becoming yellow-gray and made as unpleasant as other signs of the disease.

"What's up, Lidda?" He asked. He always called her that as if he couldn't pronounce her name correctly.

The girl sat down on the bed next to him. She liked this not quite ordinary kinsman, whose intelligence transcended everything he had encountered so far, and got along much easier with him than with any of his companions.

"Your colleague pissed me off," she said and briefly told Never the whole story.

He listened to her with a straight face.

"Fronda is already like that," he said when she finished. "He considers pregnancy a saint, maybe because he likes children so much. Give up on him, he is harmless."

"Yes, because he is not a politician. He has such a narrow worldview that he could be successfully in the Polish government."

The Indian made a faint little laugh.

"Is that so bad with you?" He asked. "Sorry, it's not funny at all."

"It's not," the girl sighed. "But as far as you can understand Fronda, our rulers are probably not from the Middle Ages, are they?"

Never remained silent. Saying a few simple words exhausted him, his, who alone managed with a few thugs. He was weaker now than a small child and tired all the time. He didn't want to think what would happen if he failed to regain his strength. Will he be an eternal cripple, helpless and rely on the care of his friends? No, he didn't want it, he would rather die. The fact that he was still clinging to life was due to the never-ending hope that he would fight the effects of chemotherapy. For now, Stasiek did not manage to find a cure for him, but he did not stop searching, and Never believed in the power of science.

Lidka adjusted his pillow, checked the drip, and after saying goodbye, she finally went to her room. She was really falling from fatigue. Meanwhile, Dr. Zakrzewski, having made sure that all the wounded had adequate care, managed to clean up and went to the living room. He knew he would find Fronda sitting there in front of the television. There were French-language channels in the illegally led cable TV, and Theo made the most of it. He could not understand the TV's operation, but it did not stop.

He never considered himself a super intelligent and easily reconciled himself to the existence of things he could not comprehend with his mind. And TV has fascinated him from the beginning. Moving pictures interested in the first rehearsals of the Lumière brothers, but the phenomenon of creating a picture in the cinema was still understandable - he did not understand the television message. However, this did not bother him to love this entertainment, especially costume films. He liked them.

"What are you watching now?" Stasiek asked, sitting next to him.

"Marquis of Angelica," Theo replied. "This girl has beautiful eyes."

"We have such an actress, Kalina Jędrusik. When she was young, huh... this whole Angelika could only clean her shoes."

"Yes, yes I know. Polish women are really great." The Frenchman confessed. "There is no second place like this one where I would see so many beautiful girls on the street. They are generally poorly dressed and most of them could use a good make-up artist, but these are rough diamonds. Your men don't even know how lucky they are."

The doctor grunted in satisfaction and followed the film awning for a moment.

"Fronda," he began after a moment. "Would you do something for us? I know that Never is in a terrible state, but I think you could help him by the way. When it comes to you, you will have free thought."

"Of course, Stash," Theo replied warmly (he still couldn't speak his name correctly). "What is that?"

"It's about my brother. I will send you to the mountains. There Never will recover. There is some strange, original force in the Tatras. It is all-encompassing and has healing powers that no one understands, and doctors refuse to accept it. This force can also be deadly, so be careful."

Doctor Zakrzewski sighed and ran his fingers through his bright hair. It was obvious that this was not all he wanted to say.

"I'm sending Janek with you because..." he continued after a moment." We've with him some... I'd say trouble. He has just returned from Dresden and I am afraid he was doing bad things there. You see, German preserved are among the best organized on the globe. They adopted the name Nuntia and form a kind of paramilitary organization with fairly strict rules. Nuntia was the organization preceding the creation of the Abwehr in Nazi Germany, it probably says everything. They are not really aggressive, but they think that vampirism is a higher form of the human species... and that we are a master race."

"I think these Germans are crazy! It was like that already," Theo snorted angrily.

"Fortunately, they are relatively few. When they start brawling, Vanhelsingians will deal with them, and we will certainly not help them. Janek messed up a bit in Dresden... he demolished their headquarters and beat their leader unconscious. They will track him now. They gave him a death sentence and there is no joke with Nuntia. There is no conversation with them either. I would prefer that Janek leave here. I will be calmer when he is with you, not here. Here, danger threatens him at every turn."

Theo shrugged slightly. He had only seen Gladiator a few times before, but he liked him. The fair-haired giant with cheerful eyes the color of pure azure and the long face of the Viking seemed to be his dream companion. He had the power of a gorilla, but in essence he was gentle. Nuntia's leader must have make him hackles rise with something, since he reacted so violently. What?

"Okay," he decided. "Since you think it will be better for him... We thought that Tygier would be traveling with us, but nothing came of it. Shame. He is a good friend and a valuable comrade in arms, although we managed without him in England.

The doctor nodded absently. He was too worried about his brother to worry about the unbalanced Lambdon.

"Can I count on looking after Janek?" He asked almost pleadingly. "He's been learning English recently, you're sure to get along. He is smarter than he looks."

Theo laughed and patted him on the back so hard that the doctor almost fell off his chair. Sometimes he did not realize what great strength he had, which posed a certain threat. The people were not on their guard, because Theo, slim and reminiscent of a harmless spider, did not look so strong at all. His friends sometimes wondered where all his power and physical strength, so great that even Gladiator, a muscular giant, lay on his hand. There was something mysterious about it.

"Don't worry," he said. "He is safe with us and we are ready to go even to the moon, as long as Never recovers. Do you think mountain air will heal him by itself?"

"Yes, but not just any air: Tatra. You have to take him to Kasprowy Wierch, only on the side where there are no tourists, and let he stay there until he gathers strength."

It sounded enigmatic and smacked with magic, but Fronda didn't care.

"Like Anteus, who was recovering when he touched the ground. Okay, we'll try it, it costs us nothing. Never is terribly miserable anyway, we probably won't hurt him anymore.

\*\*\*\*\*

When they stopped in the parking lot, friends got out of the van and looked around. No one was waiting for them, but being sensitive like other vampires, they easily sensed what Stasiek was talking about. Although they were only at the foot of the mountains, they felt a change, some magnetic impact, causing the blood to circulate more strongly in their veins, and their thoughts were clearer. The mountains, majestic in the clear air, were not as high as the Himalayas or even the Alps, but there was something unique about them. Wild beauty, indefinite threat and irresistible magnetism emanated from the massifs above this town with slopes covered with dark green forests and snowy peaks.

"Beautiful," Theo sighed, the most sensitive to wildlife.

"I was raised here," said Gladiator in very lame English. "There is no more wonderful place around the world. Once you go to the Tatras, you will miss them for the rest of your days. You'll see."

Oggy shook herself and barked cheerfully. She passed the last leg of the journey as a dog, unable to master her werewolf nature any longer. Gladiator accepted her transformation with philosophical calmness, though, until he met her, he did not even suspect that werewolves exist as a separate species.

"Where are we going?" Gerard asked, barely stopping yawning.

"My brother and I have a house just outside Krupówki. This way. We will be there soon and you will be able to lie down." Said the Pole.

215

The town was just getting gray, but you could already see people on the streets. Local people, mainly old farmers, got up around four in the morning in summer and not much later in winter. Both Frenchmen were happy to see small, stylish cottages and gardens that could be covered with a hat - the fields and farms were a little further away.

Before the sun rose, they were already safe in one of these houses, modest, indistinguishable, but inside decorated like a mini-fortress. Everything was there - steel interior doors, an alarm system, solid blinds, not worse than traditional grilles, but made in such a way that they resembled ordinary sun visors. Also the walls, wooden from the outside, were reinforced with steel bars inside, masked with carved paneling. Everything was thought of as fort equipment.

Even the wooden logs that made the hut were in fact logs of synthetic heat-resistant plastic, topped with a thin layer of bast and bark, impregnated with a preparation once invented at the Octavio's research station. Several local vampires kept in touch with Spain and from here they received sporadically more useful inventions. This house could not be set on fire, even if it was spilled on gasoline. Just in case, however, a tunnel entrance was made in the floor, supposedly leading very far up to the mountains and ending in one of the natural caves. The masked, granite slab could only be moved away from the tunnel side.

The equipment of the cottage was quite Spartan - beds, benches against the walls, a table and several chairs, in addition a few old-fashioned chests of drawers. There was a small TV in the corner, an old-fashioned radio in each room. The kitchen was dominated by a freezer with a combination lock, well stocked with frozen plasma and whole blood, and a bar full of various drinks. The newcomers drank a sip of warmed blood with relief and stretched out on the beds, covered with striped rugs. They were very tired, especially Never, though he had the most comfortable place in the van, and almost carried him through the walking route to the cottage.

To be honest, the Indian vampire did not trust the strengthening treatment prescribed by Dr. Zakrzewski, but he also thought that it would not hurt to try. He had an open mind. He would have believed even in dark magic if someone had presented him with convincing evidence, which in part justified his personal experience in India. He did not share them with anyone, which is a pity, because he would have something to talk about.

As soon as it got dark, both French and Oggy, now restored to human form, followed Gladiator. For understandable reasons he had to be their guide. As a native highlander, he knew almost every stone here and led them confidently up the climbing road. The spruce forests gave out a stunning smell, the lights of flashlights danced along a rocky path and reflected off a nearby stream. Although the day was unusually hot and the stones still gave off the heat absorbed during the day, the breeze was almost chilly.

Jadwiga waited quite high for the newcomers on the mountainside. At the sight of her, Theo, though already accustomed to the fact that every second girl he met in Poland awakens in him the desire to immediately follow her, he slightly widened his eyes. The girl seemed to be a mountain goddess, without exaggeration. Quite tall and not excessively slim, although very shapely, she had long legs with full calves, visible from under the floral skirt, wrinkled at the waist. The short-sleeved white blouse had a red ribbon at the collar as its only decoration, and though it had no cleavage, it couldn't hide the perfection of the shapes it covered. Above this blouse a head rose, mounted on a proud, strong neck, and a white, thick braid of brown wheat color wound up below the waist. The girl's face matched the rest of her character - full lips, a classically sculpted nose, long eyes with cavernous depth and even arches of eyebrows above them.

"Hello, Jadwiśka, how are you?" Gladiator asked cheerfully, leaving new friends a bit behind.

"I would ask, Janiczek," said the girl. "Why are you going walkies for years?"

Gladiator sat next to her and put a friendly arm around her muscular shoulder.

"I went to the valley, to the cepers," he said. "I brought companions here, as you see. The one who's looking at you is Fronda. He's such a wolf. The other one is Gerard, and she is Oggy, their companion, and my now. You speak American?"

"A little. How are you?"

Jadwiśka said last words in English. As it turned out, she spoke a fairly clear language, much better than Gladiator. However, in his case, it was necessary to make an amendment that he also learned what he knew, by a miracle. He hated acquiring knowledge and, while his brother was a doctor, he could only boast of a diploma in military zoo-technics.

Gerard, seeing that there was nothing to count on dazzling Fronda, told the girl the reason for their visit to Podhale. The girl listened to him, nodding her beautiful head, then answered:

"You will have to use the gondola lift, because you will not bring your friends to Kasprowy in one night. This is physically impossible. Would any of you be able to handle the lift central?"

"Me," Oggy growled.

As usual, she felt a twinge of jealousy in her heart at the sight of a friend delighted with the beautiful highlander. In her mind she compared her frail figure and unsympathetic, thin face with the posture and face of a mountain goddess. Sadly, she thought that there was nothing to compare - she just lost in these competitions before the start.

Jadwiśka did not pay attention to her reluctance at all.

"That's good," she said. "The point is, we get to the top, leave your friend there and come back."

"How will he manage there?" Gerard asked helplessly.

"Oh, that won't be a problem. Tatra will take care of him."

"Who is Tatra?" Asked Theo with interest.

"That's a very old vampires," said Gladiator. "I think she's the first in these areas. She lives in the snow and ice, rarely eats, but lives in full harmony with the strength my brother mentioned to you. I would risk saying that she herself has some supernatural power, but who can know that. In any case, Never is safe under her protection. I think he's going to regain strength."

Gerard didn't look convinced. The whole thing poisoned him with black magic and superstition of primitive culture. Then he thought of Stonehenge and the ghostly dog of Bluewater's, and just sighed. If this was to help, then one should not worry about the genesis of the phenomenon. Let them call it what they want, if it really helps. He thought back to Never, waiting for them to return in a hut converted into a shelter. He was on the verge of death, emaciated, unable to eat alone, giving the impression of someone already on the other side. Even if he couldn't be helped, it probably wouldn't hurt. And so, his days, and maybe hours were numbered. Transfer to a snow-covered mountain peak could have accelerated death, but it was already inevitable.

Resigned, he sat on the grass next to Jadwiśka and listened as the girl teased Theo. After a while, their conversation deviated on personal topics - Fronda told her a little about himself, and Jadwiśka paid him back with the story about her and her friends. It turned out that the local vampire commune was not small, especially in relation to the number of officially registered population of these mountain areas. Polish and Slovak highlanders belonged to the community, even several Hungarians. They lived high in the mountains, in a place where the Polish Tatras became Czech, occupying a complex system of connected caves. Their appearance in the area did not arouse suspicion, because many Slovaks and Poles engaged in smuggling, settling suspicious interests at the green border.

There was unwritten law on these pages about minding one's own business and not cooperating with the police on any terms. When one had to arrange something, they simply went to the town on one side or the other, without worrying.

"Don't you have a hard time getting blood?" Asked Theo.

"Sometimes. But we always have sheep's milk," the girl replied with a smile.

"Milk?" Theo was surprised.

It never occurred to him that it could be a substitute for blood, though it was not illogical.

"Yes, but it must be milk straight from the milked animal, God forbid from shop." Jadwiśka explained. "That it would be without additions. You can stand it for some time."

It was a very interesting discovery and remained a mystery why vampires from other parts of the world did not come up with such a simple solution to their troubles. Maybe because they usually lived in cities, and no one keeps milking animals there.

As the darkness thickened around for good, Theo and Gladiator returned to the hut. Never greeted them with a weary look of a fatally weary man who couldn't sleep. Their explanations did not seem to reach him, but he agreed to everything without a word. He probably didn't care. He looked very bad already. His skin, usually quite dark, now resembled stale parchment, and in addition to his misfortune his eyes sank into the skull, which meant a critical condition for vampires. There really wasn't a moment to lose.

Of course, Never could go up to the cable car station. Gladiator volunteered to carry him piggyback, which was not a big difficulty - he barely weighs anything anymore. Jadwiśka and others were waiting for them at the station itself. They had already neutralized the night watchman, and Oggy was just finishing working on the control panel. At the sound of footsteps, she raised her head and smiled friendly.

"It's nothing difficult," she said. "Get in the car, I'll do the rest."

Oggy's technical talents were even a mystery to her - after all, she had never studied at the Polytechnic - but they were very useful. The computers had no secrets for her. The short course she had taken with Fronda and proper reading were enough for her to become a real genius in this field and it was a pity to think what chances she would have been as a normal, ordinary girl.

Such a night trip over the mountains had its charm, although all its participants felt a slight fear, looking into the dark abyss below them. It so happened that apart from Jadwiśka, none of them had yet used a similar invention. They were relieved when the car reached the ignition switch at the top of the mountain.

"Follow me and be careful not to stray, because if one of you falls into a crack here, it will probably be end of him." Highlander warned everyone and walked forward confidently.

Shining strangely low over the mountains, the moon flooded everything with streams of bright light, sufficient enough for the sensitive eyes of the vampires to enjoy the full color of the Tatra Mountains. The ability of vampires to see colors in the dark is the result of a mutation in the retina of their eyes - the rods become much more sensitive than in any mammal.

At one-point Jadwiśka stopped and pointed her hand forward. In front of them appeared the woman they were looking for and although they were prepared for her otherness, their hearts beat faster than before.

Tatra was high and excessively limp, like a sylphide. She had very white skin with a bluish sheen and exactly the same color of hair, covering her naked body like a coat. She was wearing nothing, not a piece of cloth, but she was as casual as she normally was. Huge eyes, reminiscent of two pieces of blue ice, saw over the newcomers carefully, and then the girl nodded carelessly and said something in Polish. Jadwiśka answered her with a long tirade, from which they did not understand a word, and then turned toward them.

"She says let us follow her," she said.

"To hell, I don't know where to look..." murmured Gerard, detonated like never before.

"I know where," Theo gave Tatra a greedy look. "Does she really have to be so naked? Not cold to her?" He corrected his clasped hands. He and Gerard made a chair from their hands and carried Never because Gladiator stayed with Oggy in the event of something unforeseen.

"Tatra unlearned to wear clothes a long time ago, because it would be difficult for her to get some with the lifestyle she led," explained the highlander. "In addition, she seems to be suffering from a specific contact allergy. Have you probably noticed the skin color? This is not normal."

Fronda grunted in reply. His thoughts were suddenly overwhelmed by the deep sensations that gripped his sensitive mind. He could feel the strong waves of force flowing through his body very clearly, whose origin he could not determine. It certainly wasn't any enemy power. Rather, he felt he was trying to be helpful. It made hope enter the heart and the mood improved significantly. Theo has been to the mountains more than once in other countries, but nowhere has he felt such a thing. Also, the air had a definitely different smell - like a spruce, but the scent was velvety and intoxicating than anywhere in the world. The sound of trees sounded different, more mysterious, at the same time luring and warning against... before or actually?

"These mountains are alive," he whispered unconsciously.

Jadwiśka looked at him and a mysterious smile blossomed on her lips. For her, born and raised in Podhale, it was not news. She liked the Frenchman, but she looked at him with a slight indulgence, like an older sister, although from what Gladiator had told her, he was much older than her. And yet his eyes had something childish naive in their eyes. She had no idea that this look was Fronda's main weapon as a seducer, a weapon that never let him down.

Tatra stopped at the entrance to the great cave, clearly reaching far into the mountain, but did not enter it. Instead, she brushed the snow off the wide rocky threshold with her bare foot and moved it with some effort. It said a lot about the difficulty, because according to Gladiator Tatra was stronger than anyone could have imagined. It could be taken for granted that no one but her would move this rock block alone. Stone steps appeared below it, leading somewhere down. Without looking at her guests Tatra said something again.

"She tells to put the patient here," Jadwiśka translated, "she says that he will go down to the sanctuary."

"What? He won't even stand," Gerard dared to protest. Unlike Fronda, he wasn't attracted by a new friend. Tatra visibly overwhelmed him with panic, so that his teeth chattered not from cold.

"I'll stand," Never whispered, barely audible.

In fact, it seemed like he had some strength back. He staggered to his feet, then began to follow Tatra below the ground without looking at his friends. The rock closed behind them, as if there had never been a passage in it.

All three stood for a moment, staring silly at the empty space.

"Will he not freeze here?" Fronda asked finally, shaking slightly.

"No, he won't freeze. You can be sure of that. Tatra was already treating ours, and moreover, apparently, even she is not healing, but these mountains," said Jadwiśka.

They slowly turned back and headed toward the station. Gerard dragged himself behind, lost in unhappy thoughts, Theo and the beautiful highlander walked hand in hand in front.

"How do you know Tatra is a vampire like us?" The actor asked suddenly, interrupting their quiet conversation.

Jadwiśka looked at him.

"We don't know," she said. "We just think so. Is it important anyway?"

He couldn't answer her. There was a silence in which only the sound of trees was heard.

"I'm starting to believe that Never will recover," Fronda said finally, quietly, with a delighted look. "I feel that I could fall in love in these mountains. They are so indescribably beautiful, but at the same time so inscrutable... I do not want to go back down."

He breathed deeply, wonderful air, full of the smell of spruces and firs, clean and almost unspoiled by civilization. The night was exceptionally beautiful and calm.

"If you wish, we will go down on foot," Jadwiśka suggested. "You'll see things only available to the vampire's eyes that you didn't suspect existed before."

Theo thought for a moment, then looked at Gerard.

"You return to the wagon alone, Fanfan," he said aloud. "I and this beautiful lady want to discover together all available natural wonders."

"I don't doubt it," Gerard muttered sourly and included everything in this short statement.

This is not the first time something similar has happened. Theo was constantly disappearing all night in the company of one or another beauty. Danger didn't stop him; he wasn't terrified of the trouble he was getting into - he just couldn't live without love adventures. Never grunted at him because of that, but he actually thought it was better that way. Making love every week at another, Theo wasn't exposed to anything far more destructive to a vampire: great, true love.

Without protest, Gerard went alone to the cable car, just waving goodbye to his friends. A lonely road to the station was waiting for him through the black void, but he was no longer afraid. Now all he was worried about was Never, whom he had left on the highest peak, along with some naked madwoman. When he pulled his thoughts away from the Indian with some effort, he suddenly wondered:

"And how do I explain this to Oggy?"

That their friend was in love with Theo was no secret to him. He wondered how Fronda could be so blind - he loved Oggy, but like a sister, while every stupid person would realize that she had no sister affection for him. Theo saw nothing. Maybe it was more convenient for him?

"I have enough of this erotomaniac," Gerard muttered to himself angrily, tripping over snow-covered stones.

He welcomed the warm, illuminated interior of the wagon with some relief. Oggy looked at him uneasily from under her squatted mane.

"And where is Fronda and that highlander?" She asked.

"They decided to go down on foot. I didn't feel strong enough," he answered her reluctantly.

Oggy sighed sadly. She had long known that Theo would not give up his love affairs until they bury him for good, and she suffered so much. She could not become one of the flames of her ideal, because it would be too dangerous for him, so she was content with what friendship could offer her. However, jealousy could not completely suppress.

"Leave it," Gerard advised her warmly. "It's not worth thinking about it. You know what Fronda is like, he always gets something up and returns home in the morning like a tomcat roaming the rooftops. That's the way he is and we can't help it."

"He just knows how to use life. Let's go back now. We must be careful not to enter the devil's forest, because at night various things happen there. Luckily, I know which way to go," Gladiator said lightly, dragging his large body until his bones cracked.

The cable car was trembling and jumping, gliding through the darkness, and the actor suddenly felt terribly lonely. It was not the first time he regretted that he was persuaded by Never, instead of accepting his fate with dignity - what was his life now, overwhelmed him and often frightened him. He wasn't a bloodsucker from horror movies. He was an ordinary man with ordinary desires, entangled in matters he did not understand. He was not a typical vampire.

The wagon tapped slightly, stopping at the station at the foot of the mountain.

They moved through the dark subalpine forest. Nobody knows how it happened, but instead of going down the road to town, they went up the hill and did not notice it at all. They felt safe. It was still night and there was enough time until dawn so that they would not have to hurry. They scanned the path with beams of flashlights, though their eyes glimmering red in the darkness could use every faintest ray of light. Gerard once asked Never why their eyes take on this color in deep darkness and shine, and then the older vampire explained to him that the factor that changes the transformation also affects the retina of the eyes. It strengthens and thickens them, and also multiplies their ability to capture light, which causes the same visual effect as in night animals. It scares ordinary people, but it is completely harmless in itself.

They usually found what they wanted easily thanks to their eyes, but the mountains had a strange effect - the darkness seemed denser, as if all the light from the stars, the moon and their flashlights sucked out the trees growing around. Nevertheless, such a walk among firs and spruces, creating an unmistakable atmosphere, was very pleasant. Gerard was already beginning to forget what bothered him when Gladiator stopped suddenly and called out:

"We lost our way! I don't know where I am!"

There was a fear in his voice that he couldn't hide. At first, Gerard and Oggy did not understand what he was afraid of, after all they could wait until it will be brightly a bit and then find the right path, but after a while they realized that they had taken to some strange place. The trees were buzzing steadily, but nothing was heard. No shouts of hunting night birds, no murmur, as if there was no life in this part of the mountains. Nothing but the silent trees and the suffocating smell of forest litter, mixed with something they couldn't identify.

"Relax," Oggy said, trying to control her trembling voice. "I will become a dog and find the right direction. Don't panic, boys."

Gerard knew that the girl was probably right, but he could not control his anxiety. He felt that he was in a place he should avoid, and that he might never leave it again. He couldn't say where that feeling came from, but it was strong and over everything else. There was something lurking in this silent space that no intruders wanted in their area. Behind him he heard a strangled sob.

"I can't transform myself," Oggy said, "I can't..."

"Take it easy. We can do it without it. Let's just move on, we must finally go somewhere," Gerard croaked, not knowing his own voice.

They took a dozen more steps, holding each other as close as possible when Oggy stumbled over something and started screaming. Gladiator hastily clapped her mouth with his hand. She bit him so that he screamed himself and threw himself blindly among the trees. The actor at the last moment grabbed her by the dress and pulled her to him, while Gladiator shook his wounded hand cursing on. Then he leaned over to see what Oggy had stumbled over and immediately jumped away with a strangled cry.

Gerard, reassuring the girl as much as possible, turned the light of his flashlight on the mysterious object. The flashlight trembled in his hand and almost fell out. On the ground lay a brown skeleton the size of a small child. A disproportionately large skull was covered by the remnant of mummified skin, showing a face so terribly distorted, as if in life this creature was a demon from folk legends.

"Take it easy. Whatever it is, it's dead," the Frenchman choked, gasping for breath.

"We must get out of here at all costs," Gladiator muttered.

Gerard looked at him.

"You grew up in this area. Tell us what threatens us here," he demanded categorically.

The highlander shook his bright hair and looked around fearfully in the silent forest.

"Once, when I was young, I heard stories about a devil from the mountains," he said. "He is said to be so terrible that if anyone looks at him, he loses his mind with terror. However, if someone has a strong will, he can ask the devil for help, and then the devil will give him a piece of his skin. Whoever has this skin always wins cards, the most beautiful girls love him, and his herds multiply without hesitation and so on. The only condition is putting the devil's skin on your shoulder where it grows."

"And what's next?" Oggy asked, trembling like an aspen leaf.

"If somebody has some reason, after getting what he wants, he should cut the devil's skin from his shoulder with a knife and bury it in the cemetery. If he doesn't, he turns into a monster and steals people's souls until someone with a pure heart and great courage defeats him. However, I do not know how."

"Girlish tales," Gerard muttered, but he felt an unpleasant shiver.

Hug to his side, Oggy was shivering as if she had a malaria attack. The actor felt that he had to do something, so he moved forward vigorously, not caring where he was going. He just wanted to leave the cursed place. He still didn't believe in "haunting" or "possession," although the facts he learned spoke for themselves. However, even if we assume that all these strange phenomena were natural, they remained something incomprehensible and frightening. Clenching his teeth, he brushed away the branches of trees that blocked their way, branches that seemed to have their own lives.

He had the impression that the forest was reaching out after them, silently, with cruel consequence. He felt that the ground he was wading on was not moss or typical forest litter, but sticky yarn, as if he were walking on a deck of overlapping layers of giant cobwebs. His imagination gave him a picture of a giant spider lurking with predatory patience somewhere in the middle of this snare, on which victims' unconscious doom circulate. Pushing the branches away, he also felt his fingers stick to sticky shreds. He was wiping them with disgust on his clothes, but his hands were still getting new.

The forest ended abruptly and before the three wanderers a great house grew out of the ground, clung to the mountainside. Behind it was another forest wall, black and menacing. The house resembled an old building, it was different from typical highlander buildings and at the sight of it Gerard experienced another thrill. He hesitated. This house seemed more dangerous to him than the forest, though he couldn't justify this impression.

"Are we coming in?" Asked Gladiator nervously. "It will be dawn soon, and the sun in the mountains is dangerous even for marten. Apparently, the shape of the mountains creates a kind of aerial lens that multiplies the strength of the rays. That is, the part of the light that is harmful to us."

"We're coming in," Gerard decided, deciding he would not be afraid of ghosts of popular beliefs. His materialistic worldview did not allow such a thing to happen and he was ashamed of himself that foolish fear that was now tearing him.

He touched the carved door that opened, obeying his fingers. The interior of the house was quiet and dark. The old appliances stood as if their owners went out only for a moment, but nothing scraped at the corners, nothing creaked, even this door, undisturbed for a long time, and quiet, like freshly oiled. Holding on to the wall, friends entered uncertainly inside, and then the door closed silently behind them, as if pushed with an invisible hand.

Behind the short hallway was a large room, from which an open door led somewhere further. The interior of the house smelled of dust and mold, but it would be in vain to look for the smell of mice and rats, typical of old houses. Certainly not a single living creature lived here. It was cold like a cold room. The shutters were deaf to death, letting in not the faint glow or breeze. The lights of flashlights brought out the outlines of furniture, some old upholstery, numerous candlesticks...

Gerard took a lighter out of his pocket, lit all the candles one after the other and it got brighter immediately.

"We will wait here calmly west, and then we will try to find the right path." Gladiator took one of the candles and began to look at the paintings on the walls, bringing the trembling flame in turn. They all depicted some monstrous beings, faces twisted with insane fear, or eyes that seemed to live their own lives.

"Whoever lived here must have been crazy," he said finally, in an uncertain voice. Heavy footsteps on the stairs echoed him somewhere deep in the house. It sounded as if the one who was walking had lead soles. The steps sounded for a moment, then stopped.

"Is anyone here?" Gerard asked quietly.

Oggy sniffed for a moment, then shook her head and silently clung to the actor's hand. Her sense of smell could put your faith, he remained doggy even when she was human.

"I'll check it out." Gladiator stepped out into the corridor, raising the candle high.

His friends hurried after him, fearing that the group would be separated by a force they did not yet know. A faint flame illuminated the wooden stairs leading upstairs, surrounded by a rotten balustrade. The thick deck of dust on each step left no doubt - no one had gone that way for years. And yet, when they looked at them in silence, clear marks of hooves, similar to the tracks of a goat in the snow, began to form in the brown dust. The gladiator shook so that the candle almost fell out of his hand.

His left hand went to his neck, as if something suddenly caught his throat.

"I don't care about the sun," he whispered. "I'd rather burn myself to death than stay here for a while. Let's run away while we can."

"Okay," moaned Oggy. She bared her teeth aloud, saying goodbye again and again and muttering passages of Italian prayers.

Friends withdrew into the room, ran through it and stood helplessly. There was no exit to the hall. It just disappeared. Gladiator ran to the window and jerked the window shut with all his might. It broke with a snap, remaining in his hand, but beyond it there was no window, only a brick wall, from which a musty wind blew. They were trapped, locked in with something monstrous that they couldn't even see.

"I want to get out of here! Let me out!" Oggy shouted hysterically, throwing herself at the wall and punching her with her fists.

"Calm down!" Gerard grabbed her in the strong grip that Fronda had taught him. "Nothing here but mass hysteria, understand?! Nobody will hear you except us."

He paused, because a hairy paw came out of the air, clenched thick fingers on each of the candles in turn, crushing and extinguishing them, and then dissipated into nothingness. This simply could not be, but crumbled candles lying on the floor could serve as a silent testimony of some physical force. Whatever it was, it could boast a sufficiently high degree of materialization to destroy a particular thing.

"A house where evil lurks," Oggy said, suddenly calming down in an instant. "It's a horror title that Fronda once took me to. This is one of those homes and what has seized it will not let us go unless it wants to. No screams will help anything here, but self-control can help."

"Take it easy," Gerard growled, wiping sweat from his brow. This struggle, combined with fear, exhausted him a lot and he felt that he couldn't breathe. It was getting colder, the air seemed to freeze inside the house. It felt like time had stopped flowing.

"Think logically. If we could come in here, we will be able to go out," Gladiator said after a moment. "At present, we simply do not see the exit, because something or someone acts directly on our brains. Whatever it is, we must remain calm and..."

He paused, staring into the corner of the room. Gerard followed his gaze and saw a female figure reviewing the papers on the frame of the fireplace.

The woman was wearing a long, flowing dress from the previous era and a lace cap. When she turned around, they saw her wrinkled monkey face and glowing small eyes. She raised a bony finger upward, nodded it sideways, and disappeared as if it had dissolved in the dark. Nothing happened for a moment, then they heard heavy footsteps again. They did not go down the stairs anymore, but circled behind the closed door, as if unable to decide to enter. They finally stopped, as they had been the previous time.

"We're in the power of the devil," said Gladiator in a resigned voice. "Are any of you baptized?"

"I am," Oggy replied a little indistinctly, because her teeth stuck in fear like castanets.

"And I'm an atheist," Gerard said firmly. "And I will not change my worldview because of any haunted hut. I don't believe in any devils."

Somewhere inside the house came his name, uttered in a hollow voice, as if from the depth of a thick iron pipe. This unlike normal voice shook him terribly. Next to the actor, Oggy shuddered violently, and then, without warning, threw herself to the ground. Her small body, erect as in an epilepsy attack, smashed against the walls and floor to the accompaniment of a high-pitched shrill and screaming inarticulate scream. When they tried to hold her, she broke free with them, as if she were not a werewolf, but several wrestlers melted into one. The attack lasted for several minutes, then the girl stopped and calmed down without regaining consciousness.

"Listen, Mr. Marxist and Leninist, you can have the views you want, but here you need an exorcist. We can't do it alone," said Gladiator firmly.

"Where will you get him? Even if we agree with you, we can't leave to bring in a priest, and it must not be a normal priest," said Gerard wearily. He was starting to lose hope and all his materialistic worldview.

"I will try to communicate with Jadwiśka telepathically," Gladiator sat down, touched his temples with his fingertips and froze in this pose, while the Frenchman watched him with mixed feelings.

He has heard that some vampires have extrasensory perception, but he has not seen any of them with his own eyes. And Gladiator, a great man with a small brain, looked like a telepath to him the least. It always seemed to him that the phenomenon of telepathy, if it exists at all, must be associated with people with some higher intelligence. Besides, he did not believe in paranormal phenomena, and although he witnessed some of them, he took it very reluctantly. Either way, he couldn't do anything else.

He left Gladiator and took care of Oggy, still in lethargy. She still did not regain consciousness, but from time to time her body shook with severe convulsions. It didn't look good. Looking at her and at the gladiator in trance, Gerard realized that he was on his own. In the darkness, illuminated only by the now darkening flashlight, he had to find a solution to the mystery of this ghostly household, if they were to come out alive.

After searching the room thoroughly, he discovered a pattern: there was not a single right angle in it. All the corners of the room were certainly less than 90 degrees, the same was true for the corners of paintings and furniture. The consequence of this was that the walls collapsed slightly in the middle, the same applied to the sides of the furniture and even the paintings. Someone had to work hard. Gerard began to suspect that after extending the arms of the angles they form a cycle of pentagrams, and although for obvious reasons he could not check it, he was convinced that this is the case.

Having realized this, he understood that this house was specially built for certain purposes, it is not an ordinary chalet, possessed by Evil. For the first time, he thought of it in capital letters as if he were an independent being. He felt his eyes sharpen. He understood that the table is not a table, but a kind of altar, and what is stored in wardrobes is definitely not someone's clothes. Overcoming fear, he opened one of them and barely suppressed the scream. The wardrobe contained a partially unfolded and then mummified corpse of a woman of indefinite age. If the other wardrobes contained similar "exhibits", then this house was indeed a real museum of horror.

Glowing to the floor, Gerard noticed that there was a frozen puddle under the second cabinet, black in that light, but looking completely fresh. He didn't manage to open the door. Summing up what he already knew, he came to the conclusion that he still did not know which of the things registered by his senses were real and which illusion were. His experience has taught him that one should not trust the senses one hundred percent. Only that here there was rather no apparatus generating vibration or electromagnetic field. They were in the mountains, civilization seemed to be hundreds of miles away. So, what caused sensory disturbances? Were they disturbances or real paranormal phenomena? And what caused them? Devil? Nonsense, there are no devils. What then?

There were footsteps again, very close this time, right behind him. Gerard turned abruptly but didn't notice anything. No one was physically there, only the steps circling him slowly, as if deliberately. After a while a ghostly figure leaned out of the corner, drew some marks on the wall and disappeared. The wall rippled like a vertical pitch, and one of the heavy porters hanging by the window fell on Gerard's head. The actor gave a shout of terror. Thick, dust-filled matter wrapped his head tightly, stopping his breath, he fought her like a live opponent, and when he finally managed to break the doorman from his head, he was exhausted as if after a marathon run.

At the same time, the ghostly light shone under the large lampshades on the ceiling and immediately went out. After a while, the phenomenon repeated, then again, as if someone was playing with the switch. Gerard noticed with horror that there were no bulbs in the lampshades - they were empty, covered with cobwebs. He did not know how long he stood in this icy room, staring at the regularly flashing and dying ceiling, when the phenomenon finally stopped and the steps stopped. The whole house froze again, awaiting the order of its dark master.

Gerard rolled up the gatekeeper in his hands and threw her into the corner. He wasn't afraid anymore. To be honest, he was astonished himself, so great peace came over him. He knew the danger as well as before, but the fear that paralyzed him had vanished, replaced by something akin to resignation. He looked around the room.

"I'm Gerard Phil," he said aloud. "I was buried in November 1959 and I died for the world. Whatever happens here, I will not be afraid, because what lives here is not able to overwhelm me."

He walked over to Oggy, who was still, and hit her on the thin face several times.

"Stand up, sleeping beauty," he said sharply.

The girl opened her eyes and bluffed with a stream of curses in a dozen or so different languages. Her left hand shot forward, sharp fingernails on the actor's face. In the last second, he managed to dodge the blow and grabbed her wrist. She writhed, shouting sharply in an unknown language to the actor and tense like a snake, but he did not release her, repeating all the time:

"Calm, Oggy, calm. It is our fear that makes THIS so strong. You must control your fear and then it will weaken and will not be able to hurt us."

Gladiator was still sitting in the position in which he had left him, fingers of both hands pressed to his temples, indifferent to the scene. Gerard had no idea how to get out of the world to such an extent, but he did not have time to consider it now. He strained to keep screaming Oggy. How could this fragile body contain such layers of wild power? Finally, the words repeated like a mantra had the desired effect - the muscles of the girl fabled, her voice broke in a pitiful sow, and after a moment Oggy looked at Gerard completely conscious.

She gasped for a few minutes, as if it had flowed from the bottom of the lake, then she began to cry and hugged her friend tightly.

"It's okay," Gerard said, stroking her comfortingly. "It's okay. Remember, you need to control your emotions and THIS will not have a point of attachment."

"What is THIS? Is that the devil?" Oggy asked, trying to control her trembling body and sobbing.

"I do not know. If there is Hell, then it certainly is from there. I, the atheist, have no doubt about that."

"And you say not to be afraid?!!"

"Yes, that's what I'm saying. And don't shout, dear. Even abstract Evil is not all-powerful. It draws strength from our negative emotions. It can't work without them. That is why exorcisms are so effective. They cleanse the soul and heart, cleanse thoughts, and bring peace. And inexplicable phenomena disappear. Come on, baby."

Oggy obediently rose from the floor, but her legs were trembling under her so much that she had to hold on to her friend's hand so as not to fall. She was exhausted, and she was completely confused. She couldn't remember what was happening to her, all she knew was that it was grim and scary.

Gladiator moved and sighed.

"Something terrible," he said, finally lowering his arms. "Background noise is so strong that I can't break through. Once it almost succeeded, maybe Jadwiśka caught something? What's new?"

We're trying to survive," Gerard answered him succinctly. "If you've finished pretending to be the Dalai Lama, we'll go exploring the house. For now, we only know this room, it will be good to find out what is in others. Maybe we'll find out how to get out of here."

"Or never get out of nowhere again," Oggy murmured grimly.

Gladiator thought for a moment, then nodded, stood up and opened the door. However, he quickly closed them, pushing them with his great body. There was only darkness behind the door - consolidated, impenetrable, giving the impression of being alive and trying to pour through the open door to the room. Gerard hurried to help and the two of them managed to close the door somehow, closing the heavy bolt placed on them. Somewhere deep inside the house an inhuman voice came again. It repeated the words they couldn't understand, then fell silent.

"It's talking like from the bottom of an iron barrel. Look, French, if you're so smart, think about what to do to get out of here. I'm not thinking," said the highlander, wiping sweat with his sleeve from forehead.

"It's even visible... I don't know what to do to let this house leave us, but our main worry is to survive," Gerard replied calmly. "If we don't get home, Theo and this girl will start looking for us, regardless of whether she received your telepathic message that I don't even believe."

"Do you think they'll find us here?" Oggy asked in a shaky voice.

"If Miss Jadwiga has all her marbles at least, then penetrating the area, she will guess where we got. And Theo will certainly find a way to get us out of here," friend replied.

Although Never was the brain of their team, Fronda was always counted on in emergency situations. His timing, courage and strategy were worth more than Never's intelligence. Gerard was sure that if Theo were here with them, he would have long ago found a way to outsmart what had imprisoned them. Outsmarting... This word had some vague association in his brain. He looked around the dark room and suddenly understood. If his earlier calculations were accurate, then they must to make that THIS would want to get rid of them. And if the previous guesses were correct, this could be achieved.

"Listen," he said softly. "We have to do this: everything in the room, equipment, paintings, everything must be turned 180 degrees. I don't know if I'm thinking correctly, but if so, then everything is in a particular place. When we destroy this order, we will disrupt the flow of bad power. Don't pay attention to anything that happens, just do what I said. OK? To the work."

Not only friends listened to these instructions, because flames suddenly surrounded them. Oggy screamed, even Gladiator panicked and it took Gerard a good moment to bring them to order. Vampires are afraid of fire much more than people, so they needed all their internal discipline not to fall into a state in which they would be susceptible to possession. Whatever caused this condition was deadly, no matter what it was. As soon as they controlled themselves, the flames disappeared and no trace was left of them.

"If you want to know my opinion, we'll get hit, but I don't have any other idea," said the highlander, when he managed to gather his nerves, and then got to work.

Oggy began to hang up the paintings, though she had the impression that they were still trying to bite her, and Gerard took up the rolling of the carpet, covered with intricate geometric patterns. It was not easy, for the house swayed and staggered as if a giant were shaking it, and the walls seemed to press on them from all sides. Various objects hovered and hit the equipment with a monstrous force, and avoiding the collision with them became a matter of life and death. There were other phenomena, such that had already eluded logical summary, as if the dictionary had no terms, but suddenly the room was clear.

"Over there!" Shouted Oggy, throwing herself towards the gap, so faint that only animal eyes could see it.

The men followed her. They felt as if they had hit the wall of hot air, and after a while they were outside, under the starry sky, in the gusts of the night wind. Inside the house, it was still roaring and rattling, as if the infernal mill had stones there, and through the windows you could see flashes of strong, reddish light.

"Let's get out of here," moaned Oggy.

She was afraid of the thought of entering the forest again, but it was better than that terrible house. Something was puzzling her, and she quickly understood what.

"It was supposed to be dawn when we got in, and it is now around midnight," she said, looking skyward.

"Apparently our struggles lasted all day," said Gerard. "Subjective time is something that easily distorts."

"How did you know what to do?" Gladiator asked curiously.

"Looking at the room, I realized that all the corners in it were the tops of giant pentagrams, forming a kind of network," the Frenchman explained to him. "It was enough to change their mutual position so that the whole network changed its properties. It's logical, as long as magic that doesn't exist at all can be logical."

The highlander nodded pityingly.

"You're not reformable. After all that has happened to us, you still deny the existence of strange phenomena..."

"You know what? We'll talk about it some other time." Gerard sighed, not feeling able to engage in such discussions now.

He looked around and started down the road. It was certain that they had to go down instead of go up if they wanted to get to town. He managed to realize that everything here, and the house and its surroundings, was controlled by the same force, so it was not to be expected that it would release them so easily from its clutches. He plunged into the trees not without fear.

"Come on, go ahead...!" He called to hesitating friends and a voice stuck in his throat with terror.

Something heavy, cold and sticky, giving off a strong stench of rot, fell on his back, wrapping it in fragile but amazingly strong limbs. His slimy forearm blocked his mouth so that he couldn't even scream. He fell on the moss, fighting with all his might to get rid of the choking abomination. He felt himself rolling down a slope and lost his mind in horror at the thought of what awaited him down there, where that ramp led. He had no more strength or hope for rescue, when finally, somebody's strong hands grabbed him and pulled him away from the sticky lump. The black abyss that sucked him in, disappeared, sealed like a wound in space-time.

"Breathe deeply. Pick up the pieces," he heard Fronda's commanding voice and almost burst into tears at the sight of his concerned face bent over his own.

"How lucky you found us," he whispered with difficulty through his battered throat.

He looked around. The forest was buzzing around, calm and indifferent, and there was no sign of anything unusual. He couldn't understand where it had gone, what was trying to pull him into the abyss, and where it had disappeared. After a moment, he thought that it was better not to understand it and not to ask about anything.

"It's thanks to Jade. At one point, she said you were in trouble and we must find you. All in all, a pity, because we had a great time then...

but when she told me what happened here sometimes, I got scared myself, a friend answered him cheerfully.

Gerard sat up, struggling to control his dizziness and nausea. The experience he had was so terrible that his mind rejected it, confronting the memory battle in which all these memories were stuck.

"What was that?" He choked out after a moment.

"I don't know," said Theo. "I saw only some shapeless mass."

Crouched beside him, Oggy looked around nervously, holding his elbow.

"And why did IT let go now?" She asked tearfully.

Theo smiled and gave her a protective hug.

"Maybe because this type of force usually attacks individuals or small groups," he replied. "The more people, the less likely they are to attack. Or maybe because there is finally a believer among you, materialistic disbelievers."

"But also, Oggy believes in God, and besides... I don't understand what faith has to do with it," Gerard was still unconsciously groping his throat.

"It has, my dear, a lot, but you will not understand it, because it is beyond your modest possibilities," Theo handed him a flat bottle with cognac.

The actor eagerly took a long sip, wiped his mouth with his sleeve and looked around. The forest was silent all around, and although the same threat lurked in that silence as before, it felt at the same time that IT prefers to stay away now. It was hard to suppose that this was because of Fronda, so maybe the number of people in the group actually played a role?

"We must leave as soon as possible," said Jadwiśka, emerging from the bushes. "You know, Janiczek, I can't believe you were so stupid. Why didn't you warn them about this haunted cottage?"

Gladiator shrugged powerful arms. He could not find the answer to this question - after all, he knew about the gloomy fame of this place, so why, when approaching it, forgot about it? Was THIS smarter than they thought?

"As usual, nobody believes in folk tales," Theo said, rising from his knees. "And in many of them there is something more than the proverbial grain of truth. For example, the legend of the fern flower. Why was the fern selected from many non-flowering plants, the only one that actually flourished? There were no people in the Carboniferous, no mammals. And yet, somehow, the legend got through the news that there was such a thing as a fern flower."

"What does this have to the haunted property?" Gerard asked helplessly.

"That it is sometimes worth believing if the natives tell you that there is a place where something's been scaring," Fronda replied with pontifical tone.

"Let's go," Jadwiśka urged everyone, shaking restlessly. "The atmosphere is awkward. Hey where you go? We have to go up the hill."

"What?" Gerard stared at her.

"Only seemingly this path leads to the mountains," the girl explained to him. "Just as apparently that one goes down. If we follow it, we can get to an even worse place than a haunted house. We have to follow a path that we would not take in common sense."

Gerard had the impression that the girl was talking nonsense, but he decided not to protest. So many inexplicable things happened that this could be true. He stood up and followed his friends sluggishly, still feeling nauseous and a terrible headache.

"Theo, does that mean that there is really dark magic in the world?" He asked quietly.

"No, I don't think so," Fronda replied after reflection. "The thing is, I've never met a man with real magical power. But there is Evil,

Impure Forces and Powers of Darkness, even if different sages do not like it. The more we deny it, the more we are exposed to direct attack and the more defenseless we are."

"Why?"

"If someone does not acknowledge the existence of a volcano, do not run away from it, but die in the first eruption, like the inhabitants of Pompeii and Herculaneum," Theo put his arm around him warmly. "Head's up. As long as I'm with you, I won't let you hurt even Lucifer."

*****

Zakopane was slowly falling asleep. In the small house behind Krupówki, four vampires were playing bridge, while Oggy was sitting with her laptop. It was one of the first laptops ever built, but its technology was ahead of its official achievements by some twenty years. The Octavio di Mauro's research station had great technological results, only a few of which were sold to reputable institutes.

Oggy, a natural talent in the field of computer science, was able to do almost anything with this device. In the era of rapidly growing computerization, her skills became invaluable. This time, however, the girl was doing something that Fronda usually did - she prepared a report for the department of matters considered supernatural. Still no one had a good idea of what really happened in the mountains and the only acceptable explanation seemed to be a paranormal factor. The trouble was that this theory was extremely difficult to back up with any evidence. Perhaps they could be obtained by returning to the haunted place with the right equipment, but they did not have it, and besides, no one could guarantee that anything would happen the second time. No one could guarantee that what was there would not be more effective this time. Returning to a haunted property would be very risky.

"Perhaps the fact that we are not humans, but vampires, confused this IT," Theo summed up their long reflection. "That's why it wasn't as effective as usual. If that is the case, returning there would mean suicide."

"But what exactly was that?" Gerard asked him.

Fronda shrugged and made a wise face.

"Don't ask unnecessary questions and you won't learn unnecessary things," he said meaningfully. "Sometimes it's better not to know and sleep peacefully. My green-eyed friend, for millennia people have been dealing with the dark side of our world and have not yet found an explanation for certain matters, and you expect someone to explain everything to you in a minute? I personally think that the explanation understandable to us simply does not exist, and if someone has a different opinion, then please, the freeway."

There was no such a person. It was not worth the risk just to let a few scientists in faraway Spain have something to discuss. It was better to acknowledge that not everything can be explained by human logic, "Euclidean logic," as Octavio used to say. After all, their very existence denied reason, so it seemed that they could best understand various unexplained phenomena. In the meantime, they were more cautious in this matter than anyone else.

Oggy tried to describe everything honestly, without emotions, coldly, like a real scientist, although her fingers trembled on the keys. The knowledge that she had been taken over for some time by an unidentified demon was extremely frustrating for her and filled her soul with a fear she would never get rid of - the fear of being possessed again. The ease with which IT gained control over her terrified her and awakened her awareness of her own weakness. It was something that no one would want to know about herself and she got sad evidence for it. She always thought she was stronger, and meanwhile something incomprehensible overwhelmed her body and mind with contemptuous ease.

Theo explained to her that she was surprised, and Evil always chooses the most vulnerable person as his victim, but Oggy still felt guilty, she felt that she had disappointed friends. What is worse, it occurred to her that she could pose a threat to them as a weaker and less resistant person, and who knows if it would be better if she left them. So, she wrote and tears rolled from her eyes to the keyboard. Absorbed in her work and suffering, she did not notice when Fronda stood behind her.

"Are you going?" He asked cheerfully. "Jade promised to show us something less frightening than a haunted house, but very interesting."

"I'll be ready in a minute," Oggy promised him, wiping her tears slightly.

Theo called Jadwiśka "Jade" - the name was easier for him to say, and the highlander didn't mind. The charming Frenchman seemed to like her. She hadn't had such a hot affair for a long time, and she reminded the years when she was just a simple village maiden.

This time they went not to Kasprowy, but to the slope of Giewont, along a prohibited route for tourists. Jadwiśka led them to a small waterfall, behind which, as it turned out, was a passage through which one could squeeze one by one. Behind the passage was a rocky corridor, followed by a grotto that shone with mica. It did not look particularly peculiar, but after a while they noticed what the highlander meant.

"We don't have to breathe here!" Cried Oggy in amazement.

It was indeed so. Standing in this cave, you could forget about breathing - no one lacked air, as if something was breathing for them.

"This is one of the wonders of the Tatra Mountains," Jadwiśka said. "But what comes next will interest you more. I only discovered this recently, and completely by accident. Follow me."

She began to walk along the mica belt, embedded in the wall, touching the stones with her hand, until she felt the hidden spring. The rock wall parted with a creek, revealing a cave that was probably artificial because its shape was similar to a cube. It was illuminated by stones glowing in the dark, set into the walls and ceiling.

"They're probably radioactive," Gerard whispered.

"No," said Theo. "Look, bats are sleeping under the ceiling. They would not be here if there was even a trace radiation."

However, strange, unlike similar stones were least unusual here. The cave was filled with rows of hills resembling catafalques. On each of them stood a heavy, sarcophagus forged in stone with mysterious symbols carved on it for the age. The lid of one of them was moved away and one could see the figure resting inside. Gerard sniffed the air. The figure lying in the sarcophagus looked familiar to him - it was almost identical to Vandis. It was characterized by the same smoothness of the face, the hair was similar, and the final proof was four-fingered hands, devoid of nails.

"Now I know nothing." Fronda said after a moment of silent contemplation.

"Are they dead?" Oggy asked, no less surprised than men.

"Not really," said Jadwiśka. "They seem to be sleeping. I mean, I just opened the sarcophagus, but there is no reason to suppose that there is something else in the others. You see, a very old application speaks of Sleeping Knights who will one day rise... I think it's about them."

Theo nodded, looking at the still man with fascination and trying to guess whether he had wings, unlike Vandis. He reached out to touch his face, but a strong electrical discharge threw him with incredible force to the far wall. He hit his back painfully and sank to the ground.

"Be careful," the highlander helped him to his feet. "They knew what they were doing. Who do you think they are?"

"I don't know," Theo rubbed a broken elbow and winced slightly. "We knew someone similar; his name was Vandis. He considered himself an angel, but is that true? Maybe it is just the race that lived in the world before us, that is, before homo sapiens? Or maybe... aliens?"

"Not again..." Gerard snorted with pity.

"It's not so stupid," said Gladiator. "Many people believe in UFOs, and even more are looking for traces of cosmic knowledge in prehistory and ancient history. Who knows if these sleeping brothers are not the answer to most of the puzzles that bother us?"

The actor thought that if the researchers found this grotto, it would be shock in the scientific world as never before. Although not at all? Perhaps recognized authorities would prefer to destroy the cave so as not to change the truths already established. It was very likely. Perhaps there were also enemies that the "Angels" had to hide from - eventually chasing Vandis, which the detective did not want to talk about. Was it because, unlike others, he didn't hide from the world?

Suddenly Gerard understood something: Vandis loved people, he wanted to help them, and he felt a bond with them, a bond that probably others lacked. He looked at the face of the still Angel. In spite of his first impression, he wasn't really like Vandis. He had dark navy-blue hair and very long, rolled up eyelashes, and his eyebrows seemed to rise obliquely upwards. The ears visible from under the hair were very small and pointed. The delicate nostrils had a classic drawing, like those on Michelangelo's sculptures, and the expressive lips looked tight.

"Let them tie me and prick my ass if I know what kind of guy he is," Gladiator said quietly, looking at him with astonished eyes.

"I don't know either, but just in case I didn't tell anyone about him. You are the first, and because you deal with such matters. As far as I know, no one but me, and now you, know about this cave, and for the most part it is flooded to the height of one meter," Jadwiśka thoughtfully stroked the side of the sarcophagus. She was well aware that she was facing a secret older than any vampire and did not even try to guess what the solution was.

"These mountains hide extraordinary puzzles," Fronda looked around the cave as if he were looking around the church. "Naked healer, haunted house in the devil's forest, and now this. What else can we expect...?"

"Poland, brother, is even more interesting than you think in the world," Gladiator patted him friendlily in the back, almost knocking him over. He wasn't fully aware of his strength, which was sometimes embarrassing.

After leaving the cave, friends realized another phenomenon - although nothing unusual was happening there, they experienced the same missing time phenomenon as in the demonic residence. Although it seemed to them that only tens of minutes had passed since they had plunged into the depths of the mountain, the sky in the east was already pink. Jadwiśka hastily led everyone to a small hut, hidden between densely growing spruces.

"This is our emergency shelter," she explained. "We'll sleep here safely, then think what else you could visit. There is a lot to choose from."

The hut was almost empty, only a few sheepskins lay on the floor of unplanned boards.

"I don't like going to bed hungry, but what to do..." Gladiator grunted and stretched out on one of the skins.

Others followed him. There was no need to put up the guard, because the vampire-marten's dream is very light and even the softest sound of footsteps would certainly wake up everyone.

"Maybe I will take the guard? I could be useful, at least," Oggy suggested, not trusting the vigilance of her friends.

"No need, girl. Sleep better," the highlander advised her in a sleepy voice.

Oggy looked at her reluctantly. What would she do to be like her - strong, beautiful and arousing desire? Unfortunately, she was thin and inconspicuous, and the strength of her psyche left much to be desired. She was well aware of this.

"Oggy," said Theo from his bed. "Come here."

She came to him with some surprise. Fronda reached out and embraced her, forcing her to lie down next to him.

"Don't be jealous," he whispered in her ear. "It's just an experience. I wouldn't trade you for any other. You are unique."

"Do you really think so or do you just want to cheer me up?"

"You know, Oggy? I never lie to my friends. Hug and sleep, baby."

He kissed the girl's forehead and hugged her tightly to him. Calmed, Oggy curled up in her habit and closed her eyes. She knew that Theo really wasn't lying to her. He was a bit strange, but he gave her a real, warm feeling, which meant a lot to her. She was already falling asleep when something rocked the house in a strangely familiar way.

"What's happening?!" Gerard shouted, leaping from his seat.

"Aww snap! It seems like something has clung to us," Gladiator grunted, ripping the sheepskin from his face, which wrapped his head as if she were alive.

"We could have expected that. A devil would be miserable if he only worked in one parish. But don't worry, Fronda is with you," said Theo.

He yawned twice, then stood up and looked around. It was dark in the hut and the temperature was clearly dropping.

"Admit it to me immediately: who took something from the haunted house?" He asked sternly, rolling his eyes over his friends.

Gerard stared at him, Oggy shrugged, so Theo stopped his accusing glance at Gladiator. He sat for a moment with an innocent face, then he couldn't stand and growled:

"Well, I took it. Happy?"

He took an openwork pentagram, cut from one piece of stone, out of his pocket and threw it on his bed with an offended face. The sinister object gleamed on sheep's clothing like a silent accusation, glittering in purple, black and green. The banks were covered with sintered glaze. It looked very old and very valuable, but they could not identify the stone from which it was made. Equally incomprehensible as the origin of the raw material was the method that cut such a complicated shape out of the crystal without damaging the crystal lattice. It seemed impossible.

"Did you not know Janek is a kleptomaniac?" Jadwiśka asked, not taking her eyes from the shimmering object.

"We don't know a lot of things. In any case, it must be taken into place," Theo said firmly. "And if I was a skunk, I'd have you do it, blonde, alone, you would have learned a lesson. However, I will go there alone, just visit the nearest church first."

Gerard sighed with obvious impatience.

"Fronda, do you really believe that this case is religious and that you will overcome IT with religious symbols?" He asked pityingly.

"I don't expect a godless person like you to understand this... But for your message, Fanfan: it's not a religious symbol that holds back evil, but the faith of those who use that symbol. You wouldn't do anything, even if you wear yourself with rosaries like a Christmas tree, but I have a chance," Theo replied as if he were talking to a moron. He would take it every time they discussed religious matters.

Somehow, they waited for dusk, although the hut was shaking from time to time, and everything that was not attached was flying, as if someone invisible were throwing it. However, the terror was definitely less, maybe because they were here together. When the sun hid behind the mountains, Theo went to the haunted mansion, and the rest went down to the quarters. So far, they have had enough of all inexplicable phenomena, even those not dangerous.

In Zakopane, luckily, nothing "frightened" - everything that was strange or dangerous was happening high in the mountains. Native highlanders knew this, but they didn't mind. Whatever was in these mountains favored the indigenous people, turning all sinister force against visitors or dissenters. Another thing is that highlanders never go to the mountains unnecessarily, and never where they really don't have to go. The situation is different with the visitors and maybe there was a problem here.

Along the way, they began at one of the many pubs to satisfy the drunken blood of hunger customers. It was only when they had satiated that they went to a house where there was blissful peace. It was warm, everything was in place, and the light shone evenly and peacefully. No one wanted to sleep somehow, so they sat down at the bridge, waiting for Fronda to return. He categorically did not agree to anyone's company. They were worried about him, although everyone knew that he could do the best of them all and did not need anyone's help.

The bidding went sluggish, the participants of the game were wrong every now and then and they made mistakes until the front door slammed. Theo did not recognize the silent closing of the door, he always slammed it open as if to announce his arrival.

"End of the trouble," he said cheerfully. Imagine that nothing is happening there now. Whatever was there was quiet as a grave. A quiet, quiet home, complete relaxation.

He looked very lively, apparently, and he ate on the way. He took a quick shower, then persuaded Gerard to play a game of chess before bed. He always had a small chessboard and magnetic pawns with him. Then everyone finally went to sleep with a nice feeling that for now the trouble is over.

It would seem that the matter of devilish wilderness was definitely ended, but in the following days it turned out not quite so. Gladiator, usually cheerful and full of life, strangely became apathetic. He began to give the impression that he was afraid of something, constantly looked back and seemed as if he was listening to something that only he could hear. And one day, when Theo and Jadwiśka returned from one of their trips, they found him staring blankly at a crystal star lying on the table.

"Yanek!" Theo boomed sharply, for the first time using the real name of Gladiator. He looked up at him.

"I didn't bring it," he said hollowly. "I found it under my pillow this morning. Before, it was in the bathroom near the mirror."

"Before?"

"Yes. I threw into the stream because I didn't have the courage to go to the wilderness."

"I went, but apparently it did not help more than you're throwing into the stream," Theo took the sinister object in his hand and studied it carefully. "The same, no doubt. Well, we'll try a radical method. Jade, be so good and light the oven."

Jadwiśka nodded. She took a bucket of coal and poured a large portion into the kitchen stove. When the fire roared for good, Theo threw in a few pieces of chalk, extracted from his inseparable haversack, and put a purple pentagram on top. He closed the door carefully.

"Do you think it will help?" Asked Gladiator anxiously.

"I don't know. Such are the effects of moron antics. We'll see."

However, the next day, waking up, friends saw Gladiator, looking helplessly at the pentagram, lying in a decorative ashtray on the table.

"It's already getting alarming," said Gerard. "Even I begin to believe in impure power when I see something like that."

"I believed it a long time ago. Theo, you, the only one of us, have an idea of hauntings, possessions and the like. Your medieval experience can be helpful here. What do you advice?" Oggy asked, trying to stop her teeth chattering.

Theo rubbed his forehead with the back of his hand, staring at the shimmering star. Indeed, he alone knew how serious the situation was, but what could be done he did not know. He was never an exorcist; he never even saw such a ceremony.

"Taking this trash from the house of the Evil, Gladiator has personally endangered it," he said finally. "I have some vague idea of the whole thing, an association with something I once heard... If we can't get rid of this pentagram for good, Gladiator will die in a certain time, I don't know when. It can be three months, or maybe three days... We have to somehow solve the equation with the unknowns themselves."

"Ah, Janiczek, why did you do that?" Jadwiśka wrung her hands in horror.

"Don't torment him," Fronda admonished her. "Nothing will help. We need to find out how to get the legitimate owner of the ornament to accept it."

There was a heavy silence. Gerard touched his breasts with his fingers mechanically, where there was an inverted pentagram scar beneath the thin canvas of his shirt - a souvenir of a meeting with Satanists. He was convinced then that there was really no Satan, only drugged, demoralized people. Now he wasn't so sure. Who knows, wasn't this pentagram protected by a haunted mansion? Evil could have taken him for one of his own.

"Fronda, do you remember our delusions at the institute?" He asked. "Maybe here we are dealing with a phenomenon scientifically explainable?"

Theo shook his head slowly, without taking his eyes off the strange ornament.

"I don't think so, Fanfan... For example, this stone. I know gems, mineralogy is my hobby and I swear to you that I've never seen a similar crystal. Besides, you see, for centuries I had enough time to say that we know nothing about the world that surrounds us. We are able to think about every possible topic, and in the face of a really big secret we are helpless as cavemen in the face of thunder. How does it happen that I understand it and you don't?"

"You one of us are tame with such secrets. You take the existence of demons, ghosts and devils for boring certainty, it's phantasmagoria to us," Oggy said in a tone of justification.

He looked at her thoughtfully and his eyes brightened.

"Wait," he said. "Phantasmagoria... That's right. What is happening is not logical from a human point of view. We have to try to think as IT thinks, i.e. in a manner inconsistent with our logic."

"It's hopeless... we can't think otherwise than Euclidean," said Gladiator with tired voice.

"And you know a lot about this?" Oggy raised her eyebrows doubtfully. The young highlander was the last person to look like a philosopher.

"I read Henry Kuttner's short story "Mimsy Were the Borogroves" and that's where it is described. I also read something more than newspapers, you know?"

"Okay, then what?"

"The fact that since our birth we have been conditioned to use one logical system and we cannot think otherwise. It was written like that, and I think it's true."

"You look bad," Jadwiśka said sympathetically.

"Because I do not feel well. I still have the impression that every step of my life is being watched and even when I am with you, I feel as if I was alone."

"You didn't have to steal. The seventh commandment is clear and understandable," Theo got up and began to walk around the room, muttering to himself in Old French.

"Right, drive the knife deeper," Gladiator growled.

"Don't play the victim now. You made your bed. Fronda takes risks for you and you're still whining," Oggy got on him, always ready to defend her beloved friend.

"Don't argue, faith. I think I know what to do and I don't like it, but... Jade, are they robbing tourists here?" Asked Theo, stopping in front of the beautiful highlander who looked at him in surprise.

"For sure, but what does this have to do with our problem?"

"Think: Gladiator stole this damn thing and that's why Evil got stuck to him. You can't get rid of it by the usual methods, but you can probably get around the fate of our buddy. The curse will be diverted to whoever repeats his act."

That sounded reasonable.

"You think that..."

"Yes. Someone has to take on the punishment that awaits Gladiator for reaching out for Hell's property... or anything else. I do not know if we have the right to "let" the demon on some human being... but on the other hand, whoever harms someone is harming himself. Jade, you have to get the gold chain so that Gladiator can hang this gem around his neck. It must look precious enough for someone to steal it," Fronda finished his tirade.

"But who will attack Yanek? It's such a colossus that they will be afraid of him," protested Gerard.

"No problem if he will be drunk. He can do it, and there are plenty of robbers here, especially in fleabag pubs. When they see a drunk guy, they will treat him to his pants," Jadwiśka said authoritatively, breathing with relief.

"Do you think it will work?" Asked Gladiator with weak hope.

"If I fail, I shave my head to zero," Theo patted his shoulder reassuringly.

He wasn't sure of his reasoning, but somewhere in the recesses of his consciousness there was a memory of a similar accident in which the so-called "Curse projection" - with good results. He still didn't know what forces they were dealing with - everything seemed to indicate that he was dealing with the authentic forces of pure Evil - but he didn't care. Above all, he wanted to save the reckless highlander, because he had no doubt that if he could not get rid of the mysterious pentagram, Gladiator would die, perhaps in a terrible way. Whatever the forces he was dealing with, they were not joking.

"For thousands of years people have been talking about strange, often monstrous phenomena. If they were just ordinary bytes, no one would deal with them at a time when humanity barely began to write. It was too difficult art and too valuable writing material to waste it on obvious untruth," Never said once.

Theo regretted that their leader was not with them now. This one would know what to do as always. His extraordinary intelligence coped well with virtually every threat, though, which must be admitted, they have never encountered anything like this before.

Every adventure, even the most mysterious one, could be explained somehow, and what Theo was dealing with now eluded all logic. He did not know what exactly haunted Gladiator and would be afraid of inquiring about this issue, but from fragments of "secret knowledge" that, willingly or unwillingly, assimilated his tramp around the world for centuries, resulted in terrifying conclusions. There were forces on Earth that were denied by science, and these forces were able to interfere in human life in a terrible way. However, man was not vulnerable. His weapon was strength of will and mind, but hardly anyone had a strong and clear mind to fight.

Theo didn't even try it. He decided to use the "curse projection" method, because it seemed to him the only reasonable way out, the only one that could succeed. He believed that, despite everything, the events taking place here are governed by some logic - although not the one on which he was raised, but still logic, and if so, it was enough to "shoot at it." Of course, the question was whether his plan would adhere to this logic, but it could only be checked by putting it into practice.

Jadwiśka expedited very quickly. As it turned out, she had a large collection of various jewelry, mostly stolen - in this respect she was not better than Gladiator. As she admitted with her disarming honesty to her new friends, she had a magpie mentality, and every glitter could tempt her. Rather, she rarely decorated herself, she just liked to have these things. The chain she brought resembled a double twisted string, but it was visible from afar that it was made of pure gold. It must have been worth a fortune, although it was not his friends who wanted it now.

Theo, having attached the pentagram to the chain, threw the whole thing around the neck of Gladiator, who at that moment looked like a condemned man to the gallows.

"I just hope it will work out," he said, touching the ornament as if it burns.

"Me too," Fronda replied curtly. "You have the money? You have to chuck your money about to lure robbers. Of course, we will go with you, we will observe you discreetly and in case of real danger we will help you."

"No danger is as great as the one that threatens my soul now."

Gerard barely suppressed a pitying snort.

"Maybe it will teach you something... although there are little chances. You have to be completely crazy to steal something in a haunted house," Jadwiśka interjected, handing Gladiator a thick roll of banknotes.

"I think it's too late now for moral teachings," Oggy grumbled, who still could not like this girl, nice and interesting in her own way. For her, she was simply a rival and saw her in this way.

Gladiator put the money in his back pocket and sighed heavily. Although tall and athletically built, he now seemed helpless like a child. Oggy felt so sorry for him now that she wanted to offer him her company. She did not believe that Fronda's plan would have the desired effect and that in her eyes the young highlander was a lost man. She managed to like him - it would be hard to do otherwise, because he had this special gift of winning people's hearts - and she trembled at what awaited him.

So, around midnight, three strange-looking men and a large shepherd found themselves at a dingy pub called "Gawra," They whispered their last remarks, then one of them went inside, and the others went for a walk with the dog. If someone were watching them, he might be surprised why these two "cepers" with a beautiful Alsatian are wandering around the night in such a dangerous area. And that they move freely in the dark without the help of flashlights. The dog behaved quietly, sometimes only slightly barked and sniffed very carefully, staring at the door of the pub with brown, black-eyed eyes.

It was three in the morning when a massive row broke out in the pub. The two observers immediately hid with the dog in the nearby bushes, observing the fight from there, which soon moved beyond "Gawra". Soon, the participants of the adventure scattered, leaving someone on the ground. They hurried toward him. A silent sheepdog followed them.

"Are you alive, giant?" Theo embraced Gladiator, helping him to stand up.

The highlander was beastly drunk, his designer clothes hung in tatters and it was clear that in this state he would not be able to answer any question. He only gave curses that they didn't understand but guessed at their meanings.

"They robbed him though?" Gerard asked anxiously.

Fronda groped the Gladiator efficiently and nodded with satisfaction.

"They took everything from him," he replied. "Watch, wallet, this is an abomination and even shoes. They beat him well, but that's the least of his worries. I hope that all this will work."

"Do you think it really will work?"

"Not excluded. I have never dealt with such a thing, but I have heard stories from which such a conclusion came. It didn't hurt to try."

Theo supported a drunk colleague and with the help of Gerard dragged him home, where Jadwiśka was upset, waiting for them.

"Oh my, they beat him... Well, the highlander boys are beating when they are beating. Put him on the bench, I run for the first aid kit," she said, conceding with relief that neither the pentagram nor the chain was around her friend's neck. Someone tore him violently, because there was a long cut on Gladiator's neck.

"Whoever did this will be punished," she murmured, washing the wound with hydrogen peroxide.

"I don't think to regret him," Theo said sharply, as if to drown out remorse. If his plan was successful, a man would face a terrible death. And he, though not very sensitive, did not wish anyone so much bad things.

"Your knightly conscience seems to exaggerate, judging by the look on your face," said Gerard, watching him from under his eye. "Head's up. Whoever stole the pentagram was not an innocent. Just look how Yanek looks. If he were an ordinary man, they would beat him to death and would not even look at him."

Gladiator got tannings. A man somewhat frailer could pay for his life with the band that attacked him, and he looked as if he was close enough.

"He must lie for at least a few days," Jadwiśka said. "You know what? I will bring Jaro Jachima here."

"Who is it?" Oggy asked, who had already taken on a human form.

"One of us, only from the Slovak side. The vet, he knows how to help.

The highlander wound up so quickly, because Jaro, as she knew well, had been playing in the village of Harenda for several days, pretending to be a holiday-maker. It was assumed that one of the highlander's villagers caught his eye, but no one was certain of that. He never refused to help anyone, so he did not. He examined Gladiator, who was sleeping drunkenly, without closing his mouth for a moment.

"Broken ribs and left collarbone, concussion, probably subarachnoid hematoma, and lots of minor wounds," he said. "Ho, ho, they were not joking with him. I can bet any amount of internal damage that would kill every person. Fortunately, it's one of us. Don't you think we should come up with a less offensive word to describe ourselves than "vampire"? You will have to work on it. And returning to Jasiek, there is no fear for his health. Let him not get up for a week and drink a lot of blood and will pull through."

"Do you have a bottle one here?" Gerard asked.

"It's probably in the hospital, but we can't take it away. You have to go to Krakow. I'll handle it," said Jadwiśka.

"And I with you," Fronda suggested.

"And me too," Oggy joined him immediately and looked anxiously at Gerard.

He smiled at her comfortingly. He didn't mind staying with Gladiator. He was no longer afraid, as if what he had survived so far had exhausted all his fear. If IT, as Fronda claimed, was based on human fear, it could not affect him now, so he was safe. And even if he wasn't... it couldn't scare him somehow.

*****

Krakow made a huge impression on Fronda. Old buildings and lots of ancient churches, a specific mood filling this city... he felt as if he had returned home. This fleeting impression was so pleasant to him that he stopped on the street to breathe in that atmosphere for a moment.

"What a wonderful place," he whispered, looking around.

"Probably, but now come, because Professor Donat does not like to wait," Jadwiśka pulled his sleeve.

"Is that one of us?"

"No, but he's okay. He sometimes uses our services, and in return he arranges for us to supply blood."

A few streets from the parking lot, where they left the van, a Chevrolet was waiting for them. The silent driver drove them to an ordinary house, standing among other similar houses. There they were greeted by an elderly man, somewhat gray, but still handsome, dressed in a black, sporty tracksuit.

"Sorry about this outfit, but I just got back from jogging," he said, shaking hands with the arrivals one after the other. "You need blood, right? We're temporarily having problems with this, but I will try to get a supply for you. In return, however, I am asking for a favor."

"Sure," Fronda sarcastically said. "As in the American cartoon: the dog will tell me how to catch a rooster, but he wants a bone. The cat knows where the bone is, but I have to bring him fish. The mouse will give me fish when he gets cheese. I wonder what cheese will want."

The professor smiled.

"Funny," he admitted. "But I'm serious. I need some data from a military base for my work. I will not break into such a guarded building myself, but if you help me, it may work."

"Well, I don't mind."

"What the hell do you want any data from a military base for?" Jadwiśka was surprised. "You want to do espionage, right? It's supposedly a profitable business, but you die early."

"What an idea. Simply military scientists always have the best information on new discoveries and new technologies. You see, my cousin works creatively. He is a bio technician and has some interesting concepts, but he lacks some data. I want to get them for him."

"The last time you broke into a military facility, you lost your memory for six months, and Gerard went crazy. I protest," Oggy said warily, turning to Fronda.

"I promise I won't blow anything up this time," a friend embraced her warmly and kissed her forehead. He understood that the girl could be hurt after what happened at the military research facilities they destroyed, but he did not intend to change his mind.

"How do you want us to get there?" Jadwiśka asked skeptically.

"Very simply," said Professor Donat. "Every evening, a truck with supplies for the next day, new crew members, etc. arrives at the base. I know that after unloading they lock the car in the garage. The difficulty is hiding in the truck and then getting out of the lock. Of course, and then not to turn on the alarm in the base. Easy isn't it?"

"As easy as winking. Let me think, man. Strategy is probably not your strongest side?"

"Think how much you want. Jadwiśka and I will go for the blood, then she will return to Zakopane, and we will be able to get to the point," the professor was clearly of the opinion that the matter was simple and probably nothing would convince him that it was a serious military operation, not on the skills of an ordinary human.

Fortunately, Fronda had military preparation, a volatile mind and was able to think strategically. He could have put together some sensible action plan without any particular problem. He thought it was a good idea to get to the base in the truck, though it needed to be developed. It was unthinkable, for example, to get to a truck on the road. It had to be done at the place where it was loaded. Other matters also seemed uncomfortable.

"Getting there is one thing, and getting out, quite another," he said finally, grammatically, archaizing the syntax, and started writing out what was threatening them, as well as what had to be done. He worked on it until dawn, then went to bed, and when he woke up, he had a crystallized plan. He shared it with friends who accepted it without a word.

It was impossible to hide in a military truck other than under the benches. There was desperate little space there, but thanks to the tarpaulin they could feel relatively safe so that they could withstand without moving. There was so little space that every move could expose them - after all, soldiers were sitting in the shack, on those benches. Fortunately, three conspirators managed to withstand cataleptic stillness until the truck, unloaded from the imported goods, was locked in a garage at the base. When they finally decided they were safe, they eased out of benches and straightened their bones.

"The first stage is over," whispered the professor. "What now?"

In the black tracksuit and black balaclava, he looked more like a terrorist or ninja warrior than a serious scientist.

"Now we have to get out of the garage," Theo replied. "There is definitely an internal exit to the building, so we must open it."

With meticulous tenderness, he took his wallet from his pocket and counted the lock picks by touching each of them with his fingertips. Finding the inner door was not a big difficulty for the sensitive eyes of the three of them, and Fronda's skillful fingers quickly coped with a not very complicated lock. Friends found themselves in a top-secret area where ordinary mortals had no access.

Professor Donat took a small device from a shoulder bag and hung it on his shoulder.

"It's a telephony jammer. Preview will get off wherever we go," he explained in a whisper.

"Technics," Oggy murmured in awe.

She also had no empty hands. She carried her laptop, which she did not part with, and which was now to be very useful. The doors from research laboratories were electronically secured and these safeguards had to be broken without raising the alarm.

"The data is in studio number six," the professor said quietly. "That's all I know. It is enough if we copy the files from the computer. I'll take care of decoding them at home, but will you be able to crack the password?"

This last question was obviously directed at Oggy, who nodded in response. Her laptop was equipped with a futuristic program that allowed you to crack every password and any security, but only she could use it. Not counting, of course, its creator.

Studio six was closed by a complicated combination lock. Oggy connected her laptop to it and in a few minutes a green light shone on the console and the door opened slightly. The professor pushed them aside and they found themselves in a laboratory, equipped with several computers and connecting in an experimental way to the experimental laboratory. He turned on one of the computers. Oggy, who finally had the opportunity to show off the decoding program, set to work eagerly and after a quarter of an hour she proudly presented the professor with the result of her work - open access to all files.

"Thanks, baby. It will take a while for me to copy it, watch the door and make no noise," Donat sat at the computer and sank into work.

Fronda took the genetics manual in French from his desktop and began to browse it interestingly, while Oggy, succumbing to irresistible temptation, went to the laboratory. She was always interested in such places, although the sight of experimental animals immediately aroused in her desire to release them all into the wild. She still couldn't understand how people could be so cruel and unfair to other beings. She was just looking at the security features of the frames, wondering how they could also be breached when she heard a murmur behind her. She turned abruptly and her eyes met another cage, resembling a rather large terrarium.

Behind the solid, probably armored glass was a fairly spacious room, in it a bed, bowls with food and a drinker with water and..."

"Theo!" The girl squeaked in an uncomfortable voice.

Fronda burst into the laboratory, looking for an enemy. Shaky Oggy pointed a finger forward, unable to pronounce the words. Theo looked in the direction indicated and felt that his speech was also taken away, and his hair bristled on his head as if it were alive.

A creature was huddling inside the cage. It was naked, the height of a small child, almost white, with a disproportionately large head without a pinna, with tiny nostrils, narrow lips and huge, very black eyes. It touched the windshield with a thin paw, the palm of which split into a thumb and two thick finger-like processes.

"UFOs," Theo whispered in amazement; "UFOs are alive. So, I was right."

He came closer, fascinated by the view. He put his hand on the glass, and then the creature moved his paw in front of his hand. Big eyes looked at him from behind the glass sadly and somehow terribly vulnerable.

"Do you think they are experimenting here?" Oggy asked quietly.

"No, they keep him as an adviser," he said impatiently. "Sure, they do. We have to get him out of here. If this thing came from space, it is intelligent and has no less rights than we do."

He began to look carefully at the locks at the cage window. The creature followed him with its impenetrable eyes, still making no sound - as if it were dumb. Theo chose one of his lock picks and began tinkering cautiously at the locks. After a long moment he managed to open the cage. The creature behaved strangely: he did not escape or try to hide, but jumped on his arms and embraced him around the neck with a confident movement of the child.

Fronda looked at Oggy from above his head.

"I don't understand anything," he confessed. "But there is no time for combinations. Donat, are you finished?"

"Almost!" Professor answered him briskly, looked back froze at the sight of the creature on his hands.

It took him a moment to regain speech.

"Don't say anything, I don't want to know... let's get out of here, then we'll talk."

"I only hope you two know how," Oggy whispered softly.

Suddenly she was afraid of this laboratory. She always hated places where animals were harmed, even in the name of humanity's best-understood good, and life-saving measures were hardly ever developed. Rather the opposite. After all, the military always needs weapons, and as versatile as possible. If they were caught here... She didn't even want to think about it.

Fortunately, it turned out that Theo had already figured out how to get out of the base without causing unnecessary anxiety. As he admitted with disarming honesty, it wasn't even his idea, and being an avid moviegoer, he suspected it of "Star Wars." The idea was that the collector would leave the base, in which all the debris would land - the door lock, through which the garbage spilled into the garbage truck, could be easily undermined from the inside. Another thing was that getting through the piles of trash was neither easy nor pleasant. Their appearance and consistency were at least uninspiring, and the smell almost catastrophic.

The collector ended with a solid flap, opened from the outside with a code. Already in battle, Oggy easily found the blinded internal entrance to the control panel, opened it and using the laptop quickly worked out the code.

"You really didn't have a better idea? We won't wash the smell away for a week," she moaned when they were finally outside the base walls.

"Princess Leia could, we can," answered Fronda, unimpressed. "Now we quickly run away before someone can figure out what they lack in the laboratory."

Professor Donat said nothing. He was silent at all, even when they were already in his house and with great effort washed away the dirt and bad smell. It was only when they gathered in the living room with glasses full of a bloody cocktail that he took the creature saved from the base on his lap. He behaved very calmly, as if he felt safe with them, especially at Fronda, who did not let him go away from him, not even in the shower.

"And what have you done the best?" Asked Donat, watching the creature intently.

"We saved him," Fronda said cheerfully. "It's an alien, right?"

"They've experimented with him to learn about his planet," Oggy added.

"Take a bath," said the professor emphatically. "It's not more alien than we are. I'll tell you what it is: it's a monkey. Judging by the general form and movement, the Tibetan langur."

Deaf silence followed this statement.

"Eee, you kidding," Theo finally said, offended. "I haven't seen a monkey that looks like this, and I'm over six hundred years old and I've traveled around the world."

"Genetic mutation?" Oggy asked uncertainly.

"Not necessarily. Maybe the effect of certain chemicals on a pregnant female," Donat patted the langur on the bald head. "Only... only that the existence of this monkey arouses terrible suspicion in me. Maybe somewhere... they breed... people?"

"That they would pretend to be UFOs?" Oggy said to him. "That would explain why the descriptions of aliens are so homonymous. Thanks to such creatures, unscrupulous scientists could carry out experiments with people with impunity that no one would later believe."

"Monstrosity," Fronda murmured and drank greedily.

"I will know when I work out the data we stole from the database. You go back to Zakopane before the bomb bursts, because then they can lock the city, and its better not to search you too closely. Take this monkey with you, it wouldn't be safe here."

This remark made sense, although both friends had the impression that the professor was trying to get rid of them so that he could work calmly. Still, they didn't delve into the subject. They said goodbye politely and left, heading for the parking lot. Along the way, Fronda bought some fruit in the night shop (they had some Polish money) and half-relieved, half-disappointed he saw that the mysterious creature threw himself at it vigorously, like any ordinary monkey.

"I think this Donat was right. It's just a laboratory animal," he muttered to himself, not knowing if he should enjoy it or regret it.

"Sit in the kennel," Oggy instructed him curtly. "We probably won't be able to get there before sunrise, so I'll lead."

"Okay." Fronda didn't mind resting a bit, and the van kennel was cool and dark as he liked.

He lay down on the reclining seat. A langur curled up next to him, full and content. It was obvious that this creature liked him, as did all the animals with which he was in contact. But what would happen to him next? It was impossible to bring this freak around the world with them, and without him they had enough trouble with camouflage. They had to leave the monkey in the care of the locals, but would they want to take care of it?

It was already there that Fronda's worries were unfounded. In the house on Krupówki, in addition to Gladiator and Gerard, they also found Jadwiśka, Jaro and an unknown girl, a tall blonde with an impressive breasts and a round face with doll eyes. Jadwiśka introduced her as Karola, her friend, who decided to visit them as "the fourth to the bridge". As all four played with enthusiasm, but at the sight of newcomers they stopped the auction. An unusual find surprised them a lot, but after a short explanation they took the case "simply".

"Sure, we'll take care of this poor thing," said Jaro, who couldn't play bridge, but he was eager for it. "We'll have a mascot. You just have to make some clothes for it, it's cold."

"Indeed, it has no hair. I will take care of it," Karola offered cheerfully, stroking the langur on the back.

Fronda felt weight off his mind. The monkey was cared for, Gladiator had already managed to recover a little, and during their absence nothing unusual happened. Anything that clung to the careless highlander seemed to leave him alone now. It was very comforting news, because he really did not know what to do in the event of the failure of an intricate plan. Now he could really sleep soundly and took advantage of this opportunity, because he was very tired.

During those days he hardly thought about Never, and he didn't want to think about him now. If Tatra couldn't help him, he was already dead, and if she could... well, you would have to wait for him to release. There was nothing else to be done. Theo closed his eyes and after a while he was sleeping like a log. The emotions of the previous forty-eight hours had caused him to sleep through the rest of the day, the night and the whole next day.

The next night, when Fronda finally woke up, everyone else was up and joking happily with Jadwiśka, who brought them some Polish cognac and sheep's milk to try, as well as a handful of news. The monkey immediately acclimatized in the headquarters of the vampire enclave, and although it still did not make any sounds, it looked pleased. Its amazing appearance was very interesting to everyone and Jaro even proposed to use it to make a piece of several drunken gazdoms. Fortunately, he was voted out.

Cheered up with the vision of an "alien" prowling in Podhale, Theo took a cold shower, changed his clothes and at the prompting of Jadwiśka drank some milk.

"Awfulness," he said, pouring the glass of cognac hurriedly. "Certainly, very healthy, nutritious and all like that, but I feel sorry for those who have to drink it."

"You can get used to it," the girl assured him.

"Help me take a bath," said Gladiator to Gerard. "I think I'll stay on my feet, but you better protect me."

He stood up, though he did it a little uncertainly, and disappeared in the bathroom with Gerard. Fronda, taking advantage of the fact that Oggy is a dog again, took a brush and began combing it carefully. The girl ran for half a day in her dog form around the area and her hair was thoroughly folded. Jadwiśka took the opportunity to sit in an armchair and read the current newspaper calmly.

"Relax, Oggy, don't hang around," Fronda reproved his friend cheerfully, skillfully using brush. "You've got a lot of quilts. Fortunately, you didn't catch fleas this time, but I see a tick here. Wait a minute, I will delete it soon."

"Isn't it funny having a friend who turns into a dog?" Jadwiśka asked, turning the page in the newspaper.

"I don't know. Sometimes, yes, it can be funny... Although much more often troublesome and sometimes also useful. A dog can be an invaluable help, don't you think? Do you like dogs, Jade? Jade?"

Not receiving an answer, Theo looked at the highlander expectantly. She was sitting in the armchair, newspaper down on her knees, looking somewhere to a dead end.

"Don't be nervous, Fronda," she said slowly, with a dull sound in her voice.

"What happened?"

She handed him the newspaper. Theo picked it up mechanically, but then shook his head helplessly. He could not read Polish, he understood very few words.

"Professor Donat was murdered yesterday," said Jadwiśka. "The house was looted, though you don't see anything missing."

"Murdered?! For sure?!"

"He got two dum-dum bullets in his brain. Do you think you can live after this?"

"I do not know."

"So, I'll tell you: you can't. Those who did this were not Vampire Hunters. They don't use dum-dum bullets. So, who do you think it was?"

She fixed her beautiful eyes in him. Theo was silent, frozen by what he heard. He had no idea where they had made the mistake, which led the military to the professor's house, because there was no doubt who the attackers were and what they were looking for. He did not expect such a turn of events.

"They were probably looking for data floppy disks and this fake alien," he said finally. "If Donat didn't tell us to come back, there would probably be three corpses. I don't think they hesitate. Do you know what, Jade? Poland is a country of all miracles. You can find absolutely everything here."

Gladiator who had just returned from the bathroom was wiping himself with a rough towel and looking at them, not understanding this sudden change of mood. When he was going to bathe, they were both happy, and now... Gerard turned out to be smarter.

"Bad news?" He asked, eyeing the newspaper.

"Yes, but we cannot help it," Jadwiśka sighed sadly.

She liked Professor Donat, although their relationship was rather complicated. He always let her know what intellectual divide separates him, a companion man with a university degree, and her, a simple highlander, barely able to read and write.

"I'll get them, those bastards," Theo muttered, punching his knee.

"Come on, Frenchman. You will probably not fight with the entire Polish army. Although, if I know you, it might come to your mind. You'd better forget about this case. You won't bring Donat back to life, and you could put others at risk."

"I suppose you're right, Jade... But my blood is sagging when I think punishment will get away from them."

"Given your age, it's not your blood that is swaying, it's all lime," said Gladiator, who had already understood something. "And as for the getaway, it is so and always has been. In a world of people like us, they have no rights, have you forgotten?"

"The professor died not because he was a vampire, but because he stole something very important and super-secret. This confirms the thesis that we should not interfere in typically human affairs. They should solve their problems themselves. If they want to kill each other, it's not our business," said Theo cloudily.

The highlander nodded without looking at him.

"Unfortunately, it loses us," she said. "We are still trying to help, because we are mostly worthy creatures, and at least not worse than others. Other diet does not make us monsters immediately, as ordinary people would like to see.

Oggy put her head on her lap and squealed quietly, trying to attract attention. Her friend scratched her lightly behind her ears, but he did it absentmindedly - he was clearly thinking about something else. At one point, he pushed Oggy aside and left, slamming the door behind him.

He was gone long enough. He returned only the next day after dusk, tired and angry.

"Where have you been?" Jadwiśka asked sharply.

"I was trying to find out something," he murmured. He took off his shoes and threw himself on the bed. "But I didn't look for anything. The police are hanging around there."

He stared at the ceiling.

"I had more luck in the base," he added after a moment.

"You went alone to the base?! Alone?!" The girl's amazement had no limits.

"What's so strange about that? What am I, a child, you have to hold my hand?"

"You could to get caught."

"Jade, honey, have mercy... I can eavesdrop so that nobody notices me."

She waved her hand in discouragement.

"Keep talking."

"I didn't understand everything, but it seems that the professor left one of the blank diskettes in the database. It was signed, and they found him."

"But they went so far as to murder..." Gerard shook his head in disbelief.

"You don't know yet what the army is capable of?"

"We shouldn't accept this action," Oggy whispered. She was sitting by the mirror and tried to correct her messy hair with small scissors.

"Probably you are right."

The harsh atmosphere was interrupted by the door creaking. Everyone turned as per command and froze with their mouths half-open. Never came inside - skinny, ragged and overgrown, but apparently healthy. Even his head was already covered with regrown hair, just as thick and shiny as before.

"And what are you staring at?" He yelled. "Do you see me for the first time or something?"

"I'll go crazy... It worked!" Cried Fronda happily, leaping up from his seat.

"I said it would work," Jadwiśka murmured with satisfaction.

"How was it?" Gerard asked curiously, hugging his friend despite his protest.

"Come on, you know I don't like such caresses," Never grumbled, pushing him aside. "How was it? I have no idea. Something was going on there, but I don't remember much except that I was terribly cold. And today at sunset I woke up on the mountain slope, feeling like a newborn. Not much of it. And what happened to you, crazy people?"

"A lot," Fronda replied, not going into the details yet.

Never's return was a great excuse to move away from this place and return to Warsaw, where they could still wait for the next order from Octavio. Somehow, he was silent lately. Either nothing happened or something happened to him. This had to be determined, and it could not be done from here, from a mountain town where incredible things were happening. It was possible to try to explain them, but Theo instinctively felt that this task would be beyond their strength.

There was nothing to do here anymore. The forces that revealed their destructive activity to them here were older and more vicious than could have been understood by the ordinary human mind, even rich in centuries-old memories. It was nice to see that once they got in their way, they got out of it at such a low cost. Still, he felt a bit of shortage and sadness. He did not want to part with the Tatras. They were beautiful, mysterious and had magnetism about which he had no idea till now. He felt that he could stay here forever, but he had enough sense to know that this was not possible with his lifestyle.

The time has come to say goodbye to these mysterious, beautiful and threatening mountains, having accepted that they cannot be understood.

THE END

www.ingramcontent.com/pod-product-compliance
Lightning Source LLC
Chambersburg PA
CBHW031341020726
47499CB00005B/1353